THE TEMPTATION OF SAINT ANTHONY

GUSTAVE FLAUBERT

THE TEMPTATION OF SAINT ANTHONY

Translated by Lafcadio Hearn

Introduction by Michel Foucault

Foreword, Glossary, Notes, Appendix, and
Revisions to the Translation by Marshall C. Olds,
UNIVERSITY OF NEBRASKA-LINCOLN

THE MODERN LIBRARY

NEW YORK

LIBRARY OF CONGRESS CATALOGING-IN-PUBLICATION DATA
Flaubert, Gustave, 1821–1880.
[Tentation de saint Antoine. English]
The temptation of Saint Anthony / Gustave Flaubert ; translated by Lafcadio
Hearn ; introduction by Michel Foucault ; foreword, glossary, notes, appendix,
and revisions to the translation by Marshall C. Olds.
p.   cm.
Includes bibliographical references.
ISBN 0-375-75912-3
1. Anthony, of Egypt, Saint, ca. 250–355 or 6—Fiction.   2. Christian saints—
Egypt—Fiction.   I. Hearn, Lafcadio, 1850–1904.   II. Foucault, Michel.
III. Olds, Marshall C.   IV. Title.

PQ2246.T4 E5 2001
843'.8—dc21   2001044480

Gustave Flaubert

Gustave Flaubert was born on December 12, 1821, in Rouen, France, where his father was head of the local hospital; until he was eighteen he lived with his family in a residence within the hospital building. He then spent three years studying law in Paris ("which only just failed to kill me with bottled-up fury"), but due in part to an epileptic condition, he went home to devote himself to writing. He wrote, though did not publish, several works of fiction and drama, and began to envision a novel of provincial life: "One likes to imagine some deep, great, intimate story being lived here amid these peaceful dwellings, a passion like a sickness, lasting until death."

Following the death of his father in 1846 and of his sister soon after, Flaubert lived with his mother and his young niece Caroline in a country house in Croisset, in the vicinity of Rouen. Although his lover of many years, the poet Louise Colet, lived in Paris, and although he maintained close friendships in the Parisian literary world—with George Sand, the Goncourts, Théophile Gautier, Ivan Turgenev, Alphonse Daudet, and the young Guy de Maupassant, among others—most of his life was spent in the relative isolation of Croisset. "He never stirs," wrote the Goncourts, "but lives in his writing and his study." In 1849 he embarked with his friend Maxime Du Camp for a journey of a year and a half in Egypt and the Near East. (During this trip he wrote to his mother: "After my return I shall resume my good and splendid life of work, in my big study, in my comfortable armchairs, near you, my darling, and that will be all. So don't speak about pushing myself ahead. Push myself toward what? What is there that can satisfy me except the voluptuous joy I always feel when I sit at my round table?") On his return he began the slow process of writing *Madame Bovary*, which appeared serially in the *Revue de Paris* in 1856 and was promptly the object of legal persecution "for offenses against morality and religion"; Flaubert stood trial but was acquitted with a reprimand.

Flaubert made a brief journey to Tunisia to research his next book, *Salammbô* (1862), a luxuriant re-creation of ancient Carthage, which was followed by *Sentimental Education* (1869), a novel that he called a "moral history of the men of my generation"; *The Temptation of Saint Anthony* (1874), a long and extravagantly erudite drama on which he had worked since early youth; and *Three Tales* (1877). He worked for many years on a compilation of the clichés and truisms of bourgeois conversation, the *Dictionary of Accepted Ideas*, of which he wrote to George Sand: "To dissect is a form of revenge." An attempt to assist in the business affairs of his niece's husband resulted in Flaubert's financial ruin late in life. His final work, the mock-encyclopedic satirical novel *Bouvard and Pécuchet*, left unfinished, was published posthumously in the year following his death on May 8, 1880.

Contents

Foreword

Marshall C. Olds

It is generally the practice, when offering a new edition of a classic literary work written in a foreign language, for publishing houses to present a newly translated text. After all, new translations with an ear for contemporary idiom are among the principal means by which such works can cross the combined gulfs of time and culture. Each generation deserves its own translation of *Madame Bovary*. Yet crossing those gulfs effortlessly and transparently does not always provide the recommended access to the work in question, particularly if there is a strangeness about it that was felt even by its first readers and in the original language. With that in mind, a different approach is being used for the present volume, and the reader of this new edition of Gustave Flaubert's *Temptation of Saint Anthony* (1874) may be surprised to learn that the text here presented is, in fact, the *oldest* of the three translations of this work into English. Surprise should not entail alarm, however; justification for the decision is twofold. First and foremost, the translation begun by Lafcadio Hearn in 1875 or 1876 has an incomparable beauty and elegance that is a perfect match for the very particular language adopted by Flaubert in this, the most curious of his works. In the choice of an English Romantic idiom, a highly literary one at a re-move from all other usage of the day, Hearn found the equivalent to the French of the *Tentation de saint Antoine,* a language markedly different from that of Flaubert's own Realist novels. But there is more: Hearn's translation not only matches the strangeness sensed by the reader of 1874, it has weathered so well that it communicates to the reader of English in 2001 the same distance communicated by Flaubert's text to the contemporary reader of French. Unlike *Madame Bovary, The Temptation of Saint Anthony* cannot best be ap-preciated by being in some sense linguistically contemporary and so culturally relevant. It never was either, really, or at least not in any obvious way.

———

If Flaubert did not write his *Temptation of Saint Anthony* with mod-ern life and language foremost in mind, this did not mean that the haunting work fell on deaf ears. To the contrary: A young genera-tion comprised largely of poets and artists greeted the *Temptation* avidly. There have always been two readerships of Flaubert's works (in fact, there still are), who, more often than not, are quite distinct. There are those readers who much prefer the contemporary real-ism of *Madame Bovary* and the *Sentimental Education* to the works that attempt to resurrect a distant past. Among the younger writers of Flaubert's day who had this view were Émile Zola and Guy de Maupassant, who would follow the path leading to Naturalism and psychological Realism. Then there were those who admitted to having a weakness for *Salammbô,* the novel of ancient Carthage, and for the *Temptation.* It is revealing to see how many young *poets,* after the publication of the *Temptation,* wrote to Flaubert "in respectful homage," sending copies of their work for him to notice. This was the generation that would bring forth Symbolism and the fin-de-siècle Decadent movement. Among these was the young Stéphane Mallarmé, who in 1876 sent Flaubert a copy of his poem "The Afternoon of a Faun," printed on impossibly expensive paper with Manet's engravings, and personalized "To Gustave Flaubert, the Master." It was to the author of the *Temptation* that Mallarmé wished to pay his respects, for having given to this generation, as Mallarmé wrote in his preface to *Vathek*, a totally unique work "blending epochs and races in a prodigious celebration" of the literary imagination, and capturing the distinct scent of "bouquins hors de mode," of old and rarely frequented books. There was no higher praise.

Only eight years younger than Mallarmé, Lafcadio Hearn (1850–1904) may be thought of as the French poet's contemporary in every sense but that of place. He was born Patricio Lafcadio Tessima Carlos Hearn, on the Greek island of Santa Maura (today Levkás), which in ancient times was called Levkádhia, the source of his given name. His mother was Greek, and his father was a British army surgeon. Handed over for his education to a doubting and not especially wealthy aunt in Dublin, young Patrick was sent to school with the priesthood in mind, attending Irish and French Jesuit institutions. Doubtless to alleviate the torment of the strict and largely rote education he was receiving, he read voraciously in contemporary and ancient literatures, in mythology, and on all Oriental topics. A schoolyard accident cost him his left eye, and his right was said to have grown disproportionately large from overuse. He was rebellious, it seems, running away from school on at least one occasion. His aunt finally gave him up for lost and paid his passage to America in 1869, where he made his way to Cincinnati and found work as an assistant in the public library. He became a feature writer for the Cincinnati newspapers, and then continued journalistic work in New Orleans, where he moved in 1877. In 1887 Hearn began writing for *Harper's* magazine; postings took him to the West Indies and then, in 1890, to Japan, where he chose to remain for the rest of his life.

Hearn was drawn by nature to the peculiar and the exotic, and as a journalist, often wrote about violent crime and vice. In the United States at midcentury, these were topics that could only be handled by the newspapers, certainly not in magazines or novels, prompting Malcolm Cowley's observation that journalism was the Realism and Naturalism of American writers, and was the sole medium through which American writers could explore in their own way what writers in France were able to develop in more substantial literary forms. While living in New Orleans, and during his two-year stay in the West Indies, Hearn developed a passion for the French Creole people, their language and their literary and folk cultures. In Japan it was to be the same, and his voluminous writings of this period embrace all aspects of Japanese culture: social, religious, folkloric, historical, and literary. In Japan, Hearn finally married, to a woman of the Samurai class, and converted to Buddhism. He published much during his lifetime, beginning with translations of Théophile Gautier (*One of Cleopatra's Nights*, 1882) and two books of collected legends (*Stray Leaves from Strange Literatures*, 1884, and *Some Chinese Ghosts*, 1887), several books from his time in Louisiana and the Caribbean (notably *Youma*, 1890, about a slave insurrection), and then more than a dozen books in Japan (especially *Glimpses of Unfamiliar Japan*, 1894, and *Japan: An Attempt at Interpretation*, 1904). Not just family members (especially his son and wife) but also admirers from the literary world continued to publish Hearn's original material well after his death. He has had at least a half-dozen biographers. His collected articles, essays, and letters are voluminous. E. C. Hill has observed that "Hearn was a writer who combined the *fin-de-siècle* love of the exquisite with a touch of primitive vigor that led him to strange places and gave his writing a hardness that that of his British contemporaries often lacked."*

It should be clear from this thumbnail literary biography that, even at an early age, Lafcadio Hearn would have been drawn to a work like *The Temptation of Saint Anthony*.† One might venture to say that he was, in a very special sense, the reader in that first generation that this book demanded. He had traveled from East to West,

---

* *The Reader's Encyclopedia*, W. R. Benét, ed., 2d ed. (New York: Crowell, 1965).

†As a schoolboy, he confessed to a priest the hope that a temptress would come to him as she had to the anchorites in the desert. He looked forward to succumbing, however. (O. W. Frost, *Young Hearn*, Hokuseido Press, 1958, p. 57. Readers interested in Hearn might well start with this lively biography.)

been born to a Greek Orthodox mother, educated into the Catholic faith through his aunt, and then educated further in Catholicism, church history, the Gospels, the lives of the saints, Latin, Greek.... At least as much as his French contemporaries, Lafcadio Hearn was immediately attuned to the intellectual and historical perspective acquired by Flaubert over some thirty years in order to finish his work.*

Newly arrived at the Cincinnati public library in 1869, the nineteen-year-old Hearn freely indulged his passion for books (so much so that he was fired for reading too much). He passed much time with midcentury French authors: Charles Baudelaire, Gautier, and Flaubert. One may be impressed with the accuracy of his taste and judgment, which aimed unerringly at major figures. (Hearn's interest in contemporary French writing would be ongoing and would lead to many short translations published in newspapers and in *Harper's;* Hearn played an important role in introducing American readers to these authors.) According to Elizabeth Bisland,† an intimate during the New Orleans years and Hearn's first biographer, it was in 1875 or 1876 that Lafcadio Hearn began his translation of *The Temptation of Saint Anthony,* only a year or two after its first publication in Paris. It was to be a labor of love, finished in New Orleans in 1882 as he fought off malaria. Hearn's immense erudition—his knowledge of Scripture and of Church history, of the early saints and martyrs, all so painfully acquired in his seminary schools, joined with his wide reading in Orientalism, in ancient religions and mythologies, as well as his command of

* It is ironic and suggestive that the French school Hearn attended, known as *le petit séminaire,* was in Normandy, in the small town of Yvetot. Guy de Maupassant, whom Hearn would later translate, was a pupil there at the same time, 1863. There is no record of their having met. Yvetot is very close to Flaubert's house at Croisset, where the novelist had just finished *Salammbô.*

† Elizabeth Bisland (1861–1929) was a poet and magazine editor in New Orleans and was Hearn's editor at the *Times-Democrat.* She published Hearn's posthumous *Life and Letters* (1906) and his *Japanese Letters* (1910). She wrote the introduction to the first edition of the *Temptation* (1910) and may well have overseen its publication. Her lively introduction has often been reprinted in English editions of the work and is of historical interest.

classical languages—gave him privileged access to the world of the third-century anchorite that Flaubert had set himself to resurrect.

If we are to believe the confidence made to Willa Cather by Caroline Franklin Grout, Flaubert's niece and literary heir, *The Temptation of Saint Anthony* was the work that the author loved best.* Flaubert himself called it "the work of my entire life." Indeed, it spanned nearly the whole of the novelist's life: from its germ in the marionette shows of Flaubert's childhood, depicting a ludic version of the hermit and his temptations, to the partial figurations in some of the juvenilia (*Smarh,* for example), to an encounter in Genoa with Pieter Breughel's painting of the subject, to a full-blown first version of the work, written as a play and finished in 1849. Flaubert was dissuaded by his friends from doing anything further with the dramatic work. In 1856, as he was completing *Madame Bovary,* Flaubert came back to that imposing manuscript, cutting it by half but venturing only so far as to publish a few excerpts, among them the episode with the Queen of Sheba. Baudelaire noticed the publication and, in the close of his 1857 essay on *Madame Bovary,* referred to the *Temptation* as "the secret chamber of Flaubert's mind," a work at once very personal and very different from the novel that had just appeared. Finally, in 1869, after completing the *Sentimental Education,* Flaubert returned again to the abandoned work, in a three-year revision that would protect its essence yet change it profoundly. In 1871, a brief interruption: the Prussian army occupied the Flaubert house at Croisset, downstream from Rouen on the Seine, and the manuscript was buried in the garden for safekeeping. Flaubert finished in 1872 but still hesitated, finally going ahead with publication in 1874.

The *Temptation* was indeed the work of a lifetime, and in senses other than just chronological. As has often been pointed out, Flaubert lived the life of a recluse, generally shunning Parisian life and remaining holed up in Normandy, at Croisset, receiving only the friends he chose, maintaining a massive correspondence, read-

---

* See Cather's *A Chance Encounter.*

ing, writing brutally long hours, and pacing up and down in his study declaiming at full volume all that he had composed. Anthony's solitary life and his visions appear to us today, as they doubtless did to Flaubert, as the very image of the author's own life. And then there was the sheer personal investment. Flaubert was no stranger to intensive research. In 1857 he had thrown himself into gathering information on ancient Carthage for *Salammbô,* following the work he had already done on the world's religions for the *Temptation* of 1849. For the *Temptation* of 1872, as Michel Foucault observes, the preparation was of a different magnitude entirely: The library was ablaze. In the manuscripts for the final version, one can find the following notation: "From early July, 1870 until June 26, 1872, I read, for *The Temptation of Saint Anthony,* the following works...." What follows is a list of some 134 titles, in French and in Latin, on topics that cover the ancient and early medieval worlds from Greece, Palestine, and Egypt to India and China; from Chaldean astronomy to Talmudic studies and the history of the Jews, to the history of the early Christian church and its heresiarchs, to philosophy, and to ancient geography. This does not include his voluminous correspondence with specialists, such as the exchange of letters with Léon Heuzey, the noted archaeologist and founder of the Oriental Antiquities Department at the Louvre, from whom Flaubert sought information about ancient Alexandria.

One can only imagine what it must have been like to encounter this work in 1875. There had certainly been great works of the imagination heralding the height of the Romantic revolution throughout Europe, works like Goethe's *Faust* or the poetry of Samuel Coleridge or Baudelaire, that appealed to both a hieratic sense of initiation and a poetic sense of the rare. But works like the *Temptation* were far less common, in their appeal also to a kind of voluptuousness of the life of the mind, a nearly orgiastic self-indulgence within a seemingly infinite library, where meaning is at the heart of the book but understanding is challenged on every page. In the twentieth century, we had to wait for writers like James Joyce and Samuel Beckett to give us something similar.

As has been mentioned, the reader of Hearn's translation will find a poetic idiom reminiscent of that of the English Romantic poets, even of the Pre-Raphaelites (Hearn was to write articles on both). This is a language that also evokes Scripture, and Hearn's ear picks up strains of both the English Vulgate and the King James. The reader will also notice some innovation. A Latinist with a superb command of French and, if not a Hellenist, at least able to read ancient Greek quite well, Hearn was necessarily attentive to the interplay between languages. He has been called a literalist, which, in the jargon of translators, means that his tendency was to seek equivalencies that echoed the original as closely as possible. Thus, for instance, he will opt for "diverting" instead of "amusing" to render *divertissant,* and will sometimes stay with a familiar French word, as with "flambeaux" instead of "torches." O. W. Frost points out that the choice is occasionally a neologism, a curiously anglicized form of a French term—"demilune," instead of "half-moon," for *demi-lune*—or even a Latinism: "necropoli" as the plural of necropolis. All of Hearn's choices seem to have been made for prosodic reasons, or for the purposes of maintaining diction at a proper level, as with "Lo!" to render *voilà.* The original text to translate is not always a French one at its origin, however, as with biblical expressions, and so Hearn will resort to his knowledge of Scripture; where Flaubert was obliged for the same reason to use the rare *hémorroïdesse,* Hearn will use "a woman with an issue of blood."

A further word concerning the translation is necessary. After finishing it in 1882, Hearn found no publisher who was even interested in reading the manuscript; not only was the work deemed too arcane for the reading public, but, because of the painterly tradition (especially of Anthony and his seductresses), that it recalled, too scandalous. As Elizabeth Bisland wryly observed, in the United

---

* As Pierre-Louis Rey has observed, the northern painters of the *Temptation* tended to concentrate on beasts and monsters, the southern painters on temptations of the flesh (Préface, *La Tentation de saint Antoine,* Pocket, 1999).

States of the 1870s, even piano legs wore clothes. Be that as it may, when the Hearn translation was at last published in 1910, it was not complete. The editors indicated that three passages had been excised, ostensibly for the sake of decorum, but that none of the deleted material was central to an understanding or appreciation of Flaubert's masterpiece. In the second edition, the passages in question were given in the appendices, in French. The three passages were a heretical argument in favor of onanism, a heretical account of Jesus' birth having resulted from a willing union between Mary and a Roman soldier, and the extended lamentation given by Crepitus, the Roman house god of flatulence.

It is most unlikely that Hearn would have cut those passages (if indeed it was he) for any reason other than to make his translation more palatable to potential editors. What is less clear is the motivation behind the nearly dozen other excisions. These passages are predominantly single clauses consisting of several words; in most instances, their content is sexual. They may have been quietly deleted by Hearn in an attempt to present a translation that seemed less mutilated than it really was, or clandestinely by the publisher, or even possibly by Elizabeth Bisland. There are several other equally brief omissions that are inexplicable on the grounds of taste and can only be understood as involuntary oversights on Hearn's part, or as mistakes in the deciphering of his manuscript by Bisland or by the typesetter.

With new translations supplied for all of these omitted passages, *The Temptation of Saint Anthony* has been restored to a state that both Flaubert and Hearn would have recognized, and in a manner that I hope will be found consonant with Hearn's practice. The translation has also been copyedited for the first time with the original French text in mind, and for minor inconsistencies in punctuation that were probably introduced in the early editing of Hearn's manuscript. This was notably the case in the unspoken descriptive passages. In the first versions of the *Temptation,* from 1849 and 1856, Flaubert wrote these as stage directions. He changed these passages considerably in the final version, making them far more nuanced than mere scenic indications. (The author himself never knew what to call his book, seeing that it was neither a play nor a novel.) Still, Flaubert was careful to keep the descriptive passages objective and free from overt association with the point of view of any one character. This is *not* Flaubert's usual practice; he is known for his subtle use of indirect discourse imbedded within narrative passages. In the *Temptation,* he varied from this in just one instance, in the sixth chapter or tableau, where one reads, in the passage describing the universe as modern science will know it, no fewer than three exclamation marks tying the sight of the planets to Anthony's astonishment.

Hearn was perhaps somewhat more generously disposed toward his readers than was Flaubert. The translator wrote an elegant summary of the *Temptation,* which he called the Argument. It follows Michel Foucault's essay here and serves as a preface to the work. Hearn also supplied some notes, which are preserved as footnotes in the current edition. I have supplied a few additional notes, which are presented as endnotes, along with a glossary of the proper and place names and other terms that might be unfamiliar or that require a remark beyond what is generally known. This is true especially for the divergent views of the heresiarchs. For these I have relied on the immense scholarly resources brought to bear on the *Temptation* over the past century. More than with any other work of Flaubert's, study of the *Temptation* has been a collective affair spanning generations, as new findings and insights have been added to the old (rather than replacing them). For the purposes of this edition, I have also consulted the many French editions. One, however, stands out, and I would be remiss not to acknowledge my debt to Claudine Gothot-Mersch, whose 1983 edition remains the choice of scholars throughout the world. Her edition has inspired many aspects of this one, especially where the glossary is concerned. I have verified the entries of her edition that I use; changed spellings to conform to both English norms and those preferred by Hearn that are at times erudite and at variance with everyday practice; and modified the content of the entries on those occasions when my sources were at variance with hers. It should be noted, moreover, that the present edition is intended as an enriched reader's edition of Lafcadio Hearn's translation. Consequently, I have avoided references to the earlier versions of the *Temptation* and, with one notable exception, to curiosities found in the manuscript. For that exception, the reader will find in an appendix a revealing passage that Flaubert considered for inclusion and then discarded at the eleventh hour: "The Death of Christ in a Modern City."*

—

The historical Saint Anthony was born in Egypt, in 251. The only contemporary account of the saint's life is Athanasius's *Life of Anthony*, written between 356 and 362. Athanasius, who was to became bishop of Alexandria, knew Anthony and was his disciple. Intended as a source for meditation, the work was "written and sent to the monks in foreign parts by Athanasius, the bishop to the brethren in foreign parts." For his biography, Athanasius drew on material related to him directly by Anthony himself and by the anchorite disciples who lived near him.

Anthony grew up in a wealthy Christian household. His parents died when he was about eighteen, leaving him with his younger sister. In imitation of the apostles, he gave the family's earthly possessions to the needy and confided his sister to the care of "known and faithful virgins." Then, following the example of an old hermit, Anthony set out on an ascetic life of constant prayer and self-abnegation. After some wandering, he lived for a time in an empty tomb, and then withdrew further for some twenty years, immuring himself in an abandoned fort on a mountain by the Nile called Pispir (now Dayr al-Maymun). He came to Alexandria to protest

---

* Readers with French who wish to delve deeper into this fascinating work are referred to Professor Gothot-Mersch's edition and to Gisèle Séginger's critical study *Naissance et métamorphoses d'un écrivain* (Champion, 1998). All readers will profit from the entries pertaining to the *Temptation,* written by Allan Pasco and Laurence M. Porter, in the recent *A Gustave Flaubert Encyclopedia* (L. M. Porter, ed., Greenwood, 2001). Beyond this, a fine selected bibliography, with annotations in English, is to be consulted in the Flaubert chapter (E. F. Gray and L. M. Porter) of *A Critical Bibliography of French Literature: The Nineteenth Century* (D. Baguley, ed., Syracuse University Press, 1994).

the Arian heresies; he also temporarily renounced his solitude to organize into a community the monks who had come to live near him. He is thus recognized as the founder of Christian monasticism. Again seeking solitude, he withdrew "to the inner desert" east of the Nile and was led to Mount Colzim, near the Red Sea, where he stayed for nearly fifty years, attended in his last years by several disciples, and where he died in 356 at the age of 105. A monastery bearing his name (Der Mar Antonios) stands on that site.

For Athanasius, Anthony's life was exemplary because of the extreme discipline, understood as purity, that he brought to his asceticism. He ate little, never washed even his feet, and gave his thoughts over entirely to holy subjects, to the soul's preparation for eternity, and to the mortification of the flesh done to purify the body in anticipation of its final resurrection. Athanasius attributes several long sermons to Anthony, as he speaks to his disciples. Despite Anthony's near total seclusion, he was widely renowned as a holy man. The emperor Constantine wrote to him, and magistrates tried in vain to have Anthony adjudicate difficult cases.

The rigor of Anthony's life was all the more necessary because he was besieged by demonic visions, beginning in his early days of retreat and lasting throughout his life. He understood these visions as transformations of the devil, who, jealous of the hermit's goodness, came to seduce or otherwise awe him with satanic power. Anthony was tempted with piles of gold, with food, with women, with "a black boy" who was "the spirit of lust." Bands of wild animals made as if to attack him and tried to terrify him with their ferocious cries. Monstrous creatures appeared to him, having shapes half animal, half human; learned men came with beguiling heresies. Anthony was at times transported outside of himself and was able to watch his own actions. Athanasius recounts how a group of monks came to see Anthony while he was living in the fort on Mount Pispir. The din coming from within was such that they were alarmed and climbed into the fort with ladders. Anthony was calm; he had become immune to the demons. He was able to defend himself with prayer and was, at times, given celestial visions. Athanasius attributes great thaumaturgic powers to Anthony's later life and relates instances of healing and of knowledge of both future events and happenings taking place at great distances. At the time of his death, Athanasius informs us, Anthony's saintliness was known throughout Egypt, in Rome, in Spain, and into Gaul.

Flaubert's treatment of Anthony is not a little indebted to the portrait given by Athanasius. For his setting, the novelist clearly had in mind Anthony's final mountain retreat—which Athanasius says had a few old palm trees, and where the saint spent his time praying and weaving mats—mixed with elements of the retreat on Mount Pispir. Most categories of Flaubert's dramatization of the temptations and visions are mentioned by the devoted biographer—lust, gluttony, greed, wise men (the heresiarchs), the pagan gods—which Athanasius, in his conclusion, counts among the demons, as he warns the brethren against the Greek influence that was still strong in the third century. Athanasius's descriptions of Anthony's thaumaturgy account for the visions in Flaubert's text that are set in far-off places and in the future; the historical Anthony was also assailed by the apparition of a gigantic Satan.

For the details to be supplied to this broad outline, Flaubert relied on the cross-fertilization between his many sources and his powerful imagination. For other accounts about Anthony, he read Jerome's *Life of Saint Hilarion* (390), which chronicles the life of one of the hermit's most illustrious disciples (a satanic apparition of whom plays an important role in Flaubert's book), and the brief account—taken largely from Athanasius—included by Jacobus de Voragine in his compilation of the saints' lives, *The Golden Legend* (1275). There were of course other sources, much less direct, comprising the folklore surrounding Saint Anthony that grew up during the Middle Ages. This is the version of the saint's temptations that eventually would have found its way into the marionette shows that Gustave had so enjoyed as a child, Anthony the familiar of Guignol, who lived with a talking pig as his only companion and was tormented by devils, pursued by beasts, and vamped by none other than the notorious Queen of Sheba. There is indeed some of this puppet show in the *Temptation* (though less than in the earlier versions of the work). The medieval Anthony is further transmitted by the painterly tradition to which Flaubert was so attuned—combining as it did the erotic with the monstrous—and yet strangely indifferent. It is true that in 1845, in Genoa, he stood transfixed before Breughel's painting; it is also true that, having returned to Croisset, he bought an engraving by Jacques Callot to keep the strange vision before his mind's eye. It was a very different work, but for Flaubert the two images served the same function, which was to recall *his own* Anthony. To catch a first glimpse of this Anthony, we must in turn recall that the historical figure given to us by Athanasius could neither read nor write. As a boy, "he could not endure to learn letters."* He listened carefully as Scripture was read, "and afterwards his memory served him for books." Flaubert's Anthony is an anchorite of a more bookish order. He muses that he might have become a priest, or "a grammarian, a philosopher. I would have then had in my chamber a sphere of reeds, and tablets always ready at hand, young men around me, and a wreath of laurel suspended above my door, as a sign." Yet in this respect, his life is not so different from the one imagined: On a lectern, always open for consultation, is the Bible from which he soon will begin reading and in which the germ of his visions is found. Flaubert's Anthony is not the medieval marionette dashing madly to and fro between beasts and beguilements. He is a creation at once more ancient than that and more modern. We must be grateful to Lafcadio Hearn for having so gracefully captured that truth in his English translation of Flaubert's "prodigious celebration."

---

* Quoted in H. Ellershaw, *Life of Antony, Select Writings of Athanasius,* Library of Nicene and Post-Nicene Fathers II.4 (New York, 1924, repr. 1957).

INTRODUCTION

Michel Foucault

(*translated by Donald F. Bouchard and Sherry Simon*)

I

The Temptation of Saint Anthony was rewritten on three different occasions: in 1849, before *Madame Bovary;* in 1856, before *Salammbô;* and in 1872, while Flaubert was writing *Bouvard and Pécuchet.* He published extracts in 1856 and 1857. Saint Anthony accompanied Flaubert for twenty-five or thirty years—for as long, in fact, as the hero of the *Sentimental Education.* In these twin and inverted figures, the old anchorite of Egypt, still besieged by desires, responds through the centuries to a young man of eighteen, seized by the apparition of Madame Arnoux while travelling from Paris to Le Havre. Moreover, the evening when Frédéric—at this stage, a pale reflection of himself—turns away, as if in fear of incest, from the woman he continues to love recalls the shadowed night when the defeated hermit learns to love even the substance of life in its material form. "Temptation" among the ruins of an ancient world populated by spirits is transformed into an "education" in the prose of the modern world.

The *Temptation* was conceived early in Flaubert's career—perhaps after attending a puppet show—and it influenced all of his works. Standing alongside his other books, standing behind them, the *Temptation* forms a prodigious reserve: for scenes of violence, phantasmagoria, chimeras, nightmares, slapstick. Flaubert successively transformed its inexhaustible treasure into the grey provincial reveries of *Madame Bovary,* into the sculpted sets of *Salammbô,* and into the eccentricities of everyday life in *Bouvard.* The *Temptation* seems to represent Flaubert's unattainable dream: what he wanted his works to be—supple, silky, delicate, spontaneous, harmoniously revealed through rapturous phrases—but also what they must never be if they were to see the light of day. The *Temptation* existed before any of Flaubert's books (its first sketches are found in *Mémoires d'un Fou, Rêve d'Enfer, Danse des Morts,* and, particularly, in *Smahr*), and it was repeated—as ritual, purification, exercise, a "temptation" to overcome—prior to writing each of his major texts. Suspended over his entire work, it is unlike all his other books by virtue of its prolixity, its wasted abundance, and its overcrowded bestiary; and set back from his other books, it offers, as a photographic negative of their writing, the somber and murmuring prose which they were compelled to repress, to silence gradually, in order to achieve their own clarity. The entire work of Flaubert is dedicated to the conflagration of this primary discourse: its precious ashes, its black, unmalleable coal.

II

We readily understand the *Temptation* as setting out the formal progression of unconfined reveries. It would be to literature what Bosch, Breughel, or the Goya of the *Capricios* were at one time to painting. The first readers (or audience) were bored by the monotonous progression of grotesques: Maxime Du Camp remarked: "We listened to the words of the Sphinx, the chimera, the Queen of Sheba, of Simon the Magician.... A bewildered, somewhat simpleminded, and, I would even say, foolish Saint Anthony sees, parading before him, different forms of temptation." His friends were enraptured by the "richness of his vision" (François Coppée), "by its forest of shadows and light" (Victor Hugo), and by its "hallucinatory mechanism" (Hippolyte Taine). But stranger still, Flaubert himself invoked madness, phantasms; he felt he was shaping the fallen trees of a dream: "I spend my afternoons with the shutters closed, the curtains drawn, and without a shirt, dressed as a carpenter. I bawl out! I sweat! It's superb! There are moments when this is decidedly more than delirium." As the book nears completion: "I plunged furiously into *Saint Anthony* and began to enjoy the most terrifying exaltation. I have never been more excited."

In time, we have learned as readers that the *Temptation* is not the product of dreams and rapture, but a monument to meticulous erudition.* To construct the scene of the heresiarchs, Flaubert drew extensively from Tillemont's *Mémoires Ecclésiastiques,* Matter's four-volume *Histoire du gnosticisme,* the *Histoire de Manichée* by Beausobre, Reuss's *Théologie chrétienne,* and also from Saint Augustine and, of course, from Migne's *Patralogie* (Athanasius, Jerome, and Epiphanus). The gods that populate the text were found in Burnouf, Anquetil-Duperron, in the works of Herbelot and Hottinger, in the volumes of the *Univers Pittoresque,* in the work of the Englishman, Layard, and, particularly, in Creutzer's translation, the *Religions de l'Antiquité.* For information on monsters, he read Xivrey's *Traditions tératologiques,* the *Physiologus* re-edited by Cahier and Martin, Boaïstrau's *Histoires prodigieuses,* and the Duret text devoted to plants and their "admirable history." Spinoza inspired his metaphysical meditation on extended substance. Yet, this list is far from exhaustive. Certain evocations in the text seem totally dominated by the machinery of dreams: for example, the magisterial Diana of Ephesus, with lions at her shoulders and with fruits, flowers, and stars interlaced on her bosom, with a cluster of breasts, and griffins and bulls springing from the sheath that tightly encircles her waist. Nevertheless, this "fantasy" is an exact reproduction of plate 88 in

* As a result of the remarkable studies by Jean Seznec.

Creutzer's last volume: if we observe the details of the print, we can appreciate Flaubert's diligence. Cybele and Atys (with his languid pose, his elbow against a tree, his flute, and his costume cut into diamond shapes) are both found in plate 58 of the same work; similarly, the portrait of Ormuzd is in Layard and the medals of Oraios, Sabaoth, Adonaius, and Knouphus are easily located in Matter. It is indeed surprising that such erudite precision strikes us as a phantasmagoria. More exactly, we are astounded that Flaubert experienced the scholar's patience, the very patience necessary to knowledge, as the liveliness of a frenzied imagination.

Possibly, Flaubert was responding to an experience of the fantastic that was singularly modern and relatively unknown before his time, to the discovery of a new imaginative space in the nineteenth century. This domain of phantasms is no longer the night, the sleep of reason, or the uncertain void that stands before desire, but, on the contrary, wakefulness, untiring attention, zealous erudition, and constant vigilance. Henceforth, the visionary experience arises from the black-and-white surface of printed signs, from the closed and dusty volume that opens with a flight of forgotten words; fantasies are carefully deployed in the hushed library, with its columns of books, with its titles aligned on shelves to form a tight enclosure, but within confines that also liberate impossible worlds. The imaginary now resides between the book and the lamp. The fantastic is no longer a property of the heart, nor is it found among the incongruities of nature; it evolves from the accuracy of knowledge, and its treasures lie dormant in documents. Dreams are no longer summoned with closed eyes, but in reading; and a true image is now a product of learning: it derives from words spoken in the past, exact recensions, the amassing of minute facts, monuments reduced to infinitesimal fragments, and the reproductions of reproductions. In the modern experience, these elements contain the power of the impossible. Only the assiduous clamor created by repetition can transmit to us what only happened once. The imaginary is not formed in opposition to reality as its denial or compensation; it grows among signs, from book to book, in the interstice of repetitions and commentaries; it is born and takes shape in the interval between books. It is a phenomenon of the library.

Both Michelet (in the *Sorcière*) and Edgar Quinet (in *Ahasvérus*) had explored these forms of erudite dreams, but the *Temptation* is not a scholarly project that evolved into an artistically coherent whole. As a work, its form relies on its location within the domain of knowledge: it exists by virtue of its essential relationship to books. This explains why it may represent more than a mere episode in the history of Western imagination; it opens a literary space wholly dependent on the network formed by the books of the past: as such, it serves to circulate the fiction of books. Yet, we should not confuse it with apparently similar works, with *Don Quixote* or the works of Sade, because the link between the former and the tales of knight-errantry or between the *Nouvelle Justine* and the virtuous novels of the eighteenth century is maintained through irony; and, more importantly, they remain books regardless of their intention. The *Temptation*, however, is linked in a completely serious manner to the vast world of print and develops within the recognizable institution of writing. It may appear as merely another new book to be shelved alongside all the others, but it serves, in actuality, to extend the space that existing books can occupy. It recovers other books; it hides and displays them and, in a single movement, it causes them to glitter and disappear. It is not simply the book that Flaubert dreamed of writing for so long; it dreams other books, all other books that dream and that men dream of writing—books that are taken up, fragmented, displaced, combined, lost, set at an unapproachable distance by dreams, but also brought closer to the imaginary and sparkling realization of desires. In writing the *Temptation*, Flaubert produced the first literary work whose exclusive domain is that of books: following Flaubert, Mallarmé is able to write *Le Livre* and modern literature is activated—Joyce, Roussel, Kafka, Pound, Borges. The library is on fire.

Déjeuner sur l'herbe and *Olympia* were perhaps the first "museum" paintings, the first paintings in European art that were less a response to the achievement of Giorgione, Raphael, and Velázquez than an acknowledgment (supported by this singular and obvious connection, using this legible reference to cloak its operation) of the new and substantial relationship of painting to itself, as a manifestation of the existence of museums and the particular reality and interdependence that paintings acquire in museums. In the same period, *The Temptation* was the first literary work to comprehend the greenish institutions where books are accumulated and where the slow and incontrovertible vegetation of learning quietly proliferates. Flaubert is to the library what Manet is to the museum. They both produced works in a self-conscious relationship to earlier paintings or texts—or rather to the aspect in painting or writing that remains indefinitely open. They erect their art within the archive. They were not meant to foster the lamentations—the lost youth, the absence of vigor, and the decline of inventiveness— through which we reproach our Alexandrian age, but to unearth an essential aspect of our culture: every painting now belongs within the squared and massive surface of painting and all literary works are confined to the indefinite murmur of writing. Flaubert and Manet are responsible for the existence of books and paintings within works of art.

III

The presence of the book in the *Temptation*, its manifestation and concealment, is indicated in a strange way: it immediately contradicts itself as a book. From the start, it challenges the priority of its printed signs and takes the form of a theatrical presentation: the transcription of a text that is not meant to be read, but recited and staged. At one time, Flaubert had wanted to transform the *Temptation* into a kind of epic drama, a *Faust* capable of swallowing the entire world of religion and gods. He soon gave up this idea but retained within the text the indications marking a possible performance: division into dialogues and scenes, descriptions of the place of action, the scenic elements and their modifications, blocking directions for the "actors" on stage—all given according to a traditional typographical arrangement (smaller type and wider margins for stage directions, a character's name in large letters above the speeches, etc.). In a significant redoubling, the first indicated setting—the site of all future modifications—has the form of a natural theater: the hermit's retreat has been placed "at the summit of a mountain, upon a platform, rounded off into the form of a demilune and enclosed by huge stones." The text describes a stage that, itself, represents a "platform" shaped by natural forces and upon which new scenes will in turn impose their sets. But these indications do not suggest a future performance (they are largely incompatible with an actual presentation); they simply designate the specific mode of existence of the text. Print can only be an unobtrusive aid to the visible; an insidious spectator takes the reader's place and the act of reading is dissolved in the triumph of another form of sight. The book disappears in the theatricality it creates.

But it will immediately reappear within a scenic space. No sooner have the first signs of temptation emerged from the gathering shadows, no sooner have the disquieting faces appeared in the night, than Saint Anthony lights a torch to protect himself and opens a "large book." This posture is consistent with the iconographic tradition: in the painting of Breughel the Younger, the painting that so impressed Flaubert when he visited the Balbi collection in Genoa and that he felt had incited him to write the *Temptation*, the hermit, in the lower right-hand corner of the canvas, is kneeling before an immense volume, his head slightly bowed, and his eyes intent on the written lines. Surrounding him on all sides are naked women with open arms, lean Gluttony stretching her giraffe's neck, barrel-like men creating an uproar, and nameless beasts devouring each other; at his back is a procession of the grotesques that populate the earth—bishops, kings, and tyrants. But this assembly is lost on the saint, absorbed in his reading. He sees nothing of this great uproar, unless perhaps through the corner of his eye, unless he seeks to protect himself by invoking the enigmatic powers of a magician's book. It may be, on the contrary, that the mumbling recitation of written signs has summoned these poor shapeless figures that no language has ever named, that no book can contain, but that anonymously invade the weighty pages of the volume. It may be, as well, that these creatures of unnatural issue escaped from the book, from the gaps between the open pages or the blank spaces between the letters. More fertile than the sleep of reason, the book perhaps engenders an infinite brood of monsters. Far from being a protection, it has liberated an obscure swarm of creatures and created a suspicious shadow through the mingling of images and knowledge. In any case, setting aside this discussion of the open folio in Breughel's painting, Flaubert's Saint Anthony seizes his book to ward off the evil that begins to obsess him and reads at random five passages from Scriptures. But, by a trick of the text, there immediately arises in the evening air the odors of gluttony, the scent of blood and anger, and the incense of pride, aromas worth more than their weight in gold, and the sinful perfumes of Oriental queens. The book—but not any book—is the site of temptation. Where the first passage read by the hermit is taken from the "Acts of the Apostles," the last four, significantly, come from the Old Testament*—from God's Scripture, from the supreme book.

The two earlier versions of the *Temptation* excluded the reading of sacred texts. Attacked by the canonical figures of evil, the hermit immediately seeks refuge in his chapel; goaded by Satan, the Seven Deadly Sins are set against the Virtues and, led by Pride, they make repeated assaults upon the protected enclosure. This imagery of the portal and the staging of a mystery are absent from the published text. In the final version, evil is not given as the property of characters, but incorporated in words. A book intended to lead to the gates of salvation also opens the gates of Hell. The full range of fantastic apparitions that eventually unfold before the hermit— orgiastic palaces, drunken emperors, unfettered heretics, misshapen forms of the gods in agony, abnormalities of nature—arise from

---

* Acts of the Apostles 10:11; Daniel 2:46; 2 Kings 20:13; 1 Kings 10:1.

the opening of a book, as they issued from the libraries that Flaubert consulted. It is appropriate, in this context, that Flaubert dropped from the definitive text the symmetrical and opposing figures of logic and the swine, the original leaders of the pageant, and replaced them with Hilarion, the learned disciple who was initiated into the reading of sacred texts by Saint Anthony.

The presence of the book in the *Temptation,* initially in a theatrical spectacle and then more prominently as the source of a pageant, which, in turn, obscures its presence, gives rise to an extremely complicated space. We are apparently presented with a frieze of colorful characters set against cardboard scenery; on the edge of the stage, in a corner, sits the hooded figure of the motionless saint. The scene is reminiscent of a puppet theater. As a child, Flaubert saw *The Mystery of Saint Anthony* performed numerous times by Père Legrain in his puppet theater; he later brought George Sand to a performance. The first two versions of *The Temptation* retained elements from this source (most obviously, the pig, but also the personification of sin, the assault on the chapel, and the image of the Virgin). In the definitive text, only the linear succession of the visions remains to suggest an effect of "marionettes": sins, temptations, divinities, and monsters are paraded before the laconic hermit—each emerging, in turn, from the hellish confines of the box where they were kept. But this is only a surface effect constructed upon a staging in depth (it is the flat surface that is deceptive in this context).

As support for these successive visions, to set them up in their illusory reality, Flaubert arranged a limited number of stages, which extend, in a perpendicular direction, the pure and straightforward reading of the printed phrases. The first intersection is the reader (1) —the actual reader of the text—and the book lies before him (1*a*); from the first lines (*it is in the Thebaid ... the Hermit's cabin appears in the background*) the text invites the reader to become a spectator (2) of a stage whose scenery is carefully described (2*a*); at center stage, the spectator sees the hermit (3) seated with his legs crossed: he will shortly rise and turn to his book (3*a*) from which disturbing visions will gradually escape—banquets, palaces, a voluptuous queen, and finally Hilarion, the insidious disciple (4). Hilarion leads the saint into a space filled with visions (4*a*); this opens a world of heresies and gods, and a world where improbable creatures proliferate (5). Moreover, the heretics are also capable of speech and recount their shameless rites; the gods recall their past glories and the cults that were devoted to them; and the monsters proclaim their proper bestiality. Derived from the power of their words or from their mere presence, a new dimension is realized, a vision that lies within that produced by the satanic disciple (5*a*), a vision that contains the abject cult of the Ophites, the miracles of Apollonius, the temptations of Buddha, and the ancient and blissful reign of Isis (6). Beginning as actual readers, we successively encounter five distinct levels, five different orders of language (indicated by *a*): that of the book, a theater, a sacred text, visions, and visions that evolve into further visions. There are also five series of characters, of figures, of landscapes, and of forms: the invisible spectator; Saint Anthony in his retreat; Hilarion; the heretics; the gods and the monsters; and finally, the shadows propagated by their speeches or through their memories.

This organization, which develops through successive enclosures, is modified by two others. (In actuality, it finds its confirmation and completion in two others.) The first is that of a retrospective encasement. Where the figures on the sixth level (visions of visions) should be the palest and least accessible to direct perception, they appear forcefully on the scene, as dense, colorful, and insistent as the figures that precede them or as Saint Anthony himself. It is as if the clouded memories and secret desires, which produced these visions from the first, have the power of acting without mediation in the scenic space, upon the landscape where the hermit pursues his imaginary dialogue with his disciple, or upon the stage that the fictitious spectator is meant to behold during the acting out of this semi-mystery. Thus, the fictions of the last level fold back upon themselves, envelop the figures from which they arose, quickly surpass the disciple and the anchorite, and finish by inscribing themselves within the supposed materiality of the theater. Through this retrospective envelopment, the most ephemeral fictions are presented in the most direct language, through the stage directions, indicated by the author, whose task is an external definition of the characters.

This arrangement allows the reader (1) to see Saint Anthony (3) over the shoulder of the implied spectator (2) who is an accomplice to the dramatic presentation: the effect is to identify the reader with the spectator. Consequently, the spectator sees Anthony on the stage, but he also sees over his shoulder the apparitions presented to the hermit, apparitions that are as substantial as the saint: Alexandria, Constantinople, the Queen of Sheba, Hilarion. The spectator's glance dissolves into the hallucinated gaze of the hermit. Anthony then leans over Hilarion's shoulder, and sees with his eyes the figures evoked by the evil disciple; and Hilarion, through the arguments of the heretics, perceives the face of the gods and the snarling monsters, contemplates the images that haunt them. Developed from one figure to another, a wreath is constructed that links the characters in a series of knots independent of their proper intermediaries, so that their identities are gradually merged and their different perceptions blended into a single dazzling sight.

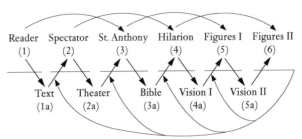

An immense distance lies between the reader and the ultimate visions that entrance the imaginary figures: orders of language placed according to degrees of subordination, relay-characters gazing over each other's shoulders and withdrawing to the depths of this "text-representation," and a population abounding in illusions. But two movements counter this distance: the first, affecting the different orders of language, renders the invisible elements visible through a direct style, and the second, which concerns the figures, gradually adopts the vision and the light fixed upon the characters and brings forward the most distant images until they emerge from the sides of the scene. It is this double movement that makes a vision actually tempting: the most indirect and encased elements of the vision are given with a brilliance compatible with the foreground; and the visionary, attracted by the sights placed before him, rushes into this simultaneously empty and overpopulated space, identifies himself with this figure of shadow and light, and begins to see, in turn, with unearthly eyes. The profundity of these boxed apparitions and the linear and naive succession of figures are not in any way contradictory. Rather, they form the perpendicular intersections that constitute the paradoxical shape and the singular domain of the *Temptation*. The frieze of marionettes and the stark, colored surface of these figures who jostle one another in the shadows offstage are not the effects of childhood memories or the residue of vivid impressions: they are the composite result of a vision that develops on successive and gradually more distant levels and a temptation that attracts the visionary to the place he has seen and that suddenly envelops him in his own visions.

IV

The *Temptation* is like a discourse whose function is to maintain not a single and exclusive meaning (by excising all the others), but the simultaneous existence of multiple meanings. The visible sequence of scenes is extremely simple: first, the memories of the aging monk, the hallucinations and sins summarized by the figure of an ancient queen who arrives from the Orient (Chapters I and II); then, the disciple who initiates the rapid multiplication of heresies through his debate on Scripture (III and IV); followed by the emergence of the gods who successively appear on the stage (V); with the depopulation of the earth, Anthony is free to return to it guided by his disciple who has become both Satan and Knowledge, free to gauge its expanse and to observe the tangled and infinite growth of monsters (VI, VII). This visible sequence is supported by a number of underlying series.

1. Temptation is conceived in the hermit's heart; it hesitantly evokes his companions during his retreat and the passing caravans; from this, it extends into vaster regions: overpopulated Alexandria, the Christian Orient torn by theological conflicts, all those Mediterranean civilizations ruled by gods who emerged from Asia, and, finally, the limitless expanses of the universe—the distant stars at night, the imperceptible cell from which life awakens. But this ultimate scintillation only serves to return the hermit to the material principle of his first desires. Having reached the limits of the world, the grand and tempting itinerary returns to its point of departure. In the first two versions of the text, the Devil explained to Anthony "that sins were in his heart and sorrows in his mind." These explanations are now inessential: pushed to the limits of the universe, the arching waves of the temptation return to those things that are nearest. In the minute organism where the primordial desires of life are awakened, Anthony recaptures his ancient heart, his badly controlled appetites, but no longer experiences their charged fantasies. Before his eyes, there lies the material truth. Under this red light, the larva of desire is gently formed. The center of temptation has not shifted: or rather, it has been displaced very slightly from the top to the bottom—passing from the heart to the sinews, from a dream to the cell, from a bright image to matter. Those things that haunted the imagination of the hermit from inside can now become the object of enraptured contemplation; and where he had pushed them aside in fear, they now attract and invite him to a dormant identification: "to descend to the very depths of matter, to become matter." It is only in appearance that the temptation wrenches the hermit from his solitude and populates his field of vision with men, gods, and monsters, for, along its curved expanse, it gives rise to a number of distinct movements: a progressive expansion to the confines of the universe; a loop bringing desire back to

its truth; a shift that causes a violent phantasm to subside in the soft repose of matter; a passage from the inside to the outside—from heartfelt nostalgia to the vivid spectacle of life; the transformation of fear into the desire for identification.

2. Sitting on the doorstep of his cabin, the hermit is obsessed by the memories of an old man: formerly, isolation was less painful, work less tedious, and the river not as distant as now. He had enjoyed his youth—the young girls who congregated at the fountain—and also his retreat, and the opportunity for companionship, particularly with his favorite disciple. His memories flood back upon him in this slight wavering of the present at the hour of dusk. It is a total inversion of time: first, the images of twilight in the city humming with activity before dark—the port, shouting in the streets, the tambourines in the taverns; followed by Alexandria in the period of the massacres, Constantinople during the Council; this suddenly gives way to the heretics whose affronts originated with the founding of Christianity; behind them are the gods who once had a following of faithful and whose temples range from India to the Mediterranean; and finally, the appearance of figures as old as time itself—the distant stars, brute matter, lust and death, the recumbent Sphinx, chimeras, all those things that, in a single movement, create life and its illusions. Further, beyond this primordial cell from which life evolved, Anthony desires an impossible return to the passive state prior to life: the whole of his existence is consequently laid to rest where it recovers its innocence and awakens once again to the sounds of animals, the bubbling fountain, and the glittering stars. The highest temptation is the longing to be another, to be all others; it is to renew identifications and to achieve the principle of time in a return that completes the circle. The vision of Engadine approaches.

An ambiguous figure—simultaneously a form of duration and eternity, acting as conclusion and a fresh start—introduces each stage of this return through time. The heresies are introduced by Hilarion—as small as a child and withered like an old man, as young as awakening knowledge and as old as well-pondered learn-

ing. Apollonius introduces the gods: he is familiar with their un-
ending metamorphoses, their creation and death, but he is also able
to regain instantly "the Eternal, the Absolute, and Being." Lust and
Death lead the dance of life because they undoubtedly control the
end and new beginnings, the disintegration of forms and the origin
of all things. The larva-skeleton, the eternal Thaumaturge, and the
old child each function within the book as "alternators" of duration; through the time of history, myth, and the entire universe,
they guarantee the hermit's recapture of the cellular principle of
life. The night of the *Temptation* can greet the unchanged novelty
of a new day, because the earth has turned back upon its axis.

3. The resurgence of time also produces a prophetic vision of
the future. Within his recollections, Anthony encountered the ancient imagination of the Orient: deep within this memory, which
no longer belongs to him, he saw a form arising that represented
the temptation of the wisest of the kings of Israel—the Queen of
Sheba. Standing behind her, he recognized in the shape of an ambiguous dwarf, her servant and his own disciple, a disciple who is
indissociably linked to Desire and Wisdom. Hilarion is the incarna-
tion of all the dreams of the Orient, but he possesses as well a perfect knowledge of Scriptures and their interpretation. Greed and
science are united in him—covetous knowledge and damnable
facts. This gnome increases in size throughout the course of the
liturgy; by the last episode, he has become gigantic, "beautiful as an
archangel and luminous as a sun." His kingdom now includes the
universe as he becomes the Devil in the lightning flash of truth.
Serving as an embryonic stage in the development of Western
thought, he first introduces theology and its infinite disputes; then,
he revives ancient civilizations and their gods whose rule was so
quickly reduced to ashes; he inaugurates a rational understanding
of the world; he demonstrates the movement of the stars and reveals the secret powers of life. All of European culture is deployed
in this Egyptian night where the spector, the ancient history, of the
Orient still haunts the imagination: the theology of the Middle
Ages, the erudition of the Renaissance, and the scientific bent of

the modern period. The *Temptation* acts as a nocturnal sun whose trajectory is from East to West, from desire to knowledge, from imagination to truth, from the oldest longings to the findings of modern science. The appearance of Egypt converted to Christianity (and with it Alexandria) and the appearance of Anthony represent the zero point between Asia and Europe; both seem to arise from a fold in time, at the point where Antiquity, at the summit of its achievement, begins to vacillate and collapses, releasing its hidden and forgotten monsters; they also plant the seed of the modern world with its promise of endless knowledge. We have arrived at the hollow of history.

The "temptation" of Saint Anthony is the double fascination exercised upon Christianity by the sumptuous spectacle of its past and the limitless acquisitions of its future. The definitive text excludes Abraham's God, the Virgin, and the virtues (who appear in the first two versions), but not to save them from profanation; they were incorporated in figures that represent them—in Buddha the tempted god, in Apollonius the thaumaturge who resembles Christ, and in Isis the mother of sorrows. The *Temptation* does not mask reality in its glittering images, but reveals the image of an image in the realm of truth. Even in its state of primitive purity, Christianity was formed by the dying reflections of an older world, formed by the feeble light it projected upon the still grey shadows of a nascent world.

4. The two earlier versions of the *Temptation* began with the battle of the Seven Deadly Sins against the three theological virtues (Faith, Hope, and Charity), but this traditional imagery of the mysteries disappears in the published text. The sins appear only in the form of illusions and the virtues are given a secret existence as the organizing principles of the sequences. The endless revival of heresies places Faith at the mercy of overpowering error; the agony of the gods, which makes them disappear as glimmers of imagination, transforms Hope into a futile quest; and nature in repose or with its savage forces unleashed reduces Charity to a mockery. The three supreme virtues have been vanquished; and turning away

from Heaven, the saint "lies flat on his stomach, and leaning upon his elbows, he watches breathlessly. Withered ferns begin to flower anew." At the sight of this small palpitating cell, Charity is transformed into dazzling curiosity ("O joy! O bliss! I have seen the birth of life; I have seen motion begin"), Hope is transformed into an uncontrollable desire to dissolve into the violence of the world ("I long to fly, to swim, to bark, to shout, to howl"), and Faith becomes an identification with brute nature, the soft and somber stupidity of things ("I wish to huddle upon these forms, to penetrate each atom, to descend to the depths of matter—to become pure matter").

This book, which initially appears as a progression of slightly incoherent fantasies, can claim originality only with respect to its meticulous organization. What appears as fantasy is no more than the simple transcription of documents, the reproductions of drawings or texts, but their sequence conforms to an extremely complex composition. By assigning a specific location to each documentary element, it is also made to function within several simultaneous series. The linear and visible sequence of sins, heresies, divinities, and monsters is merely the superficial crest of an elaborate vertical structure. This succession of figures, crowded like puppets dancing the farandole, also functions as: a trinity of canonical virtues; the geodesic line of a culture born in the dreams of the Orient and completed in the knowledge of the West; the return of History to the origin of time and the beginning of things; a pulsating space that expands to the outer limits of the universe and suddenly recedes to return to the simplest element of life. Each element and each character has its place not only in the visible procession, but in the organization of Christian allegories, the development of culture and knowledge, the reverse chronology of the world, and the spatial configurations of the universe.

In addition, the *Temptation* develops the encapsulated visions in depth as they recede, through a series of stages, to the distance; it constitutes a volume behind the thread of its speeches and under its line of successions. Each element (setting, character, speech, alteration of scenery) is effectively placed at a definite point in the linear sequence, but each element also has its vertical system of correspondences and is situated at a specific depth in the fiction. This explains why the *Temptation* can be the book of books: it unites in a single "volume" a series of linguistic elements that derive from existing books and that are, by virtue of their specific documentary character, the repetition of things said in the past. The library is opened, catalogued, sectioned, repeated, and rearranged in a new space; and this "volume" into which Flaubert has forced it is both the thickness of a book that develops according to the necessarily linear thread of its text and a procession of marionettes that, in deploying its boxed visions, also opens a domain in depth.

V

Saint Anthony seems to summon *Bouvard and Pécuchet,* at least to the extent that the latter stands as its grotesque shadow, its tiny, yet boundless, double. As soon as Flaubert completed *The Temptation,* he began his last book. It contains the same elements: a book produced from other books; the encyclopedic learning of a culture; temptation experienced in a state of withdrawal; an extended series of trials; the interplay of illusions and belief. But the general shape is altered. First, the relationship of the Book to the indefinite series of all other books has changed. The *Temptation* was composed of fragments drawn from invisible volumes and transformed into a display of pure phantasms: only the Bible—the supreme Book— shows the sovereign presence of the written word in the text and on the center of its stage; it announced, once and for all, the powers of temptation possessed by the Book. Bouvard and Pécuchet are directly tempted by books, by their endless multiplicity, by the frothing of works in the gray expanse of the library. In *Bouvard and Pécuchet,* the library is clearly visible—classified and analyzed. It can exert its fascination without being consecrated in *a* book or transformed into images. Its powers stem from its singular existence—from the unlimited proliferation of printed paper.

The Bible has become a bookstore, and the magic power of the image has become a devouring appetite for reading. This accounts for the change in the form of temptation. Saint Anthony had withdrawn into idle seclusion in his desire to avoid the disturbing presence of others; yet, neither a living grave nor a walled fortress is sufficient protection. He had exorcised every living form but they returned with a vengeance, testing the saint by their proximity but also by their remoteness. These forms surround him on every side, possess him, but disappear as he extends his hand. Their operation places the saint in a state of pure passivity: his only function was to localize them in the Book through happy memories or the force of imagination. All of his gestures, every word of compassion, and any show of violence, dissipate the mirage—proving that he had suffered a temptation (that only in his heart did an illusory image take on reality). Bouvard and Pécuchet, on the other hand, are indefatigable pilgrims: they try everything, they touch and are drawn to everything; they put everything to the test of their marginal industry. If they withdraw from the world as the Egyptian monk did, it is an active retreat, an enterprising use of their leisure where they summon, with constant recourse to their extensive reading, all the seriousness of science and the most solemnly printed truths. They wish to put into practice everything they read, and if success eludes them, as the images dissipate before Saint Anthony, it is not as a result of their initial gesture but of their persistent search. Their temptation arises from zealousness.

For these two simple men, to be tempted is to believe. It is to believe in the things they read, to believe in the things they overhear; it is to believe immediately and unquestioningly in the persistent flow of discourse. Their innocence is fully engaged in this domain of things already said. Those things that have been *read* and *heard* immediately became things *to do*. But their enterprise is so pure that no setback can alter their belief: they do not measure their truths by their success; they do not threaten their beliefs with the test of action. Possible disasters always remain outside the sovereign field of belief and their faith remains intact. When Bouvard and Pécuchet abandon their quest, they renounce not their faith but the possibility of applying their beliefs. They detach themselves from works to maintain the dazzling reality of their faith in faith. They repeat, for the modern world, the experiences of Job; stricken through their knowledge and not their possessions, abandoned by science and not by God, they persist, like him, in their fidelity—they are saints. For Saint Anthony, unlike these modern-day saints, temptation lies in the sight of the things without belief: it is to perceive error mixed with truth, the spectre of false gods resembling the true God, a nature abandoned without providence to the immensity of its spaces or the unleashing of its vital forces. And paradoxically, as these images are relegated to the shadows from which they emerged, they carry with them some of the belief that Saint Anthony had invested in them, if only for an instant—a part of the faith he had invested in the Christian God. The disappearance of those fantasies that seemed most inimical to his faith does not forcefully reinstate his religion, but gradually undermines it until it is completely taken from him. In their fanatical bloodshed, the heretics dissolve the truth; and the dying gods gather into their darkness part of the image of the true God. Anthony's saintliness was broken in the defeat of those things in which he had no faith; and that of Bouvard and Pécuchet triumphs in the downfall of their faith. They are the true elect. They were given the grace denied the saint.

The relationship between sainthood and stupidity was undoubtedly of fundamental importance for Flaubert; it can be found in Charles Bovary; it is visible in *Un Coeur simple*, and perhaps as well in the *Sentimental Education;* it is essential to the *Temptation* and *Bouvard*, but it adopts symmetrically opposite forms in these books. Bouvard and Pécuchet link sainthood to stupidity on the basis of the will-to-act, the dimension where they activate their desires: they had dreamed of being rich, of being men of leisure and independent means, men of property, but in achieving these goals, they discover that these new roles necessitate an endless cycle of tasks and not a pure and simple existence; the books that should have taught them how to exist dissipated their energies by telling them what they must do. Such is the stupidity and virtue, the sanctity and simplemindedness of those who zealously undertake to make of themselves what they already are, who put into practice received ideas, and who silently endeavor throughout their lives to achieve union with their inner selves in a blind and desperate eagerness. On the other hand, Saint Anthony links simplemindedness to sainthood on the basis of a will-to-be: he wished to be a saint through a total deadening of his senses, intelligence, and emotions, and by dissolving himself into the images that come to him through the mediation of the Book. It is from this that the temptations increase their hold upon him: he refuses to be a heretic, but takes pity on the gods; he recognizes himself in the temptations of Buddha, secretly shares the raptures of Cybele, and weeps with Isis. But his desire to identify with the things he sees triumphs when faced with pure matter: he wishes to be blind, drowsy, greedy, and as stupid as the "Catoblepas"; he wishes that he were unable to lift his head higher than his stomach and that his eyelids would become so heavy that no light could possibly reach his eyes. He wishes to be a dumb creature—an animal, a plant, a cell. He wishes to be pure matter. Through this sleep of reason and in the innocence of desires that have become pure movement, he could at last be reunited to the saintly stupidity of things.

As Anthony is about to accomplish his desire, the day returns and the face of Christ shines in the sun: the saint kneels and returns to his prayers. Has he triumphed over his temptations; has he been defeated and, as a punishment, must the same cycle be indefinitely repeated? Or has he achieved purity through the dumbness of matter; is this the moment when he achieves a true saintliness by discovering, through the dangerous space of books, the pulsation of innocent things; is he now able to *perform*, through his prayers, prostrations, and readings, this mindless sanctity he has become?

Bouvard and Pécuchet also make a new start: having been put to the test, they are now made to abandon the performance of those actions they had undertaken to become what they were initially. They can now be purely and simply themselves: they commission the construction of a large double desk to reestablish the link to their essential nature, to begin anew the activity that had occupied them for over ten years, to begin their copying. They will occupy themselves by copying books, copying their own books, copying every book; and unquestionably they will copy *Bouvard and Pécuchet*. Because to copy is *to do* nothing; it is *to be* the books being copied. It is to be this tiny protrusion of redoubled language, of discourse folded upon itself, this invisible existence transforms fleeting words into an enduring and distant murmur. Saint Anthony was able to triumph over the Eternal Book in becoming the languageless movement of pure matter; Bouvard and Pécuchet triumph over everything alien to books, all that resists the book, by transforming themselves into the continuous movement of the book. The book opened by Saint Anthony, the book that initiated the flight of all possible temptations, is indefinitely extended by these two simple men; it is prolonged without end, without illusion, without greed, without sin, without desire.

———

MICHEL FOUCAULT (1926–1984) was a French philosopher and the author of *Madness and Civilization, The Order of Things,* and *The History of Sexuality,* among other books.

Argument

FRAILTY

Sunset in the desert. Enfeebled by prolonged fasting, the hermit finds himself unable to concentrate his mind upon holy things. His thoughts wander; memories of youth evoke regrets that his relaxed will can no longer find strength to suppress,—and, remembrance begetting remembrance, his fancy leads him upon dangerous ground. He dreams of his flight from home,—of Ammonaria, his sister's playmate,—of his misery in the waste,—his visit to Alexandria with the blind monk Didymus,—the unholy sights of the luxurious city.

Involuntarily he yields to the nervous dissatisfaction growing upon him. He laments his solitude, his joylessness, his poverty, the obscurity of his life; grace departs from him; hope burns low within his heart. Suddenly revolting against his weakness, he seeks refuge from distraction in the study of the Scriptures.

Vain effort! An invisible hand turns the leaves, placing perilous texts before his eyes. He dreams of the Maccabees slaughtering their enemies, and desires that he might do likewise with the Arians of Alexandria;—he becomes inspired with admiration of King Nebuchadnezzar;—he meditates voluptuously upon the visit of Sheba's queen to Solomon;—discovers a text in the Acts of the Apostles antagonistic to principles of monkish ascetism,—indulges in reveries regarding the riches of Biblical kings and holy men. The Tempter comes to tempt him with evil hallucinations for which the Saint's momentary frailty has paved the way; and with the Evil One come also

THE SEVEN DEADLY SINS

Phantom gold is piled up to excite Covetousness; shadowy banquets appear to evoke Gluttony. The scene shifts to aid the temptations of Anger and of Pride....

Anthony finds himself in Alexandria, at the head of a wild army of monks slaughtering the heretics and the pagans, without mercy for age or sex. In fantastic obedience to the course of his fancy while reading the Scriptures a while before, and like an invisible echo of his evil thoughts, the scene changes again. Alexandria is transformed into Constantinople.

Anthony finds himself the honoured of the Emperor. He beholds the vast circus in all its splendour, the ocean of faces, the tumult of excitement. Simultaneously he beholds his enemies degraded to the condition of slaves, toiling in the stables of Constantine. He feels joy in the degradation of the Fathers of Nicæa. Then all is transformed.

It is no longer the splendour of Constantinople he beholds under the luminosity of a Greek day; but the prodigious palace of Nebuchadnezzar by night. He beholds the orgies, the luxuries, the abominations;—and the spirit of Pride enters triumphantly into him as the spirit of Nebuchadnezzar....

Awaking as from a dream, he finds himself again before his hermitage. A vast caravan approaches, halts; and the Queen of Sheba descends to tempt the Saint with the deadliest of all temptations. Her beauty is enhanced by oriental splendour of adornment; her converse is a song of witchcraft. The Saint remains firm.... The Seven Deadly Sins depart from him.

THE HERESIARCHS

But now the tempter assumes a subtler form. Under the guise of a former disciple of Anthony,—Hilarion,—the demon, while pretending to seek instruction, endeavours to poison the mind of Anthony with hatred of the fathers of the church. He repeats all the scandals amassed by ecclesiastical intriguers, all the calumnies created by malice;—he cites texts only to foment doubt, and quotes the evangels only to make confusion. Under the pretext of obtaining mental enlightenment from the wisest of men, he induces Anthony to enter with him into a spectral basilica, wherein are assembled all the Heresiarchs of the third century. The hermit is confounded by the multitude of tenets,—horrified by the blasphemies and abominations of Elkes, Corpocrates, Valentinus, Manes, Cerdo,—disgusted by the perversions of the Paternians, Marcosians, Montanists, Serptians,—bewildered by the apocryphal Gospels of Eve and of Judas, of the Lord, and of Thomas.

And Hilarion grows taller.

THE MARTYRS

Anthony finds himself in the dungeons of a vast amphitheatre, among Christians condemned to the wild beasts. By this hallucination the tempter would prove to the Saint that martyrdom is not always suffered for purest motives. Anthony finds the martyrs possessed by bigotry and insincerity. He sees many compelled to die against their will; many who would forswear their faith could it avail them aught. He beholds heretics die for their heterodoxy more nobly than orthodox believers.

And he finds himself transported to the tombs of the martyrs. He witnesses the meetings of Christian women at the sepulchres. He beholds the touching ceremonies of prayer change into orgies,— lamentations give place to amorous dalliance.

THE MAGICIANS

Then the Tempter seeks to shake Anthony's faith in the excellence and evidence of miracles. He assumes the form of a Hindoo Brahmin, terminating a life of wondrous holiness by self-cremation;— he appears as Simon Magus and Helena of Tyre,—as Apollonius of Tyana, greatest of all thaumaturgists, who claims superiority to Christ. All the marvels related by Philostratus are embodied in the converse of Apollonius and Damis.

THE GODS

Hilarion reappears, taller than ever, growing more gigantic in proportion to the increasing weakness of the Saint. Standing beside Anthony he evokes all the deities of the antique world. They defile before him in a marvellous panorama:—Gods of Egypt and India, Chaldea and Hellas, Babylon and Ultima Thule,—monstrous and multiform, phallic and ithyphallic, fantastic or obscene. Some intoxicate by their beauty; others appall by their foulness. The Buddha recounts the story of his wondrous life; Venus displays the rounded daintiness of her nudity; Isis utters awful soliloquy. Lastly the phantom of Jehovah appears, as the shadow of a god passing away forever.

Suddenly the stature of Hilarion towers to the stars; he assumes the likeness and luminosity of Lucifer; he announces himself as

SCIENCE

And Anthony is lifted upon mighty wings and borne away beyond the world, above the solar system, above the starry arch of the Milky Way. All future discoveries of Astronomy are revealed to him. He is tempted by the revelation of innumerable worlds,—by the refutation of all his previous ideas of the nature of the Universe,—by the enigmas of infinity,—by all the marvels that conflict with faith. Even in the night of immensity the demon renews the temptation of reason: Anthony wavers upon the verge of pantheism.

LUST AND DEATH

Anthony abandoned by the spirit of Science comes to himself in the desert. Then the Tempter returns under a two-fold aspect: as the Spirit of Lust and the Spirit of Destruction. The latter urges him to suicide,—the former to indulgence of sense. They inspire him with strong fancies of palingenesis, of the illusion of death, of the continuity of life. The pantheistic temptation intensifies.

THE MONSTERS

Anthony in reveries meditates upon the monstrous symbols painted upon the walls of certain ancient temples. Could he know their meaning he might learn also something of the secret lien between Matter and Thought. Forthwith a phantasmagoria of monsters commence to pass before his eyes:—the Sphinx and the Chimera, the Blemmyes and Astomi, the Cynocephali and all creatures of mythologic creation. He beholds the fabulous beings of Oriental imagining,—the abnormities described by Pliny and Herodotus, the fantasticalities to be later adopted by heraldry,— the grotesqueries of future medieval illumination made animate;—

the goblinries and foulnesses of superstitious fancy,—the Witches' Sabbath of abominations.

METAMORPHOSIS

The multitude of monsters melts away; the land changes into an Ocean; the creatures of the briny abysses appear. And the waters in turn also change; seaweeds are transformed to herbs, forests of coral give place to forests of trees, polypous life changes to vegetation. Metals crystallize; frosts effloresce; plants become living things, inanimate matter takes animate form, monads vibrate, the pantheism of nature makes itself manifest. Anthony feels a delirious desire to unite himself with the Spirit of Universal Being....

The vision vanishes. The sun arises. The face of Christ is revealed. The temptation has passed; Anthony kneels in prayer.

L. H.

THE TEMPTATION OF SAINT ANTHONY

I

It is in the Thebaid, at the summit of a mountain, upon a platform, rounded off into the form of a demilune, and enclosed by huge stones.

The Hermit's cabin appears in the background. It is built of mud and reeds, it is flat-roofed and doorless. A pitcher and a loaf of black bread can be distinguished within also, in the middle of the apartment a large book resting on a wooden stela; while here and there, fragments of basketwork, two or three mats, a basket, and a knife lie upon the ground.

Some ten paces from the hut, there is a long cross planted in the soil; and, at the other end of the platform, an aged and twisted palmtree leans over the abyss; for the sides of the mountain are perpendicular, and the Nile appears to form a lake at the foot of the cliff.

The view to right and left is broken by the barrier of rocks. But on the desert-side, like a vast succession of sandy beaches, immense undulations of an ashen-blond color extend one behind the other, rising higher as they recede; and far in the distance, beyond the sands, the Libyan chain forms a chalk-colored wall, lightly shaded by violet mists. On the opposite side the sun is sinking. In the north the sky is of a pearl-gray tint, while at the zenith purple clouds disposed like the tufts of a gigantic mane, lengthen themselves against the blue vault. These streaks of flame take darker tones; the azure *spots turn to a nacreous pallor; the shrubs, the pebbles, the earth, all now seem hard as bronze; and throughout space there floats a golden dust so fine as to become confounded with the vibrations of the light.*

SAINT ANTHONY

who has a long beard, long hair, and wears a tunic of goatskin, is seated on the ground cross-legged, and is occupied in weaving mats. As soon as the sun disappears, he utters a deep sigh, and, gazing upon the horizon:

Another day! another day gone! Nevertheless formerly I used not to be so wretched. Before the end of the night I commenced my orisons; then I descended to the river to get water, and remounted the rugged pathway with the skin upon my shoulder, singing hymns on the way. Then I would amuse myself by arranging everything in my hut. I would make my tools; I tried to make all my mats exactly equal in size, and all my baskets light; for then my least actions seemed to me duties in nowise difficult or painful of accomplishment.

Then at regular hours I ceased working; and when I prayed with my arms extended, I felt as though a fountain of mercy were pouring from the height of heaven into my heart. That fountain is now dried up. Why?...

He walks up and down slowly, within the circuit of the rocks.

All blamed me when I left the house. My mother sank to the ground, dying;[1] my sister from afar off made signs to me to return; and the other wept, Ammonaria, the child whom I used to meet every evening at the cistern, when she took the oxen to drink. She ran after me. Her foot rings glittered in the dust; and her tunic, open at the hips, fluttered loosely in the wind. The aged anchorite who was leading me away called her vile names. Our two camels galloped forward without respite; and I have seen none of my people since that day.

At first, I selected for my dwelling place the tomb of a Pharaoh. But an enchantment circulates through all those subterranean palaces, where the darkness seems to have been thickened by the ancient smoke of the aromatics. From the depths of Sarcophagi, I heard doleful voices arise, and call my name; or else, I suddenly beheld the abominable things painted upon the walls live and move; and I fled away to the shore of the Red Sea, and took refuge in a ruined citadel. There my only companions were the scorpions dragging themselves among the stones, and the eagles continually wheeling above my head, in the blue of heaven. At night I was torn by claws, bitten by beaks; soft wings brushed against me; and frightful demons, shrieking in my ears, flung me upon the ground. Once I was even rescued by the people of a caravan going to Alexandria; and they took me away with them.

Then I sought to obtain instruction from the good old man Didymus. Although blind, none equalled him in the knowledge of the Scriptures. When the lesson was finished, he used to ask me to give him my arm to lean upon, that we might walk together. Then I would conduct him to the Paneum, whence may be seen the Pharos and the open sea. Then we would return by way of the port, elbowing men of all nations, even Cimmerians clad in the skins of bears and Gymnosophists of the Ganges anointed with cowdung. But there was always some fighting in the streets—either on account of the Jews refusing to pay taxes, or of seditious people who wished to drive the Romans from the city. Moreover, the city is full of heretics—followers of Manes, Valentinus, Basilides, Arius—all seeking to engross my attention in order to argue with me and to convince me.

Their discourses often come back to my memory. Vainly do I seek to banish them from my mind. They trouble me!

I took refuge at Colzim, and there lived a life of such penance that I ceased to fear God. A few men, desirous of becoming anchorites, gathered about me. I imposed a practical rule of life upon them, hating, as I did, the extravagance of Gnosis and the assertions of the philosophers. Messages were sent to me from all parts, and men came from afar off to visit me.

Meanwhile the people were torturing the confessors; and the

thirst of martyrdom drew me to Alexandria. The persecution had ceased three days before I arrived there!

While returning thence, I was stopped by a great crowd assembled before the temple of Serapis. They told me it was a last example which the Governor had resolved to make. In the centre of the portico, under the sunlight, a naked woman was fettered to a column, and two soldiers were flogging her with thongs; at every blow her whole body writhed. She turned round, her mouth open; and over the heads of the crowd, through the long hair half hiding her face, I thought that I could recognize Ammonaria....

Nevertheless ... this one was taller ... and beautiful ... prodigiously beautiful!

He passes his hands over his forehead.

No! no! I must not think of it!

Another time Athanasius summoned me to assist him against the Arians. The contest was limited to invectives and laughter. But since that time he has been calumniated, dispossessed of his see, obliged to fly for safety elsewhere. Where is he now? I do not know! The people give themselves very little trouble to bring me news. All my disciples have abandoned me—Hilarion like the rest!

He was perhaps fifteen years of age when he first came to me and his intelligence was so remarkable that he asked me questions incessantly. Then he used to listen to me with a pensive air, and whatever I needed he brought it to me without a murmur—nimbler than a kid, merry enough to make even the patriarchs laugh. He was a son to me!

The sky is red; the earth completely black. Long drifts of sand follow the course of the gusts of wind, rising like great shrouds and falling again. Suddenly against a bright space in the sky a flock of birds pass, forming a triangular battalion, gleaming like one sheet of metal, of which the edges alone seem to quiver.

Anthony watches them.

Ah, how I should like to follow them!

How often also have I enviously gazed upon those long vessels, whose sails resemble wings—and above all when they were bearing far away those I had received at my hermitage! What pleasant hours we passed!—what out-pourings of feeling! No one ever interested me more than Ammon: he told me of his voyage to Rome, of the Catacombs, the Coliseum, the piety of illustrious women, and a thousand other things!—and it grieved me to part with him! Wherefore my obstinacy in continuing to live such a life as this? I would have done well to remain with the monks of Nitria, inasmuch as they supplicated me to do so. They have cells apart, and nevertheless communicate with each other. On Sundays a trumpet summons them to assemble at the church, where one may see three scourges hanging up, which serve to punish delinquents, robbers, and intruders; for their discipline is severe.

Nevertheless they are not without some enjoyments. The faithful bring them eggs, fruits, and even instruments with which they can extract thorns from their feet. There are vineyards about Pisperi; those dwelling at Pabena have a raft on which they may journey when they go to seek provisions.

But I might have served my brethren better as a simple priest. As a priest one may aid the poor, administer the sacraments, and exercise authority over families.

Furthermore, all laics are not necessarily damned, and it only depended upon my own choice to become—for example—a grammarian, a philosopher. I would then have had in my chamber a sphere of reeds, and tablets always ready at hand, young men around me, and a wreath of laurel suspended above my door, as a sign.

But there is too much pride in triumphs such as those. A soldier's life would have been preferable. I was robust and bold: bold enough to fasten the cables of the military machines—to traverse dark forests, or to enter, armed and helmeted, into smoking cities!...
Neither was there anything to have prevented me from purchasing with my money the position of publican at the toll-office of some

bridge; and travellers would have told me strange stories, the while showing me many curious objects packed up among their baggage....

The merchants of Alexandria sail upon the river Canopus on holidays, and drink wine in the chalices of lotus-flowers, to a music of tambourines which makes the taverns along the shore tremble! Beyond, trees, made cone-shaped by pruning, protect the quiet farms against the wind of the south. The roof of the lofty house leans upon thin colonettes placed as closely together as the laths of a lattice; and through their interspaces the master, reclining upon his long couch, beholds his plains stretching about him—the hunter among the wheat-fields—the winepress where the vintage is being converted into wine, the oxen treading out the wheat. His children play upon the floor around him; his wife bends down to kiss him.

Against the grey dimness of the twilight, here and there appear pointed muzzles, with straight, pointed ears and bright eyes. Anthony advances toward them. There is a sound of gravel crumbling down; the animals take flight. It was a troop of jackals.

One still remains, rising upon his hinder legs, with his body half arched and head raised in an attitude full of defiance.

How pretty he is! I would like to stroke his back gently.

Anthony whistles to coax him to approach. The jackal disappears.

Ah! he is off to join the others. What solitude! what weariness!

Laughing bitterly:

A happy life this indeed!—bending palm-branches in the fire to make shepherds' crooks, fashioning baskets, stitching mats together—and then exchanging these things with the Nomads for bread which breaks one's teeth! Ah! woe, woe is me! will this never end? Surely death were preferable! I can endure it no more! Enough! enough!

He stamps his foot upon the ground, and rushes frantically to and fro among the rocks; then pauses, out of breath, bursts into tears, and lies down upon the ground, on his side.

The night is calm; multitudes of stars are palpitating; only the crackling noise made by the tarantulas is audible.

The two arms of the cross make a shadow upon the sand; Anthony, who is weeping, observes it.

Am I, then, so weak, O my God! Courage, let me rise from here!

He enters his hut, turns over a pile of cinders, finds a live ember, lights his torch and fixes it upon the wooden desk, so as to throw a light upon the great book.

Suppose I take . . . the Acts of the Apostles? . . .—yes!—no matter where!

"And he saw the heaven opened, and a certain vessel descending, as it were a great linen sheet let down by the four corners from heaven to the earth—wherein were all manner of four-footed beasts; and creeping things of the earth and fowls of the air. And there came a voice to him: Arise, Peter! Kill and eat!"*

Then the Lord desired that his apostle should eat of all things? . . . while I . . .

Anthony remains thoughtful, his chin resting against his breast. The rustling of the pages, agitated by the wind, causes him to lift his head again; and he reads:

---

* Acts x: 11–13.

"So the Jews made a great slaughter of their enemies with the sword, and killed them, repaying according to what they had prepared to do to them."*

Then comes the number of people slain by them—seventy-five thousand. They had suffered so much! Moreover, their enemies were the enemies of the true God. And how they must have delighted in avenging themselves thus by the massacre of idolaters! Doubtless the city must have been crammed with the dead! There must have been corpses at the thresholds of the garden gates, upon the stairways, in all the chambers, and piled up so high that the doors could no longer move upon their hinges!... But lo! here I am permitting my mind to dwell upon ideas of murder and of blood!

He opens the book at another place.

"Then King Nebuchadnezzar fell on his face, and worshipped Daniel."†

Ah! that was just! The Most High exalts his prophets above Kings; yet that monarch spent his life in banqueting, perpetually drunk with pleasure and pride. But God, to punish him, changed him into a beast! He walked upon four feet!

Anthony begins to laugh; and in extending his arms, involuntarily disarranges the leaves of the book with the tips of his fingers. His eyes fall upon this phrase:

"And Ezechias rejoiced at their coming, and he showed them the house of his aromatical spices, and the gold and the silver, and divers precious odours and ointments, and the house of his vessels, and all that he had in his treasures."‡

I can imagine that spectacle; they must have beheld precious

---

* Esther ix: 5.
† Daniel ii: 46.
‡ IV Kings xx: 13 (Vulg.).

stones, diamonds and darics heaped up to the very roof. One who possesses so vast an accumulation of wealth is no longer like other men. While handling his riches he knows that he controls the total result of innumerable human efforts—as it were the life of nations drained by him and stored up, which he can pour forth at will. It is a commendable precaution on the part of Kings. Even the Wisest of all did not neglect it. His navy brought him elephants' teeth and apes.... Where is that passage?

He turns the leaves over rapidly.

Ah! here it is:
"And the Queen of Sheba, having heard of the fame of Solomon in the name of the Lord, came to try him with hard questions."*
How did she hope to tempt him? The Devil indeed sought to tempt Jesus! But Jesus triumphed because he was God; and Solomon, perhaps, owing to his knowledge of magic! It is sublime—that science! For the world—as a philosopher once explained it to me, forms a whole, of which all parts mutually influence one another, like the organs of one body. It is this science which enables us to know the natural loves and natural repulsions of all things, and to play upon them.... Therefore, it is really possible to modify what appears to be the immutable order of the universe.

Then the two shadows formed behind him by the arms of the cross, suddenly lengthen and project themselves before him. They assume the form of two great horns. Anthony cries out:

Help me! O my God!

The shadows shrink back to their former place.

---

* III Kings x: 1 (Vulg.).

Ah!... it was an illusion ... nothing more. It is needless for me to torment my mind further! I can do nothing!—absolutely nothing.

He sits down and folds his arms.

Nevertheless ... it seems to me that I felt the approach of ... But why should *He* come? Besides, do I not know all his artifices? I repulsed the monstrous anchorite who laughingly offered me little loaves of warm, fresh bread, the centaur who sought to carry me away upon his croup, and that black child who appeared to me in the midst of the sands, who was very beautiful, and who told me that he was called the Spirit of Lust!

Anthony rises and walks rapidly up and down, first to the right, then to the left.

It was by my order that this multitude of holy retreats was constructed—full of monks all wearing sackcloth of camel's hair beneath their garments of goatskin, and numerous enough to form an army! I have cured the sick from afar off; I have cast out demons; I have passed the river in the midst of crocodiles; the Emperor Constantine wrote me three letters; Balacius, who had spat upon me, was torn to pieces by his own horses; when I reappeared the people of Alexandria fought for the pleasure of seeing me, and Athanasius himself escorted me on the way back. But what works have I not accomplished! Lo! for these thirty years and more I have been dwelling and groaning unceasingly in the desert! Like Eusebius, I have carried thirty-eight pounds of bronze upon my loins; like Macarius, I have exposed my body to the stings of insects; like Pacomus, I have passed fifty-three nights without closing my eyes; and those who are decapitated, tortured with red hot pincers, or burned alive, are perhaps less meritorious than I, seeing that my whole life is but one prolonged martyrdom.

Anthony slackens his pace.

Assuredly there is no human being in a condition of such unutterable misery! Charitable hearts are becoming scarcer. I no longer receive aught from any one. My mantle is worn out. I have no sandals—I have not even a porringer!—for I have distributed all I possessed to the poor and to my family, without retaining so much as one obolus. Yet surely I ought to have a little money to obtain the tools indispensable to my work? Oh, not much! a very small sum ... I would be very saving of it....

The fathers of Nicæa,[2] clad in purple robes, sat like magi, upon thrones ranged along the wall; and they were entertained at a great banquet and overwhelmed with honours, especially Paphnutius, because he is one-eyed and lame, since the persecution of Diocletian! The Emperor kissed his blind eye several times; what foolishness! Besides, there were such infamous men members of that Council! A bishop of Scythia, Theophilus; another of Persia, John; a keeper of beasts, Spiridion; Alexander was too old. Athanasius ought to have shown more gentleness toward the Arians, so as to have obtained concessions from them!

Yet would they have made any? They would not hear me! The one who spoke against me—a tall young man with a curly beard—uttered the most captious objections to my argument; and while I was seeking words to express my views they all stared at me with their wicked faces, and barked like hyenas. Ah! why cannot I have them all exiled by the Emperor! or rather have them beaten, crushed, and see them suffer! I suffer enough myself.

He leans against his cabin in a fainting condition.

It is because I have fasted too long! my strength is leaving me. If I could eat—only once more—a piece of meat.

He half closes his eyes with langour.

Ah! some red flesh—a bunch of grapes to bite into ... curdled milk that trembles on a plate!...

But what has come upon me?... What is the matter with me?... I feel my heart enlarging like the sea, when it swells before the storm. An unspeakable feebleness weighs down upon me, and the warm air seems to waft me the perfume of a woman's hair. No woman has approached this place; nevertheless?——

He gazes toward the little pathway between the rocks.

That is the path by which they come, rocked in their litters by the black arms of the eunuchs. They descend and joining their hands, heavy with rings, kneel down before me. They relate to me all their troubles. The desire of superhuman pleasure tortures them; they would gladly die; they have seen in their dreams God calling to them ... and all the while the hems of their robes fall upon my feet. I repel them from me. "Ah! no!" they cry, "not yet! What shall I do?" They gladly accept any penitence I impose on them. They ask for the hardest of all; they beg to share mine and to live with me.

It is now a long time since I have seen any of them! Perhaps some of them will come? why not? If I could only hear again, all of a sudden, the tinkling of mule-bells among the mountains. It seems to me ...

Anthony clambers upon a rock at the entrance of the pathway and leans over, darting his eyes into the darkness.

Yes! over there, far off I see a mass moving, like a band of travellers seeking the way. *She* is there!... They are making a mistake.

Calling:

This way! come! come!

Echo repeats: come! come!
He lets his arms fall, stupefied.

What shame for me! Alas! poor Anthony!

And all of a sudden he hears a whisper: "Poor Anthony!"

Who is there? Speak!

The wind, passing through the intervals between the rocks, makes modu-
lations; and in those confused sonorities he distinguishes

VOICES,
as though the air itself were speaking. They are low, insinuating, hissing.

THE FIRST
Dost thou desire women?

THE SECOND
Great heaps of money, rather!

THE THIRD
A glittering sword?

and

THE OTHERS
All the people admire thee! Sleep!
Thou shalt slay them all, aye, thou shalt slay them!

At the same moment objects become transformed. At the edge of the cliff, the
old palm tree with its tuft of yellow leaves changes into the torso of a woman
leaning over the abyss, her long hair waving in the wind.

ANTHONY

turns toward his cabin; and the stool supporting the great book whose pages are covered with black letters seems to him changed into a bush all covered with nightingales.

It must be the torch which is making this strange play of light... Let us put it out!

He extinguishes it; the obscurity becomes deeper, the darkness profound.

And suddenly in the air above there appear and disappear successively— first, a stretch of water; then the figure of a prostitute; the corner of a temple; a soldier; a chariot with two white horses, prancing.

These images appear suddenly, as in flashes—outlined against the background of the night, like scarlet paintings executed upon ebony.

Their motion accelerates. They defile by with vertiginous rapidity. Sometimes again, they pause and gradually pale and melt away; or else float off out of sight, to be immediately succeeded by others.

Anthony closes his eyelids.

They multiply, surround him, besiege him. An unspeakable fear takes possession of him; and he feels nothing more of living sensation, save a burning contraction of the epigastrium. In spite of the tumult in his brain, he is aware of an enormous silence which separates him from the world. He tries to speak;—impossible! He feels as though all the bands of his life were breaking and dissolving;—and, no longer able to resist, Anthony falls prostrate upon his mat.

II

Then a great shadow, subtler than any natural shadow, and festooned by other shadows along its edges, defines itself upon the ground.

It is the Devil, leaning upon the roof of the hut, and bearing beneath his two wings—like some gigantic bat suckling its little ones—the Seven Deadly Sins, whose grimacing heads are dimly distinguishable.

With eyes still closed, Anthony yields to the pleasure of inaction; and stretches his limbs upon the mat.

It seems to him quite soft, and yet softer—so that it becomes as if padded; it rises up; it becomes a bed. The bed becomes a shallop; water laps against its sides.

To right and left rise two long tongues of land, overlooking low cultivated plains, with a sycamore tree here and there. In the distance there is a tinkling of bells, a sound of drums and of singers. It is a party going to Canopus to sleep upon the temple of Serapis, in order to have dreams. Anthony knows this; and impelled by the wind, his boat glides along between the banks. Papyrus-leaves and the red flowers of the nymphæs, larger than the body of a man, bend over him. He is lying at the bottom of the boat; one oar at the stern drags in the water. From time to time, a lukewarm wind blows; and the slender reeds rub one against the other, and rustle. Then the sobbing of the wavelets be-

comes indistinct. A heavy drowsiness falls upon him. He dreams that he is a Solitary of Egypt.

Then he awakes with a start.

Did I dream?... It was all so vivid that I can scarcely believe I was dreaming! My tongue burns! I am thirsty!

He enters the cabin, and gropes at random in the dark.

The ground is wet!... can it have been raining? What can this mean! My pitcher is broken into atoms!... But the goatskin?

He finds it.

Empty!—completely empty!

In order to get down to the river, I should have to walk for at least three hours; and the night is so dark that I could not see my way. There is a gnawing in my entrails. Where is the bread?

After long searching, he picks up a crust not so large as an egg.

What? Have the jackals taken it? Ah! malediction!

And he flings the bread upon the ground with fury.

No sooner has the action occurred than a table makes its appearance, covered with all things that are good to eat.

The byssus cloth, striated like the bandelets of the sphinx, produces of itself luminous undulations. Upon it are enormous quarters of red meats; huge fish; birds cooked in their plumage, and quadrupeds in their skins; fruits with colors and tints almost human in appearance; while fragments of cooling ice, and flagons of violet crystal reflect each other's glittering. Anthony notices in the middle of the table a boar smoking at every pore—with legs doubled up under its belly, and eyes half closed—and the idea of being able to eat so formidable an animal greatly delights him. Then many things appear which he has never seen before—black hashes, jellies the color of gold, ragouts in which mushrooms float like nenuphars upon ponds, dishes of whipt cream light as clouds.

And the aroma of all this comes to him together with the salt smell of the ocean, the coolness of fountains, the great perfumes of the woods. He dilates his nostrils to their fullest extent; his mouth waters; he thinks to himself that he has enough before him for a year, for ten years, for his whole life!

As he gazes with widely-opened eyes at all these viands, others appear; they accumulate, forming a pyramid crumbling at all its angles. The wines begin to flow over—the fish palpitate—the blood seethes in the dishes—the pulp of the fruit protrudes like amorous lips—and the table rises as high as his breast, up to his very chin at last—now bearing only one plate and a single loaf of bread, placed exactly in front of him.

He extends his hand to seize the loaf. Other loaves immediately present themselves to his grasp.

For me! ... all these! But ...

Anthony suddenly draws back.

Instead of one which was there, lo! there are many! ... It must be a miracle, then, the same as our Lord wrought! ...

Yet for what purpose? Ah! all the rest of these things are equally incomprehensible! Demon, begone from me! depart! begone!

He kicks the table from him. It disappears.

Nothing more?—no!

He draws a long breath.

Ah! the temptation was strong! But how well I delivered myself from it!

He lifts his head, and at the same time stumbles over some sonorous object.

Why! what can that be?

Anthony stoops down.

How! a cup! Some traveller must have lost it here. There is nothing extraordinary . . .

He wets his finger, and rubs.

It glitters!—metal! Still, I cannot see very clearly. . . .

He lights his torch and examines the cup.

It is silver, ornamented with ovules about the rim, with a medal at the bottom of it.

He detaches the medal with his nail.

It is a piece of money worth . . . about seven or eight drachmas— not more! It matters not! even with that I could easily buy myself a sheepskin.

A sudden flash of the torch lights up the cup.

Impossible! gold? Yes! . . . all gold, solid gold!

A still larger piece of money appears at the bottom. Under it he perceives several others.

Why, this is a sum . . . large enough to purchase three oxen . . . and a little field!

The cup is now filled with pieces of gold.

What! what!... a hundred slaves, soldiers, a host ... enough to buy ...

The granulations of the rim, detaching themselves, form a necklace of pearls.

With such a marvel of jewelry as that, one could win even the wife of the Emperor!

By a sudden jerk, Anthony makes the necklace slip down over his wrist. He holds the cup in his left hand, and with his right lifts up the torch so as to throw the light upon it. As water streams overflowing from the basin of a fountain, so diamonds, carbuncles, and sapphires, all mingled with broad pieces of gold bearing the effigies of Kings, overflow from the cup in never ceasing streams, to form a glittering hillock upon the sand.

What! how! Staters, cycles, dariacs, aryandics![3] Alexander, Demetrius, the Ptolemies, Cæsar!—yet not one of them all possessed so much! Nothing is now impossible! no more suffering for me! how these gleams dazzle my eyes! Ah! my heart overflows! how delightful it is! yes—yes!—more yet! never could there be enough! Vainly I might continually fling it into the sea, there would always be plenty remaining for me. Why should I lose any of it? I will keep all, and say nothing to any one about it; I will have a chamber hollowed out for me in the rock, and lined with plates of bronze, and I will come here from time to time to feel the gold sinking down under the weight of my heel; I will plunge my arms into it as into sacks of grain. I will rub my face with it, I will lie down upon it!

He flings down the torch in order to embrace the glittering heap, and falls flat upon the ground.
He rises to his feet. The place is wholly empty.

What have I done!

Had I died during those moments, I should have gone to hell— to irrevocable damnation!

He trembles in every limb.

Am I, then, accursed? Ah! no; it is my own fault! I allow myself to be caught in every snare! No man could be more imbecile, more infamous! I should like to beat myself, or rather to tear myself out of my own body! I have restrained myself too long! I feel the want of vengeance—the necessity of striking, of killing!—as though I had a pack of wild beasts within me! Would that I could hew my way with an axe, through the midst of a multitude.... Ah, a poniard!...

He perceives his knife, and rushes to seize it. The knife slips from his hand; and Anthony remains leaning against the wall of his hut, with wide-open mouth, motionless, cataleptic. —

Everything about him has disappeared.

He thinks himself at Alexandria, upon the Paneum—an artificial moun-tain in the centre of the city, encircled by a winding stairway.

Before him lies Lake Mareotis; on his right hand is the sea, on his left the country; and immediately beneath him a vast confusion of flat roofs, traversed from north to south and from east to west by two streets which intercross, and which offer throughout their entire length the spectacle of files of porticoes with Corinthian columns. The houses overhanging this double colonnade have windows of stained glass. Some of them support exteriorly enormous wooden cages, into which the fresh air rushes from without.

Monuments of various architecture tower up in close proximity. Egyptian pylons dominate Greek temples. Obelisks appear like lances above battlements of red brick. In the middle of public squares there are figures of Hermes with pointed ears, and of Anubis with the head of a dog. Anthony can distinguish the mosaic pavements of the courtyards, and tapestries suspended from the beams of ceilings.

He beholds at one glance the two ports (the Great Port and the Eunostus), both round as circuses, and separated by a mole connecting Alexandria with the craggy island upon which the Pharos-tower rises—quadrangular, five hundred cubits high, nine storied, having at its summit a smoking heap of black coals.

Small interior ports open into the larger ones. The mole terminates at each end in a bridge supported upon marble columns planted in the sea. Sailing vessels pass beneath it, while heavy lighters overladen with merchandise, thalamegii* inlaid with ivory, gondolas covered with awnings, triremes, biremes, and all sorts of vessels are moving to and fro, or lie moored at the wharves.

About the Great Port extends an unbroken array of royal construction: the palace of the Ptolemies, the Museum, the Posidium, the Cæsareum, the Timonium where Mark Anthony sought refuge, the Soma which contains the tomb of Alexander; while at the other extremity of the city, beyond the Eunostus, the great glass factories, perfume factories, and papyrus factories may be perceived in a suburban quarter.

Strolling peddlers, porters, ass-drivers run and jostle together. Here and there one observes some priest of Osiris wearing a panther skin on his shoulders, a Roman soldier with his bronze helmet, and many negroes. At the thresholds of the shops women pause, artisans ply their trades; and the grinding noise of chariot wheels puts to flight the birds that devour the detritus of the butcher-shops and the morsels of fish left upon the ground.

The general outline of the streets seems like a black network flung upon the white uniformity of the houses. The markets stocked with herbs make green bouquets in the midst of it; the drying-yards of the dyers, blotches of color; the golden ornaments of the temple-pediments, luminous points—all comprised within the oval enclosure of the grey ramparts, under the vault of the blue heaven, beside the motionless sea.

But suddenly the movement of the crowd ceases; all turn their eyes toward the west, whence enormous whirlwinds of dust are seen approaching.

It is the coming of the monks of the Thebaid, all clad in goatskins, armed with cudgels, roaring a canticle of battle and of faith with the refrain:

"Where are they? Where are they?"

---

* *Thalamegii* (fr. Θάλαμος)—pleasure-boats having apartments.

Anthony understands that they are coming to kill the Arians.

The streets are suddenly emptied—only flying feet are visible.

The Solitaries are now in the city. Their formidable cudgels, studded with nails, whirl in the air like suns of steel. The crash of things broken in the houses is heard. There are intervals of silence. Then great screams arise.

From one end of the street to the other there is a continual eddy of terrified people.

Several are holding pikes. Sometimes two bands meet, rush into one; and this mass of men slips upon the pavement—separating, falling down. But the men with the long hair always reappear.

Threads of smoke begin to escape from the corners of edifices. Folding doors burst open. Portions of walls crumble down. Architraves fall.

Anthony finds all his enemies again, one after the other. He even recognizes some whom he had altogether forgotten; before killing them he outrages them. He disembowels—he severs throats—he fells as in a slaughter house—he hales old men by the beard, crushes children, smites the wounded. And vengeance is taken upon luxury, those who do not know how to read tear up books; others smash and deface the statues, paintings, furniture, caskets,—a thousand dainty things the use of which they do not know, and which simply for that reason exasperate them. At intervals they pause, out of breath, in the work of destruction; then they recommence.

The inhabitants moan in the courtyards where they have sought refuge. The women raise their tearful eyes and lift their naked arms to heaven. In hope of moving the Solitaries they embrace their knees; the men cast them off and fling them down, and the blood gushes to the ceilings, falls back upon the walls like sheets of rain, streams from the trunks of decapitated corpses, fills the aqueducts, forms huge red pools upon the ground.

Anthony is up to his knees in it. He wades in it; he sucks up the bloodspray on his lips; he is thrilled with joy as he feels it upon his limbs, under his hair-tunic which is soaked through with it.

Night comes. The immense uproar dies away.

The Solitaries have disappeared.

Suddenly, upon the outer galleries corresponding to each of the nine stories of the Pharos, Anthony observes thick black lines forming, like lines of crows perching. He hurries thither; and soon finds himself at the summit.

A huge mirror of brass, turned toward the open sea, reflects the forms of the vessels in the offing.

Anthony amuses himself by watching them; and while he watches, their number increases.

———

They are grouped together within a gulf which has the form of a crescent. Upon a promontory in the background towers a new city of Roman architecture, with cupolas of stone, conical roofs, gleams of pink and blue marbles, and a profusion of brazen ornamentation applied to the volutes of the capitals, to the angles of the cornices, to the summits of the edifices. A cypress-wood overhangs the city. The line of the sea is greener, the air colder. The mountains lining the horizon are capped with snow.

Anthony is trying to find his way, when a man approaches him and says:

"Come! they are waiting for you!"

He traverses a forum, enters a great court, stoops beneath a low door; and he arrives before the façade of the palace, decorated with a group in wax, representing Constantine overcoming a dragon. There is a porphyry basin, from the centre of which rises a golden conch-shell full of nuts. His guide tells him that he may take some of them. He does so.

Then he is lost, as it were, in a long succession of apartments.

There are mosaics upon the walls representing generals presenting the Emperor with conquered cities, which they hold out upon the palms of their hands. And there are columns of basalt everywhere, trellis-work in silver filagree, ivory chairs, tapestries embroidered with pearls. The light falls from the vaults above; Anthony still proceeds. Warm exhalations circulate about him; occasionally he hears the discreet clapping sound of sandals upon the pavement. Posted in the antechambers are guards, who resemble automata, holding wands of vermillion upon their shoulders.

At last he finds himself in a great hall, with hyacinth-colored curtains at the further end. They part, and display the Emperor seated on a throne, clad in a violet tunic, and wearing red shoes striped with bands of black.

A diadem of pearls surrounds his head; his locks are arranged symmetrically in rouleaux. He has a straight nose, drooping eyelids, a heavy and cun-

ning physiognomy. At the four corners of the dais stretched above his head are placed four golden doves; and at the foot of the throne are two lions in enamel crouching. The doves begin to sing, the lions to roar. The Emperor rolls his eyes; Anthony advances; and forthwith, without preamble, they commence to converse about recent events. In the cities of Antioch, Ephesus, and Alexandria, the temples have been sacked, and the statues of the gods converted into pots and cooking utensils; the Emperor laughs heartily about it. Anthony reproaches him with his tolerance toward the Novations. But the Emperor becomes vexed. Novations, Arians or Meletians—he is sick of them all! Nevertheless, he admires the episcopate; for inasmuch as the Christians maintain bishops, who depend for their position upon five or six important personages, it is only necessary to gain over the latter in order to have all the rest on one's side. Therefore he did not fail to furnish them with large sums. But he detests the Fathers of the Council of Nicæa—

"Let us go and see them!"

Anthony follows him.
And straightaway they find themselves on a terrace.
It overlooks a hippodrome thronged with people, and surmounted by porticoes where other spectators are walking to and fro. From the centre of the race-course rises a narrow platform, supporting a little temple of Mercury, the statue of Constantine, and three serpents of bronze twisted into a column; there are huge wooden eggs at one end, and at the other a group of seven dolphins with their tails in the air.
Behind the imperial pavilion sit the Prefects of the Chambers, the Counts of the Domestics, and the Patricians—in ranks rising by tiers to the first story of a church whose windows are thronged with women. On the right is the tribune of the Blue Faction; on the left, that of the Green; below, a picket of soldiers is stationed; and on a level with the arena is a row of Corinthian arches, forming the entrances to the stables.
The races are about to commence; the horses are drawn up in line. Lofty plumes, fastened between their ears, bend to the wind like saplings; and with every restive bound, they shake their chariots violently, which are shell-shaped, and conducted by charioteers clad in a sort of multi-colored

cuirass, having sleeves tight at the wrist and wide in the arms; their legs are bare, their beards full, their foreheads shaven after the manner of the Huns.

Anthony is at first deafened by the billowy sound of voices. From the summit of the hippodrome to its lowest tiers, he sees only faces painted with rouge, garments checkered and variegated with many colors, flashing jewelry; and the sand of the arena, all white, gleams like a mirror.

The Emperor entertains him. He confides to him many matters of high importance, many secrets; he confesses the assassination of his son Crispus, and even asks Anthony for advice regarding his health.

Meanwhile Anthony notices some slaves in the rear portion of the stables below. They are the Fathers of Nicæa, ragged and abject. The martyr Paphnutius is brushing the mane of one horse; Theophilus is washing the legs of another; John is painting the hoofs of a third; Alexander is collecting dung in a basket.

Anthony passes through the midst of them. They range themselves on either side respectfully; they beseech his intercession; they kiss his hands. The whole assemblage of spectators hoots at them; and he enjoys their degradation with immeasurable pleasure. Lo! he is now one of the grandees of the Court— the Emperor's confidant—the prime minister! Constantine places his own diadem upon his brows. Anthony allows it to remain upon his head, thinking this honor quite natural.

———

And suddenly in the midst of the darkness a vast hall appears, illuminated by golden candelabra.

Candles so lofty that they are half lost in the darkness stretch away in huge files beyond the lines of banquet-tables, which seem to extend to the horizon, where through a luminous haze loom superpositions of stairways, suites of arcades, colossi, towers, and beyond all a vague border of palace walls, above which rise the crests of cedars, making yet blacker masses of blackness against the darkness.

The guests, crowned with violet wreaths, recline upon very low couches and are leaning upon their elbows. Along the whole length of this double line of couches, wine is being poured out from amphoræ, and at the further end, all alone, coiffed with the tiara and blazing with carbuncles, King Nebuchadnezzar eats and drinks.

On his right and left, two rows of priests in pointed caps are swinging censers. On the pavement below crawl the captive kings whose hands and feet have been cut off; from time to time he flings them bones to gnaw. Further off sit his brothers, with bandages across their eyes, being all blind.

From the depths of the ergastula arise moans of ceaseless pain. Sweet slow sounds of a hydraulic organ alternate with choruses of song; and one feels that all about the palace without extends an immeasurable city—an ocean of human life whose waves break against the walls.

The slaves run hither and thither carrying dishes. Women walk between the ranks of guests, offering drinks to all; the baskets groan under their burthen of loaves; and a dromedary, laden with perforated water-skins, passes and repasses through the hall, sprinkling and cooling the pavement with vervain.

Beast-handlers are leading tamed lions about. Dancing girls—their hair confined in nets—balance themselves and turn upon their hands, emitting fire through their nostrils; negro boatmen are juggling; naked children pelt each other with pellets of snow, which burst against the bright silverware. There is an awful clamour as of a tempest; and a huge cloud hangs over the banquet—so numerous are the meats and breaths. Sometimes a flake of fire, torn from the great flambeaux by the wind, traverses the night like a shooting star.

The king wipes the perfumes from his face with his arm. He eats from the sacred vessels—then breaks them; and secretly reckons up the number of his fleets, his armies, and his subjects. By and by, for a new caprice, he will burn his palace with all its guests. He dreams of rebuilding the tower of Babel, and dethroning God.

Anthony, from afar off, reads all these thoughts upon his brow. They penetrate his own brain, and he becomes Nebuchadnezzar.

Immediately he is cloyed with orgiastic excesses, sated with fury of extermination; and a great desire comes upon him to wallow in vileness. For the degradation of that which terrifies men is an outrage inflicted upon their minds—it affords yet one more way to stupefy them; and as nothing is viler than a brute, Anthony goes upon the table on all fours, and bellows like a bull.

He feels a sudden pain in his hand—a pebble has accidentally wounded him—and he finds himself once more in front of his cabin.

The circle of the rocks is empty. The stars are glowing in the sky. All is hushed.

Again have I allowed myself to be deceived! Why these things? They come from the rebellion of the flesh. Ah! wretch!

He rushes into his cabin and seizes a bunch of thongs with metallic hooks attached to their ends, strips himself to the waist, and, lifting his eyes to heaven, exclaims:

Accept my penance, O my God: disdain it not for its feebleness. Render it sharp, prolonged, excessive! It is time, indeed!—to the work!

He gives himself a vigorous lash—and shrieks.

No! no!—without mercy it must be.

He recommences.

Oh! oh! oh! each lash tears my skin, rends my limbs! It burns me horribly!
Nay!—it is not so very terrible after all!—one becomes accustomed to it. It even seems to me....

Anthony pauses.

Continue, coward! continue! Good! good!—upon the arms, on the back, on the breast, on the belly—everywhere! Hiss, ye thongs! bite me! tear me! I would that my blood could spurt to the stars!—let my bones crack!—let my tendons be laid bare! O for pincers, racks, and melted lead! The martyrs have endured far worse; have they not, Ammonaria?

The shadow of the Devil's horns reappears.

I might have been bound to the column opposite to thine,—face to face—under thy eyes—answering thy shrieks by my sighs; and our pangs might have been interblended, our souls intermingled.

He lashes himself with fury.

What! what! again. Take that!—But how strange a titillation thrills me! What punishment! what pleasure! I feel as though receiving invisible kisses; the very marrow of my bones seems to melt! I die!

And he sees before him three cavaliers, mounted upon onagers, clad in robes of green—each holding a lily in his hand, and all resembling each other in feature.

Anthony turns round, and beholds three other cavaliers exactly similar, riding upon similar onagers, and preserving the same attitude.

He draws back. Then all the onagers advance one pace at the same time, and rub their noses against him, trying to bite his garment. Voices shout: "Here! here! this way!" *And between the clefts of the mountain, appear standards,—camels' heads with halters of red silk—mules laden with baggage, and women covered with yellow veils, bestriding piebald horses.*

The panting beasts lie down; the slaves rush to the bales and packages; motley-striped carpets are unrolled; precious glimmering things are laid upon the ground.

A white elephant, caparisoned with a golden net, trots forward, shaking the tuft of ostrich plumes attached to his head-band.

Upon his back, perched on cushions of blue wool, with her legs crossed, her eyes half closed, her comely head sleepily nodding, is a woman so splendidly clad that she radiates light about her. The crowd falls prostrate; the elephant bends his knees; and

THE QUEEN OF SHEBA
letting herself glide down from his shoulder upon the carpets spread to receive her, approaches Saint Anthony.

Her robe of gold brocade, regularly divided by furbelows of pearls, of jet, and of sapphires, sheaths her figure closely with its tight-fitting bodice, set off by colored designs representing the twelve signs of the Zodiac. She wears very high patterns—one of which is black, and sprinkled with silver stars, with a moon crescent; the other, which is white, is sprinkled with a spray of gold, with a golden sun in the middle.

Her wide sleeves, decorated with emeralds and bird-plumes, leave exposed her little round bare arms, clasped at the wrist by ebony bracelets; and her hands, loaded with precious rings, are terminated by nails so sharply pointed that the ends of her fingers seem almost like needles.

A chain of dead gold, passing under her chin, is caught up on either side of her face, and spirally coiled about her blue-powdered coiffure, whence, redescending, it grazes her shoulders and is attached upon her bosom to a diamond scorpion, which protrudes a jewelled tongue between her breasts. Two immense blond pearls depend heavily from her ears. The borders of her eyelids are painted black. There is a natural brown spot upon her left cheek; and she opens her mouth in breathing, as if her corset inconvenienced her.

She shakes, as she approaches, a green parasol with an ivory handle, and silver-gilt bells attached to its rim; twelve little woolly-haired negro-boys support the long train of her robe, whereof an ape holds the extremity, which it raises up from time to time.

She exclaims:

Ah! handsome hermit! handsome hermit!—my heart swoons!

By dint of stamping upon the ground with impatience, callosities have formed upon my heel, and I have broken one of my nails! I sent out shepherds, who remained upon the mountain tops, shading their eyes with their hands—and hunters who shouted thy name in all the forests—and spies who travelled along the highways, asking every passer-by: "Hast thou seen him?"

By night I wept, with my face turned to the wall. And at last my tears made two little holes in the mosaic, like two pools of water among the rocks;—for I love thee!—oh! how I love thee!

She takes him by the beard.

Laugh now, handsome hermit! laugh! I am very joyous, very gay; thou shalt soon see! I play the lyre; I dance like a bee; and I know a host of merry tales to tell, each more diverting than the other. Thou canst not even imagine how mighty a journey we have made. See! the onagers upon which the green couriers rode are dead with fatigue!

The onagers are lying motionless upon the ground.

For three long moons they never ceased to gallop on with the same equal pace, holding flints between their teeth to cut the wind, their tails ever streaming out behind them, their sinews perpetually strained to the uttermost, always galloping, galloping. Never can others be found like them! They were bequeathed me by my maternal grandfather, the Emperor Saharil, son of Iakhschab, son of Iaarab, son of Kastan. Ah! if they were still alive, we should harness them to a litter that they might bear us back speedily to the palace! But... what ails thee?—of what art thou dreaming?

She stares at him, examines him closely.

Ah, when thou shalt be my husband, I will robe thee, I will perfume thee, I will depilate thee.

Anthony remains motionless, more rigid than a stake, more pallid than a corpse.

Thou hast a sad look—is it because of leaving thy hermitage? Yet I have left everything for thee—even King Solomon, who, nevertheless, possesses much wisdom, twenty thousand chariots of war, and a beautiful beard! I have brought thee my wedding gifts. Choose.

She walks to and fro among the ranks of slaves and the piles of precious goods.

Here is Genezareth balm, incense from Cape Gardefui, labdanum, cinnamon, and silphium—good to mingle with sauces. In that bale are Assyrian embroideries, ivory from the Ganges, purple from Elissa; and that box of snow contains a skin of chalybon, the wine which is reserved for the Kings of Assyria, and which is drunk pure from the horn of a unicorn. Here are necklaces, brooches, nets for the hair, parasols, gold powder from Baasa, cassiteria from Tartessus, blue wood from Pandio, white furs from Issedonia, carbuncles from the Island Palæsimondus, and toothpicks made of the bristles of the tachas—that lost animal which is found under the earth. These cushions come from Emath, and these mantle-fringes from Palmyra. On this Babylonian carpet there is... But come hither! come! come!

She pulls Saint Anthony by the sleeve. He resists. She continues:

This thin tissue, which crackles under the finger with a sound as of sparks, is the famous yellow cloth which the merchants of Bactria bring us. They have need of forty-three translators for their voyage. I will have robes made of it for thee, which thou shalt wear in the house.

Unfasten the hooks of that sycamore box, and hand me also the little ivory casket tied to my elephant's shoulder!

They take something round out of a box—something covered with a veil—and also bring a little ivory casket covered with carving.

Dost thou desire the buckler of Dgian-ben-Dgian, who built the pyramids?—behold it!—It is formed of seven dragon-skins laid one over the other, fastened together by adamantine screws and tanned in the bile of parricides. Upon one side are represented all the wars that have taken place since the invention of weapons; and upon the other, all the wars that will take place until the end of the world. The lightning itself rebounds from it like a ball of cork. I am going to place it upon thy arm; and thou wilt carry it during the chase.

But if thou didst only know what I have in this little box of mine! Turn it over and over again! try to open it! No one could ever succeed in doing that. Kiss me; I will tell thee how to open it.

She takes Saint Anthony by both cheeks. He pushes her away at arms' length.

It was one night that King Solomon lost his head. At last we concluded a bargain. He arose, and stealing out on tiptoe ...

She suddenly executes a pirouette.

Ah, ah! comely hermit, thou shalt not know it! thou shalt not know!

She shakes her parasol, making all its little bells tinkle.

And I possess many other strange things—oh! yes! I have treasures concealed in winding galleries where one would lose one's way, as in a forest. I have summer-palaces constructed in trelliswork of reeds, and winter-palaces all built of black marble. In the midst of lakes vast as seas, I have islands round as pieces of silver, and all covered with mother-of-pearl,—islands whose shores make music to the lapping of tepid waves upon the sand. The slaves of my kitchens catch birds in my aviaries, and fish in my fishponds. I have engravers continually seated at their benches to hollow out my likeness in hard jewel-stones, and panting molders forever casting statues of me, and perfumers incessantly mingling the sap of rare plants with vinegar, or preparing cosmetic pastes. I have female dressmakers cutting out patterns in richest material, goldsmiths cutting and mounting jewels of price, and careful painters pouring upon my palace wainscoting boiling resins, which they subsequently cool with fans. I have enough female attendants to form a harem, eunuchs enough to make an army. I have armies likewise; I have nations! In the vestibule of my palace I keep a guard of dwarfs—all bearing ivory trumpets at their backs.

Anthony sighs.

I have teams of trained gazelles; I have elephant quadrigæ; I have hundreds of pairs of camels, and mares whose manes are so long that their hoofs become entangled therein when they gallop, and herds of cattle with horns so broad that when they go forth to graze the woods have to be hewn down before them. I have giraffes wandering in my gardens; they stretch their heads over the edge of my roof, when I take the air after dinner.

Seated in a shell drawn over the waters by dolphins, I travel through the grottoes, listening to the dropping of the water from the stalactites. I go down to the land of diamonds, where my friends the magicians allow me to choose the finest: then I reascend to earth and return to my home.

She utters a sharp whistle; and a great bird, descending from the sky, alights upon her hair, from which it makes the blue powder fall.

Its orange-colored plumage seems formed of metallic scales. Its little head, crested with a silver tuft, has a human face. It has four wings, the feet of a vulture, and an immense peacock's tail which it spreads open like a fan.

It seizes the Queen's parasol in its beak, reels a moment ere obtaining its balance; then it erects all its plumes, and remains motionless.

Thanks! my beautiful Simorg-Anka!—thou didst tell me where the loving one was hiding! Thanks! thanks! my heart's messenger! He flies swiftly as Desire! He circles the world in his flight. At eve he returns; he perches at the foot of my couch and tells me all he has seen—the seas that have passed far beneath him with all their fishes and ships, the great void deserts he has contemplated from the heights of the sky, the harvests that were bowing in the plains, and the plants that were growing upon the walls of cities abandoned.

She wrings her hands, languorously.

Oh! if thou wast willing! if thou wast willing!... I have a pavilion on a promontory in the middle of an isthmus dividing two oceans. It is all wainscoted with sheets of glass, and floored with tortoise shell, and open to the four winds of heaven. From its height I watch my fleets come in, and my nations toiling up the mountain-slopes with burthens upon their shoulders. There would we sleep upon downs softer than clouds; we would drink cool draughts from fruit-shells, and we would gaze at the sun through emeralds! Come!...

Anthony draws back. She approaches him again, and exclaims in a tone of vexation:

How? neither the rich, nor the coquettish, nor the amorous woman can charm thee: is it so? None but a lascivious woman, with a hoarse voice and lusty person, with fire-colored hair and superabundant flesh? Dost thou prefer a body cold as the skin of a serpent, or rather great dark eyes deeper than the mystic caverns?—behold them, my eyes!—look into them!

Anthony, in spite of him, gazes into her eyes.

All the women thou hast ever met—from the leman of the cross-roads, singing under the light of her lantern, even to the patrician lady scattering rose-petals abroad from her litter,—all the forms thou hast ever obtained glimpses of—all the imaginations of thy desire thou hast only to ask for them! I am not a woman: I am a world. My cloak has only to fall in order that thou mayest discover a succession of mysteries!

Anthony's teeth chatter.

Place but thy finger upon my shoulder: it will be as though a stream of fire shot through all thy veins. The possession of the least part of me will fill thee with a joy more vehement than the conquest of an Empire could give thee. Approach thy lips: there is a sweetness in my kisses as of a fruit dissolving within thy heart! Ah! how thou wilt lose thyself beneath my long hair, inhale the perfume of my bosom, madden thyself with the beauty of my limbs: and thus, consumed by the fire of my eyes, clasped within my arms as in a whirlwind ...

Anthony makes the sign of the cross.

Thou disdainest me! farewell!

She departs, weeping; then, suddenly turning round:

Art quite sure?—so beautiful a woman!

She laughs, and the ape that bears her train lifts it up.

Thou wilt regret it, my comely hermit! thou wilt yet weep! thou wilt again feel weary of thy life; but I care not a whit! La! la! la!—oh! oh! oh!

She takes her departure, hopping upon one foot and covering her face with her hands.
All the slaves file off before Saint Anthony—the horses, the dromedaries, the elephant, the female attendants, the mules (which have been reloaded), the negro boys, the ape, the green couriers each holding his broken lily in his hand; and the Queen of Sheba departs, uttering a convulsive hiccough at intervals, which might be taken either for a sound of hysterical sobbing, or the half-suppressed laughter of mockery.

III

When she has disappeared, ANTHONY *observes a child seated upon the threshold of his cabin.*

It is one of the Queen's servants, no doubt,

he thinks.
This child is small like a dwarf, and nevertheless squat of build, like one of the Cabiri; deformed withal, and wretched of aspect. His prodigiously large head is covered with white hair; and he shivers under a shabby tunic, all the while clutching a roll of papyrus. The light of the moon passing through a cloud falls upon him. Anthony watches him from a distance, and is afraid of him.

Who art thou?

THE CHILD

replies:
Thy ancient disciple, Hilarion.

ANTHONY

Thou liest! Hilarion hath been dwelling in Palestine for many long years.

HILARION

I have returned! It is really I!

ANTHONY

draws near and examines him closely.

Yet his face was radiant as the dawn, candid, joyous. This face is the face of one gloomy and old.

HILARION

Long and arduous labor hath wearied me!

ANTHONY

The voice is also different. It hath an icy tone.

HILARION

Because I have nourished me with bitter things!

ANTHONY

And those white hairs?

HILARION

I have endured many woes!

ANTHONY

aside:

Could it be possible?

HILARION

I was not so far from thee as thou dost imagine. The hermit Paul visited thee this year, during the month of Schebar. It is just twenty days since the Nomads brought thee bread. Thou didst tell a sailor, the day before yesterday, to send thee three bodkins.

ANTHONY

He knows all!

HILARION

Know furthermore that I have never left thee. But there are long periods during which thou hast no knowledge of my presence.

ANTHONY

How can that be? Yet it is true that my head is so much troubled—this night especially ...

HILARION

All the Capital Sins came hither. But their wretched snares can avail nothing against such a Saint as thou!

ANTHONY

Oh! no!—no! I fall at every moment! Why am I not of those whose souls are ever intrepid, whose minds are always firm,—for example, the great Athanasius?

HILARION

He was illegally ordained by seven bishops!

ANTHONY

What matter if his virtue! ...

HILARION

Go to!—a most vainglorious and cruel man, forever involved in intrigues, and exiled at last as a monopolist.*

---

* Gibbon, a sincere admirer of Athanasius, gives a curious history of these charges, and expresses his disbelief in their truth. The story regarding the design to intercept the corn-fleet of Alexandria is referred to in the use of the word "monopolist."

ANTHONY

Calumny!

HILARION

Thou wilt not deny that he sought to corrupt Eustates, the treasurer of largesses?

ANTHONY

It is affirmed, I acknowledge.

HILARION

Through vengeance he burned down the house of Arsenius!

ANTHONY

Alas!

HILARION

At the council of Nicæa he said in speaking of Jesus: "The man of the Lord."

ANTHONY

Ah! that is a blasphemy!

HILARION

So limited in understanding, moreover, that he confesses he comprehends nothing of the nature of the Word!

ANTHONY

smiling with gratification:
In sooth his intelligence is not ... very lofty.

HILARION

Should you have been placed in his stead, it would have been a great joy for your brethren, as for you. This lonely life of yours is bad.

ANTHONY

On the contrary! Being spirit, Man must retreat from material things. All action is degrading. I would have no contact with the earth,—the soles of my feet notwithstanding!

HILARION

Hypocrite! burying thyself in solitude only in order the more fully to abandon thyself to the indulgence of thy envious desires! What if thou dost deprive thyself of meats, of wine, of warmth, of bath, of slaves, or honours?—dost thou not permit thy imagination to offer thee banquets, perfumes, naked women, and the applause of multitudes? Thy chastity is but a more subtle form of corruption, and thy contempt of this world is but the impotence of thy hatred against it! Either this it is that makes such as thyself so lugubrious, or else 'tis doubt. The possession of truth giveth joy. Was Jesus sad? Did he not travel in the company of friends, repose beneath the shade of olive trees, enter the house of the publican, drink many cups of wine, pardon the sinning woman, and assuage all sorrows? Thou, thou hast no pity save for thine own misery. It is like a remorse that gnaws thee, a savage madness that impels thee to repel the caress of a dog or to frown upon the smile of a child.

ANTHONY

bursting into tears.

Enough! enough! thou dost wound my heart deeply.

HILARION

Shake the vermin from thy rags! Rise up from thy filth! Thy God is not a Moloch who demands human flesh in sacrifice!

ANTHONY

Yet suffering is blessed. The cherubim stoop to receive the blood of confessors.

HILARION

Admire, then, the Montanists!—they surpass all others.

ANTHONY

But it is the truth of the doctrine which makes the martyrdom.

HILARION

How can martyrdom prove the excellence of the doctrine, inasmuch as it bears equal witness for error?

ANTHONY

Silence!—thou viper!

HILARION

Perhaps martyrdom is not so difficult as thou dost imagine. The exhortations of friends, the pleasure of insulting the people, the oath one has taken, a certain dizzy excitement, a thousand circumstances all aid the resolution of the martyrs....

Anthony turns his back upon Hilarion and moves away from him. Hilarion follows him.

Moreover this manner of dying often brings about great disorders. Dionysius, Cyprian and Gregory fled from it. Peter of Alexandria has condemned it; and the council of Elvira....

ANTHONY

stops his ears.
I will listen to thee no longer!

HILARION

raising his voice:
Lo! thou fallest again into thy habitual sin, which is sloth. Ignorance is the foam of pride. One says, forsooth:—"My conviction is

formed! wherefore argue further?"—and one despises the doctors, the philosophers, tradition itself, and even the text of the Law whereof one is ignorant. Dost thou imagine that thou dost hold all wisdom in the hollow of thy hand?

ANTHONY

I hear him still! His loud words fill my brain.

HILARION

The efforts of others to comprehend God are mightier than all thy mortifications to move Him. We obtain merit only by our thirst for Truth. Religion alone cannot explain all things; and the solution of problems ignored by thee can render faith still more invulnerable and noble. Therefore, for our salvation we must communicate with our brethren—otherwise the Church, the assembly of the faithful, would be a meaningless word—and we must listen to all reasoning, despising nothing, nor any person. The magician Balaam, the poet Æschylus, and the Sybil of Cumæ—all foretold the Saviour. Dionysius, the Alexandrian, received from heaven the command to read all books. Saint Clement orders us to cultivate Greek letters. Hermas was converted by the illusion of a woman he had loved.

ANTHONY

What an aspect of authority! It seems to me thou art growing taller ...

And, in very truth, the stature of Hilarion is gradually increasing; and Anthony shuts his eyes, that he may not see him.

HILARION

Reassure thyself, good Hermit!

Let us seat ourselves there, upon that great stone, as we used to do in other years, when, at the first dawn of day, I was wont to salute thee with the appellation "Clear star of morning"—and thou wouldst therewith commence to instruct me. Yet my instruction is not yet completed. The moon gives us light enough. I am prepared to hear thy words.

He has drawn a calamus from his girdle, and seating himself cross-legged upon the ground, with the papyrus roll still in his hand, he lifts his face toward Saint Anthony, who sits near him, with head bowed down.
After a moment of silence Hilarion continues:

Is not the word of God confirmed for us by miracles? Nevertheless the magicians of Pharaoh performed miracles; other imposters can perform them; one may be thereby deceived. What then is a miracle? An event which seems to us outside of nature. But do we indeed know all of Nature's powers; and because a common occurrence causes us no astonishment, does it therefore follow that we understand it?

ANTHONY
It matters little! We must believe the Scriptures!

HILARION
Saint Paul, Origen, and many others did not understand the Scriptures in a literal sense: yet if Holy Writ be explained by allegories it becomes the portion of a small number, and the evidence of the truth disappears. What must we do?

ANTHONY
We must rely upon the Church!

HILARION
Then the Scriptures are useless?

ANTHONY
No! no! although I acknowledge that in the Old Testament there are some ... some obscurities ... But the New shines with purest light.

HILARION

Nevertheless, the Angel of the annunciation, in Matthew, appears to Joseph; while, in Luke, he appears to Mary. The anointing of Jesus by a woman takes place, according to the first Gospel, at the commencement of his public life; and, according to the other three, a few days before his death. The drink offered to him on the cross, is, in Matthew, vinegar mixed with gall; in Mark, it is wine and myrrh. According to Luke and Matthew, the apostles should take with them neither money nor scrip for their journey—not even sandals nor staff; in Mark, on the contrary, Jesus bids them take nothing with them, except sandals and a staff. I am thereby bewildered!...

ANTHONY

in amazement:

Aye, indeed!...in fact...

HILARION

At the contact of the woman who had an issue of blood, Jesus turned and said: "Who hath touched my garments?" He did not know, then, who had touched him? That contradicts the omniscience of Jesus. If the tomb was watched by guards, the women need have felt no anxiety about finding help to roll away the stone from the tomb. Therefore there were no guards, or the holy women were not there. At Emmaus, he eats with his disciples and makes them feel his wounds. It is a human body, a material and ponderable object; and nevertheless it passes through walls. Is that possible?

ANTHONY

It would require much time to answer thee properly!

HILARION

Why did he receive the Holy Spirit, being himself Son of the Holy Spirit? What need had he of baptism if he was the Word? How could the Devil have tempted him, inasmuch as he was God?

Have these thoughts never occurred to thee?

ANTHONY

Yes!... often! Sometimes torpid, sometimes furious—they remain forever in my conscience. I crush them; they rise again, they stifle me; and sometimes I think that I am accursed.

HILARION

Then it is needless for thee to serve God?

ANTHONY

I shall always need to adore Him!

After a long silence

HILARION

continues:

But aside from dogma, all researches are allowed us. Dost thou desire to know the hierarchy of the Angels, the virtue of the Numbers, the reason of germs and of metamorphoses?

ANTHONY

Yes! yes! my thought struggles wildly to escape from its prison. It seems to me that by exerting all my force I might succeed. Sometimes, for an instant, brief as a lightning flash, I even feel myself as thought uplifted,—then I fall back again!

HILARION

The secret thou wouldst obtain is guarded by sages. They dwell in a distant land; they are seated beneath giant trees; they are robed in white; they are calm as Gods. A warm air gives them sufficient nourishment. All about them, leopards tread upon grassy turf. The murmuring of fountains and the neighing of unicorns mingle with their voices. Thou shalt hear them; and the face of the Unknown shall be unveiled!

ANTHONY

sighing:
>   The way is long; and I am old.

HILARION

>   Oh! oh! wise men are not rare! there are some even very nigh thee!—here! Let us enter!

IV

And Anthony beholds before him a vast basilica.

The light gushes from the further end, marvellous as a multi-colored sun. It illuminates the innumerable heads of the crowd that fills the nave, and that eddies about the columns toward the side-aisles—where can be perceived, in wooden compartments, altars, beds, little chains of blue stones linked together, and constellations painted upon the walls.

In the midst of the throng there are groups which remain motionless. Men standing upon stools harangue with fingers uplifted; others are praying, with arms outstretched in form of a cross; others are lying prostrate upon the pavement, or singing hymns, or drinking wine; others of the faithful, seated about a table, celebrate their agape;* martyrs are unbandaging their limbs in order to show their wounds; and aged men, leaning upon staffs, recount their voyages.

There are some from the country of the Germans, from Thrace also, and from the Gauls, from Scythia and from the Indies, with snow upon their beards, feathers in their hair, thorns in the fringe of their garments, their

---

* Agape.—Love-feast of the primitive Christians.

sandals black with dust, their skin burnt by the sun. There is a vast confusion of costumes, mantles of purple and robes of linen, embroidered dalmaticas, hair shirts, sailors' caps, bishops' mitres. Their eyes fulgurate strangely. They have the look of executioners, or the look of eunuchs.

Hilarion advances into their midst. All salute him. Anthony, shrinking closer to his shoulder, observes them. He remarks the presence of a great many women. Some of these are attired like men, and have their hair cut short. Anthony feels afraid of them.

HILARION

Those are Christian women who have converted their husbands. Besides, the women were always upon the side of Jesus, even the idolatrous ones, for example, Procula, the wife of Pilate, and Poppæa, the concubine of Nero. Do not tremble!—come on!

And others are continually arriving.

They seem to multiply, to double themselves by self-division, light as shadows—all the while making an immense clamour, in which yells of rage, cries of love, canticles and objurgations intermingle.

ANTHONY

in a low voice:

What do they desire?

HILARION

The Lord said: "I have yet many things to say to you."* They possess the knowledge of those things.

And he pushes Anthony forward to a golden throne approached by five steps, whereon—surrounded by ninety-five disciples, all very thin and pale, and anointed with oil—sits the prophet Manes. He is beautiful as an archangel, immobile as a statue; he is clad in an Indian robe; carbuncles

---

* John xvi: 12.

gleam in his plaited hair; at his left hand lies a book of painted images; his right reposes upon a globe. The images represent the creatures that erst slumbered in Chaos. Anthony bends forward to look upon them. Then,

MANES

makes his globe revolve; and regulating the tone of his words by a lyre which gives forth crystalline sounds, exclaims:

The celestial earth is at the superior extremity; the terrestrial earth at the inferior extremity. It is sustained by two angels—the Angel Splenditeneus, and Omophorus, whose faces are six.

At the summit of the highest heaven reigns the impassible Divinity; below, face to face, are the Son of God and the Prince of Darkness.

When the darkness had advanced even to his kingdom, God evolved from his own essence a virtue which produced the first man; and he environed him with the five elements.[4] But the demons of darkness stole from him a part; and that part is the soul.

There is but one soul, universally diffused, even as the waters of a river divided into many branches. It is this universal soul that sighs in the wind—that shrieks in the marble under the teeth of the saw—that roars in the voice of the sea—that weeps tears of milk when the leaves of the fig tree are torn off.

The souls that leave this world emigrate to the stars, which are themselves animated beings.

ANTHONY

bursts into a laugh:
Ah! ah! what an absurd imagination!

A MAN

having no beard, and of a most austere aspect:
Wherefore absurd?

Anthony is about to reply when Hilarion tells him in a low voice that the questioner is none other than the tremendous Origen himself; and:

MANES

continues:

But first they remain awhile in the Moon, where they are purified. Then they rise into the sun.

ANTHONY

slowly:

I do not know of anything ... which prevents us ... from believing it.

MANES

The proper aim of every creature is the deliverance of the ray of celestial light imprisoned within matter. It finds easier escape through the medium of perfumes, spices, the aroma of warmed wine, the light things which resemble thoughts. But the acts of life retain it within its prison. The murderer shall be born again in the form of a celephus; he that kills an animal shall become that animal; if thou plantest a vine, thou shalt be thyself bound within its boughs. Food absorbs the celestial light. Therefore abstain! fast!

HILARION

Thou seest, they are temperate!

MANES

There is much of it in meats, less of it in herbs. Moreover the Pure Ones, by means of their great merits, despoil vegetation of this luminous essence; and, thus liberated, it reascends to its source. But through generation, animals keep it imprisoned within the flesh. Therefore, avoid women!

HILARION

Admire their continence!

MANES

Or rather contrive that the women shall not be fecund.—Better is it for the soul to fall on the ground than languish in fleshy shackles!

ANTHONY

Oh—abomination!

HILARION

What signifies the hierarchy of turpitudes? The Church has, forsooth, made marriage a sacrament!

SATURNINUS

in Syrian costume:

He teaches a most dismal system of the universe! The Father, desiring to punish the angels who had revolted, ordered them to create the world. Christ came, in order that the God of the Jews, who was one of those angels ...

ANTHONY

He an angel? the Creator?

CERDO

Did he not seek to kill Moses, to deceive his own prophets, to seduce nations?—did he not sow falsehood and idolatry broadcast?

MARCION

Certainly, the Creator is not the true God!

SAINT CLEMENT OF ALEXANDRIA

Matter is eternal!

BARDESANES

in the costume of the Babylonian magi:

It was formed by the Seven Planetary Spirits.

THE HERMIANS

Souls were made by the angels!

THE PRISCILLIANISTS

It was the Devil who made the world!

ANTHONY

rushing back from the circle:
Horror!

HILARION

supporting him:
Thou despairest too hastily!—thou dost misapprehend their doctrine! Here is one who received his teaching directly from Theodas, the friend of St. Paul. Hearken to him!

And at a sign from Hilarion

VALENTINUS

appears in a tunic of cloth of silver; his skull is pointed at its summit; his voice has a wheezing sound:
The world is the work of a God in delirium!

ANTHONY

bending his head down:
The work of a God in delirium!...

After a long silence:

How can that be?

VALENTINUS

The most perfect of beings, and of the Æons, the Abyss, dwelt in the bosom of the Deep together with Thought. By their union was begotten Intelligence, to whom Truth was given as a companion.

Intelligence and Truth engendered the Word and Life, who in their turn begat Man and the Church; and that doth make eight Æons!

He counts upon his fingers.

The Word and Truth also produced ten other Æons—which is to say, five couples. Man and the Church had begotten twelve more—among these the Paraclete and Faith, Hope and Charity, Perfection and Wisdom—Sophia.

The union of these thirty Æons constitutes the Pleroma, or Universality of God. Thus, even as the echo of a passing voice, as the effluvia of a perfume evaporating, as the fires of the setting sun, the Powers that emanated from the Principle, forever continue to grow weaker.

But Sophia, desirous to know the Father, darted from the Pleroma; and the Word then made another couple, Christ and the Holy Ghost, who reunited all the Æons; and all together formed Jesus, the flower of the Pleroma.

But the effort of Sophia to flee away had left in the void an image of her—an evil substance, Acharamoth.* The Saviour took pity upon her, freed her from all passion; and from the smile of Acharamoth redeemed, light was born; her tears formed the waters; by her sorrow was dark matter begotten.

Of Acharamoth was born the Demiurgos—the fabricator of worlds, the creator of the heaven and of the Devil. He dwells far below the Pleroma—so far that he cannot behold it—so that he deems himself to be the true God, and repeats by the mouths of his prophets—"There is no other God but I." Then he made man, and instilled into his soul the immaterial Seed which was the Church— a reflection of the other Church established in the Pleroma.

---

* Masheim gives *Achamoth*. I prefer to remain faithful to the orthography given by Flaubert.

One day Acharamoth shall reach the highest region and unite herself with the Saviour; the fire that is hidden in the world shall annihilate all matter, and shall even devour itself and men, becoming pure spirits, shall espouse the angels!

ORIGEN

Then shall the Demon be overthrown and the reign of God commence!

Anthony supresses a cry, and forthwith

BASILIDES
taking him by the elbow, exclaims:

The Supreme Being with all the infinite emanations is called Abraxas; and the Saviour with all his virtues, Kaulakau—otherwise, line-upon-line, rectitude upon rectitude.

The power of Kaulakau is obtained by the aid of certain words, which are inscribed upon this chalcedony to help the memory.

And he points to a little stone suspended at his neck, upon which stone fantastic characters are graven.

Then thou wilt be transported into the Invisible; and placed above all law, thou shalt contemn all things—even virtue!

We, the Pure, must flee from pain, after the example of Kaulakau.

ANTHONY

What! and the cross?

THE ELKHESAITES
in robes of hyacinth answer him:

The woe and the degradation, the condemnation and oppression of my fathers* are blotted out, through the mission which has come!

---

* The French text gives *mes pères,* not *nos pères.* Elxai, or Elkhai, who established his sect in the reign of Trajan, was a Jew.

One may deny the inferior Christ, the man-Jesus; but the other Christ must be adored—whose personality was evolved under the brooding of the Dove's wings.

Honor marriage! The Holy Spirit is feminine!

Hilarion has disappeared; and Anthony, carried along by the crowd, arrives in the presence of

THE CARPOCRATIANS

reclining with women upon scarlet cushions:

Before entering into the Only thou shalt pass through a series of conditions and of actions. To free thyself from the powers of darkness, thou must at once accomplish their works! The husband shall say to the wife: "Have charity for thy brother"—and she will kiss thee.

THE NICOLAITANS

gathered about a mass of smoking meats:

This is a portion of the meat offered to idols;—partake of it! Apostasy is permissible when the heart is pure. Gorge thy flesh with all that it demands. Seek to exterminate it by dint of debauchery! Prounikos, the Mother of Heaven, wallowed in ignominies.

THE MARCOSIANS

wearing rings of gold, and glistening with precious balm and unguents:

Enter among us that thou mayst unite thyself to the Spirit! Enter among us that thou mayst quaff the draught of immortality!

And one of them shows him, behind a tapestry-hanging, the body of a man terminated by the head of an ass. This represents Sabaoth, father of the Devil. He spits upon the image in token of detestation.

Another shows him a very low bed, strewn with flowers, exclaiming:

The spiritual marriage is about to be consummated.

A third, who holds a cup of glass, utters an invocation;—blood suddenly appears in the cup:

Ah! behold it! behold it!—the blood of Christ!

Anthony withdraws, but finds himself bespattered by water splashed from a cistern.

THE HELVIDIANS
are flinging themselves into it head foremost, muttering:
The man regenerated by baptism is impeccable!

Then he passes by a great fire at which the Adamites are warming themselves—all completely naked in imitation of the purity of Paradise; and he stumbles over

THE MESSALINES
wallowing upon the pavement, half-slumbering, stupid:
Oh! crush us if thou wilt! we shall not move! Work is crime; all occupation is evil.

Behind these, the abject

PATERNIANS
men, women, and children lying pell mell upon a heap of filth, lift their hideous faces, wine-besmeared, and they cry aloud:
The inferior parts of the body, which were created by the Devil, belong to him! Let us eat, drink, and fornicate!

ÆTIUS
Crimes are necessities beneath the notice of God!

But suddenly

A MAN

clad in a Carthaginian mantle, bounds into their midst, brandishing a scourge of thongs in his hand; and strikes violently and indiscriminately at all in his path:

Ah! imposters! brigands, simonists, heretics and demons!—vermin of the schools!—dregs of hell! Marcion, there, is a sailor of Sinopus excommunicated for incest;—Carpocrates was banished for being a magician; Ætius stole his concubine; Nicholas prostituted his wife; and this Manes, who calls himself the Buddha, and whose real name is Cubricus, was flayed alive with the point of a reed, so that his skin even now hangs at the gates of Ctesiphon!

ANTHONY

recognizing Tertullian, rushes to join him:

Master! help! help!

TERTULLIAN

continuing:

Break the images! veil the virgins! Pray, fast, weep and mortify yourselves! No philosophy! no books! After Jesus, science is useless!

All have fled away; and Anthony beholds, in lieu of Tertullian, a woman seated upon a bench of stone.

She sobs, leaning her head against a column; her hair is loose; her body, weakened by grief, is clad in a long brown simar. Then they find themselves face to face and alone, far from the crowd; and a silence, an extraordinary stillness falls—as in the woods when the winds are lulled, and the leaves of the trees suddenly cease to whisper.

This woman is still very beautiful, although faded, and pale as a sepulchre. They look at one another; and their eyes send to each other waves, as it were, of thoughts, bearing drift of a thousand ancient things, confused, mysterious. At last—

PRISCILLA

speaks:

I was in the last chamber of the baths; and the rumbling sounds of the street caused a sleep to fall upon me.

Suddenly I heard a clamour of voices. Men were shouting: "It is a magician!—it is the Devil!" And the crowd stopped before our house, in front of the Temple Æsculapius. I drew myself up with my hands to the little window.

Upon the peristyle of the temple, there stood a man who wore about his neck a collar of iron. He took burning coals out of a chafing-dish, and with them drew lines across his breast, the while crying out: "Jesus! Jesus!" The people shouted: "This is not lawful! let us stone him!" But he continued. Oh! those were unheard of marvels—things which transported men who beheld them. Flowers broad as suns circled before my eyes, and I heard in the spaces above me the vibrations of a golden harp. Day died. My hands loosened their grasp of the window-bars; my body fell back, and when he had led me away to his house ...

ANTHONY

But of whom art thou speaking?

PRISCILLA

Why, of Montanus!

ANTHONY

Montanus is dead!

PRISCILLA

It is not true!

A VOICE

No, Montanus is not dead!

Anthony turns; and sees upon the bench near him, on the opposite side, another woman sitting; she is fair, and even paler than the other; there are swellings under her eyes, as though she had wept a long time. She speaks without being questioned:

MAXIMILLA

We were returning from Tarsus by way of the mountains, when, at a turn in the road, we saw a man under a fig tree.

He cried from afar off: "Stop! stop!" and rushed toward us, uttering words of abuse. The slaves ran up; he burst into a loud laugh. The horses reared; the molossi all barked.

He stood before us. The sweat streamed from his forehead; his mantle flapped in the wind.

And calling us each by our names, he reproached us with the vanity of our work, the infamy of our bodies; and he shook his fist at the dromedaries because of the silver bells hanging below their mouths.

His fury now filled my very entrails with fear and yet there was a strange pleasure in it which fascinated me, intoxicated me.

First the slaves came. "Master," they said, "our animals are weary." Then the women said, "We are frightened," and the slaves departed. Then the children began to weep,—"We are hungry!" And as the women were not answered, they disappeared also from our view.

He still spoke. I felt some one near me. It was my husband; but I listened only to the other. My husband crawled to me upon his knees among the stones, and cried—"Dost thou abandon me," and I replied: "Yes! go thy way!" that I might accompany Montanus.

ANTHONY

A eunuch!

PRISCILLA

Ah! does that astound thee, vulgar soul! Yet Magdalen, Johanna, Martha and Susannah did not share the couch of the Saviour. Souls may know the delirium of embrace better than bodies. That he might keep Eustolia with impunity, the bishop Leontius mutilated himself—loving his love more than his virility. And then, it was no fault of mine. Sotas could not cure me; a spirit constrained me. It is cruel, nevertheless! But what matter? I am the last of the prophetesses; and after me the end of the world shall come.

MAXIMILLA

He showered his gifts upon me. Moreover, no one loves him as I, nor is any other so well beloved by him!

PRISCILLA

Thou liest! I am the most beloved!

MAXIMILLA

No: it is I!

They fight. Between their shoulders suddenly appears the head of a negro.

MONTANUS
clad in a black mantle, clasped by two cross-bones:

Peace, my doves! Incapable of terrestrial happiness, we have obtained the celestial plentitude of our union. After the age of the Father, the age of the Son; and I inaugurate the third, which is that of the Paraclete. His light descended upon me during those forty nights when the heavenly Jerusalem appeared shining in the firmament, above my house at Pepuzza.

Ah, how ye cry out with anguish when the thongs of the scourge lacerate! how your suffering bodies submit to the ardor of my spiritual discipline! how ye languish upon my breast with irrealizable longing! So strong has that desire become that it has enabled you to behold the invisible world; and ye can now perceive souls even with the eyes of the body.

ANTHONY
makes a gesture of astonishment.

TERTULLIAN

who appears again, standing beside Montanus:
Without doubt; for the soul has a body, and that which is bodiless
has no existence.

MONTANUS

In order to render it yet more subtle, I have instituted many
mortifications, three Lents a year, and prayers to be uttered nightly
by the mind only, keeping the mouth closed, lest breathing might
tarnish thought. It is necessary to abstain from second marriages, or
rather from all marriage! The Angels themselves have sinned with
women.

THE ARCHONTICS

wearing cilices of hair:
The Saviour said: "I come to destroy the work of the Woman!"

THE TATIANITES

wearing cilices of reed:
She is the tree of evil! Our bodies are but garments of skin.

And continuing to advance along the same side, Anthony meets:

THE VALESIANS

*extended upon the ground, with red wounds below their bellies, and blood
saturating their tunics.*
They offer him a knife:
Do as Origen did and as we have done! Is it the pain that thou
fearest, coward? Is it the love of thy flesh that restrains thee, hypocrite?

And while he watches them writhing upon their backs, in a pool of blood,

THE CAINITES

wearing knotted vipers as fillets about their hair, pass by, vociferating in his ear:

Glory to Cain! Glory to Sodom! Glory be to Judas!

Cain made the race of the strong; Sodom terrified the earth by her punishment, and it was by Judas that God saved the world! Yes! by Judas: without him there would have been no death and no redemption!

They disappear beneath the horde of the

CIRCUMCELLIONITES

all clad in the skins of wolves, crowned with thorns, and armed with maces of iron:

Crush the fruit! befoul the spring! drown the child! Pillage the rich who are happy—who eat their fill! Beat the poor who envy the ass his saddle-cloth, the dog his meal, the bird his nest,—and who is wretched at knowing that others are not as miserable as himself.

We, the Saints, poison, burn, massacre, that we may hasten the end of the world!

Salvation may be obtained through martyrdom only. We give ourselves martyrdom. We tear the skin from our heads with pincers; we expose our members to the plough; we cast ourselves into the mouths of furnaces!

Out upon baptism! out upon the Eucharist! out upon marriage! universal damnation!

Then throughout all the basilica there is a redoubling of fury.

The Audians shoot arrows against the Devil; the Collyridians throw blue cloths toward the roof; the Ascites prostrate themselves before a waterskin; the Marcionites baptise a dead man with oil. A woman, standing near Apelles, exhibits a round loaf within a bottle, in order the better to explain her idea. Another, standing in the midst of an assembly of Sampseans, distributes, as a sacrament, the dust of her own sandals. Upon the rose-strewn bed of the Marcosians, two lovers embrace. The Circumcellionites slaughter one another; the Valesians utter the death-rattle; Bardesanes sings; Carpocras

*dances; Maximilla and Priscilla moan; and the false prophetess of Cappado-
cia, completely naked, leaning upon a lion, and brandishing three torches,
shrieks the Terrible Invocation.*

*The columns of the temple sway to and fro like the trunks of trees; the
amulets suspended about the necks of the Heresiarchs seem to cross each other
in lines of fire; the constellations in the chapels palpitate; and the walls recoil
with the ebb and flow of the crowd, in which each head is a wave that leaps
and roars.*

*Nevertheless, from the midst of the clamour arises the sound of a song, in
which the name of Jesus is often repeated, accompanied by bursts of laughter.*

*The singers belong to the rabble of the people; they all keep time to the song
by clapping their hands. In their midst stands*

ARIUS

in a deacon's vestments.

The fools who declaim against me pretend to explain the absurd;
and in order to confound them utterly, I have composed ditties so
droll that they are learned by heart in all the mills, in the taverns
and along the ports.

No! a thousand times no!—the Son is not coeternal with the Father, nor of the same substance! Otherwise he would not have said:
"Father, remove this chalice from me! Why dost thou call me good?
God alone is good! I go to my God, to your God!"—and many other
things testifying to his character of creature. The fact is further
demonstrated for us by all his names:—lamb, shepherd, fountain,
wisdom, son-of-man, prophet, the way, the corner-stone!

SABELLIUS

I hold that both are identical.

ARIUS

The Council of Antioch has decided the contrary.

ANTHONY

Then what is the Word? ... What was Jesus?

THE VALENTINIANS

He was the husband of Acharamoth repentant!

THE SETHIANIANS

He was Shem, the son of Noah!

THE THEODOTIANS

He was Melchisedech!

THE MERINTHIANS

He was only a man!

THE APOLLINARISTS

He assumed the appearance of one! He simulated the Passion!

MARCEL OF ANCYRA

He was a development of the Father!

POPE CALIXTUS

Father and Son are but two modes of one God's manifestation!

METHODIUS

He was first in Adam, then in man!

CERINTHUS

And He will rise again!

VALENTINUS

Impossible—his body being celestial!

PAUL OF SAMOSATA

He became God *only* from the time of his baptism!

HERMOGENES

He dwells in the sun!

And all the Heresiarchs form a circle about Anthony, who weeps, covering his face with his hands.

A JEW
with a red beard, and spots of leprosy upon his skin, approaches close to Anthony, and, with a hideous sneer, exclaims:

His soul was the soul of Esau! He suffered from the Bellerophontian sickness.[5] Did not his mother, the seller of perfumes, surrender to the Roman soldier Pantherus, one harvest evening, on a bed of sheaves?

ANTHONY
suddenly raising his head, looks at them a moment in silence; then advancing boldly upon them exclaims:

Doctors, magicians, bishops, and deacons, men and phantoms, away from me! begone! Ye are all lies!

THE HERESIARCHS

We have martyrs more martyrs than thine, prayers that are more difficult, outbursts of love more sublime, ecstasies as prolonged as thine are.

ANTHONY

But ye have no revelation! no proofs!

They all at once brandish in the air their rolls of papyrus, tablets of wood, scrolls of leather, rolls of woven stuff bearing inscriptions; and elbowing, and pushing each other, they all shout to Anthony:

THE CERINTHIANS

Behold the Gospel of the Hebrews!

THE MARCIONITES

Behold the Gospel of the Lord!

THE MARCOSIANS

The Gospel of Eve!

THE EUCRATITES

The Gospel of Thomas!

THE CAINITES

The Gospel of Judas!

BASILIDES

The Treatise upon the Destiny of the Soul!

MANES

The Prophecy of Barkouf!

Anthony struggles, breaks from them, escapes them; and in a shadowy corner perceives

THE AGED EBIONITES

withered as mummies, their eyes dull and dim, their eyebrows white as frost. In tremulous voices they exclaim:

We have known him, we have seen him! We knew the Carpenter's Son! We were then the same age as he; we dwelt in the same street. He used to amuse himself by modelling little birds of mud; aided his father at his work without fear of the sharp tools, or gathered for his mother the skeins of dyed wool. Then he made a voyage to Egypt, from whence he brought back wondrous secrets. We were at Jericho when he came to find the Eater of Locusts.[6] They talked together in a low voice, so that no one could hear what was said. But it was from that time that his name began to be noised abroad in Galilee, and that men began to relate many fables regarding him.

They reiterate, tremulously:

We knew him! we others, we knew him!

ANTHONY
Ah, speak on, speak! What was his face like?

TERTULLIAN
His face was wild and repulsive; forasmuch as he had burthened himself with all the crimes, all the woes, all the deformities of mankind.

ANTHONY
Oh! no, no! I imagine, on the contrary, that his entire person must have been glorious with a beauty greater than the beauty of man.

EUSEBIUS OF CÆSAREA
There is indeed, at Paneades, propped up against the walls of a crumbling edifice surrounded by a wilderness of weeds and creeping plants, a certain statue of stone which, some say, was erected by the Woman healed of the issue of blood. But time has gnawed the face of the statue, and the rains have worn the inscription away.

A woman steps forward from the group of the Carpocratians.

MARCELLINA
I was once a deaconess at Rome, in a little church, where I used to exhibit to the faithful the silver images of Saint Paul, Homer, Pythagoras and Jesus Christ.
I have only kept that of Jesus.

She half opens her mantle.

Dost thou desire it?

A VOICE
He reappears himself when we call upon him! It is the hour!—come!

And Anthony feels a brutal hand seize him by the arm and drag him away.

He mounts a stairway in complete darkness; and after having ascended many steps, he finds himself before a door.

Then the one who is leading him—(is it Hilarion?—he does not know)—whispers in the ear of another: "The Lord is about to come"—and they are admitted into a chamber, with a very low ceiling, and without furniture.

The first object which attracts his attention is a long blood-colored chrysalis, with a human head surrounded by rays, and the word Knouphus *inscribed all around it in Greek characters. It is placed upon the shaft of a column, which is in turn supported by a broad pedestal. Hanging upon the walls of the chamber are medallions of polished iron representing the heads of various animals:—the head of an ox, the head of a lion, the head of an eagle, the head of a dog, and the head of an ass—again!*

Earthen lamps, suspended below these images, create a vacillating light. Through a hole in the wall, Anthony can see the moon shining far off upon the waves; he can even hear the feeble regular sound of lapping water; together with the heavy thud occasionally caused by the bumping of a ship's hull against the stones of the mole.

There are men crouching down, with their faces hidden by their mantles. From time to time they utter sounds resembling a smothered bark. There are women also, sleeping with their foreheads resting upon their arms, and their arms supported by their knees; they are so hidden by their garments as to resemble heaps of cloth piled up at intervals against the wall. Near them are half naked children, whose persons swarm with vermin as they watch with idiotic stare the burning of the lamps; and nothing is done: all are waiting for something.

They talk in undertones about family matters, or recommend to each other various remedies for their ailments. Some of them must embark at earliest daylight; the persecution is becoming too terrible to be endured. Nevertheless, the pagans are easily enough deceived:—

"The fools imagine that we are really adoring Knouphus!"

But one of the brethren, feeling himself suddenly inspired, takes his place before the column, where a basket has already been placed, filled with fennel and aristolochia. On the top of the basket is placed a loaf.

THE INSPIRED BROTHER
unrolling a placard covered with designs representing cylinders blending with and fitting into one another, commences to pray:
The ray of the Word descended upon the darknesses; and there arose a mighty cry, like unto the voice of Light.

ALL
swaying their bodies in unison, respond:
Kyrie Eleison!

THE INSPIRED BROTHER
Then was Man created by the infamous God of Israel, aided by those who are these

pointing to the medallions

—Astophaios, Oraios, Sabaoth, Adonai, Eloi, Iao![7]
And Man, hideous, feeble, formless and thoughtless, lay upon the slime of the earth.

ALL
in plaintive accents:
Kyrie Eleison!

THE INSPIRED BROTHER
But Sophia, compassionating him, vivified him with a spark of her own soul.

Then God, beholding Man so beautiful, waxed wroth; and imprisoned him within His own kingdom, forbidding him to touch the Tree of Knowledge.

Again did the other succor him! She sent to him the Serpent, who, by many long subterfuges, made him disobey that law of hate.

And Man, having tasted knowledge, understood celestial things.

ALL
raising their voices:
Kyrie Eleison!

THE INSPIRED BROTHER
But Iabdalaoth through vengeance cast down man into the world of matter, and the Serpent with him.

ALL
in a very low tone:
Kyrie Eleison!

Then all hold their peace, and there is silence.

The odors of the port mingle with the smoke of the lamps in the warm air. The lampwicks crepitate; their flames are about to go out, long mosquitoes flit in rapid circlings about them. And Anthony groans in an agony of anguish, as with the feeling that a monstrosity is floating about him, as with the fear of a crime that is about to be accomplished.

But

THE INSPIRED BROTHER
stamping his heel upon the floor, snapping his fingers, tossing his head wildly, suddenly chants to a furious rhythm, with accompaniment of cymbals and a shrill flute:

Come! come! come!—issue from thy cavern!

O swift one, who runneth without feet, captor who seizeth without hand!

Sinuous as the rivers, orbicular as the sun, black, with spots of gold, like the firmament star-besprinkled! Like unto the intertwinings of the vine, and the circumvolutions of entrails!

Unengendered! eater of earth! immortally young! unfailing perspicaceous! honored at Epidaurus! Kindly to man! thou who didst heal King Ptolemy, and the warriors, of Moses, and Glaucus, son of Minos!

Come! come! come!—issue from thy cavern!

ALL

repeat:

Come! come! come!—issue from thy cavern!

Nevertheless, nothing yet appears.

Why? What aileth him?

And they concert together, devise means.

An old man presents a clod of turf as an offering. Then something up-heaves within the basket. The mass of verdure shakes; the flowers fall, and the head of a python appears.

It passes slowly around the edge of the loaf, like a circle moving around an immovable disk;—then it unfolds itself, lengthens out; it is enormous and of great weight. Lest it should touch the floor, the men uphold it against their breasts, the women support it upon their heads, the children hold it up at arms' length; and its tail, issuing through the hole in the wall, stretches away indefinitely to the bottom of the sea. Its coils double; they fill the chamber; they enclose Anthony.

THE FAITHFUL

press their mouths against its skin, snatch from one another the loaf which it has bitten, and cry aloud.

It is thou! it is thou!

First raised up by Moses, broken by Ezechias, re-established by the Messiah. He drank thee in the waters of baptism; but thou didst leave him in the Garden of Olives; and then indeed he felt his own weakness.

Writhing about the arms of the cross, and above his head, while casting thy slime upon the crown of thorns, thou didst behold him die. For thou art not Jesus, thou!—thou art the Word! thou art the Christ!

Anthony faints with horror, and falls prostrate in front of his hut upon the splinters of wood, where the torch that had slipped from his hand is burning low.

The shock arouses him. Opening his eyes again, he perceives the Nile, brightly undulating under the moon, like a vast serpent winding over the sands; so that the hallucination returns upon him again, he has not left the company of the Ophites; they surround him, call him; he sees them carrying baggage, descending to the port. He embarks along with them.

An inappreciable time elapses.

Then the vaults of a prison environ him. Iron bars in front of him make black lines against a background of blue; and in the darkness beside him people are weeping and praying surrounded by others who exhort and console.

Without, there is a murmur like the deep humming of a vast crowd, and there is splendour as of a summer's day.

Shrill voices announce watermelons for sale, iced drinks, and cushions of woven grass to sit upon. From time to time there are bursts of applause. He hears the sound of footsteps above his head.

Suddenly a long roar is heard, mighty and cavernous as the roar of water in an aqueduct.

And he sees, directly opposite, behind the bars of another compartment across the arena, a lion walking to and fro, then a line of sandals, bare legs, and purple fringes. Beyond are the vast circling wreaths of people, in sym-metrical tiers, enlarging as they rise, from the lowest which hems in the arena to the uppermost above which masts rise to sustain a hyacinth-colored awning, suspended in air by ropes. Stairways radiating toward the centre divide these huge circles of stone at regular intervals. The benches disappear under a host of spectators—knights, senators, soldiers, plebeians, vestals, and courtesans—in woollen hoods, in silken maniples, in fallow-colored tunics; together with aigrettes of precious stones, plumes of feathers, the fasces of lictors; and all this swarming multitude deafens and stupefies Anthony with its shoutings, its tumultuous fury, as of an enormous boiling vat. In the middle of the arena, a vase of incense smokes upon an altar.

Anthony thus knows that the people with him are Christians condemned to be thrown to the wild beasts. The men wear the red mantle of the pontiffs of Saturn; the women, the bandellettes of Ceres. Their friends divide among themselves shreds of their garments and rings. To obtain access to the prison, they say, costs a great deal of money. But what matter! They will remain until it is all over.

Anthony notices among these consolers a certain bald-headed man, in a black tunic: Anthony has seen that face somewhere before. The consoler discourses to them concerning the nothingness of this world, and the felicity of the Elect. Anthony feels within him a transport of celestial love; he longs for the opportunity to lay down his life for the Saviour—not knowing as yet whether he himself is to be numbered among the martyrs.

But all—except a certain Phrygian, with long hair, who stands with his arms uplifted—have a look of woe. One old man is sobbing upon a bench; a youth standing close by, with drooping head, abandons himself to a reverie of sorrow.

THE OLD MAN

had refused to pay the customary contribution before the statue of Minerva, erected at the angle of the crossroads; and he gazes at his companions with a look that signifies:

Ye ought to have succored me! Communities can sometimes so arrange matters as to insure their being left in peace. Some among ye also procured those letters which falsely allege that one has sacrificed to idols.

He asks aloud:

Was it not Petrus of Alexandria who laid down the rule concerning what should be done by those who have yielded to torture?

Then, to himself:

Ah! how cruel this at my age! My infirmities make me so weak! Nevertheless, I might easily have lived until the coming winter, or longer!

The memory of his little garden makes him sad, and he gazes toward the altar.

THE YOUNG MAN
who disturbed the festival of Apollo by violence and blows, murmurs:
Yet it would have been easy for me to have fled to the mountains!

One of the brothers answers.
—But the soldiers would have captured thee!
—Oh! I would have done as Cyprian did—I would have returned, and the second time I would surely have had more force!

Then he thinks of the innumerable days that he might have lived, of all the joys that he might have known, but will never know; and he gazes toward the altar.
But

THE MAN IN THE BLACK TUNIC
rushes to his side:
What scandal! What! Thou! a victim of God's own choice! And all these women here who are looking at thee! Nay, think what thou art doing! Moreover, remember that God sometimes vouchsafes to

perform a miracle. Pionius numbed and made powerless the hands of his executioners; the blood of Polycarp extinguished the fire of the stake.

Then he turns to the Old Man:

Father, father! it behooves thee to edify us by thy death. By longer delaying it, thou wouldst doubtless commit some evil action that would lose thee the fruit of all thy good works. Remember, also, that the power of God is infinite; and it may come to pass that all the people will be converted by thy example.

And in the great den opposite, the lions stride back and forth, ceaselessly, with a rapid continuous motion. The largest suddenly looks at Anthony and roars, and a vapour issues from his jaws.

The women are huddled against the men.

THE CONSOLER
goes from one to the other.

What would ye say, what wouldst thou say if thou wert to be burned with red-hot irons, if thou wert to be torn asunder by horses, if thou hadst been condemned to have thy body smeared with honey, and thus exposed to be devoured by flies! As it is, thou wilt only suffer the death of a hunter surprised by a beast in the woods.

Anthony would prefer all those things to death by the fangs of the horrible wild beasts; he fancies already that he feels their teeth and their claws, that he hears his bones cracking between their jaws.

A keeper enters the dungeon; the martyrs tremble.

Only one remains impassable, the Phrygian, who prays standing apart from the rest. He has burned three temples; and he advances with arms uplifted, mouth open, face turned toward heaven, seeing nothing around him, like a somnambulist.

THE CONSOLER

shouts:

Back! back! lest the spirit of Montanus might come upon you.

ALL

recoil from the Phrygian, and vociferate:

Damnation to the Montanist!

They insult him, spit upon him, excite each other to beat him. The rearing lions bite each other's manes; the people howl:

To the beasts with them, to the beasts.

The Martyrs burst into sobs, and embrace each other passionately. A cup of narcotic wine is offered them. It is passed from hand to hand, quickly.

Another keeper, standing at the door of the den, awaits the signal. The den opens; a lion comes out.

He crosses the arena with great oblique strides. Other lions follow in file after him; then a bear, three panthers, and some leopards. They scatter through the arena like a flock in a meadow.

The crack of a whip resounds. The Christians stagger forward; and their brethren push them, that it may be over the sooner. Anthony closes his eyes.

He opens them again. But darkness envelopes him.

Soon the darkness brightens; and he beholds an arid plain, mamillated with knolls, such as might be seen about abandoned quarries.

Here and there a tuft of shrubbery rises among the slabs of stone, level with the soil; and there are white figures, vaguer than clouds, bending over the slabs.

Others approach, softly, silently. Eyes gleam through the slits of long veils. By the easy indifference of their walk, and the perfumes exhaled from their garments, Anthony knows they are patrician women. There are men also, but of inferior condition; for their faces are at once simple-looking and coarse.

ONE OF THE WOMEN

taking a long breath:

Ah! how good the cool air of night is, among the sepulchres! I am so weary of the softness of beds, the turmoil of days, the heavy heat of the sun!

Her maid-servant takes from a canvas bag a torch which she ignites. The faithful light other torches by it, and plant them upon the tombs.

A WOMAN

panting:

I am here at last! Oh how wearisome to be the wife of an idolator!

ANOTHER

These visits to the prisons, interviews with our brethren, are all matters of suspicion to our husbands! And we must even hide ourselves in order to make the sign of the cross; they would take it for a magical conjuration.

ANOTHER

With my husband it was a quarrel every day. I would not submit myself to the brutal exactions he required of my body; therefore he has had me prosecuted as a Christian.

ANOTHER

Do you remember Lucius, that young man who was so beautiful, who was dragged like Hector, with his heels attached to a chariot, from the Esquiline Gate to the mountains of Tibur?—and how his blood spattered the bushes on either side of the road? I gathered up the drops of his blood. Behold it!

She drags a black sponge from her bosom, covers it with kisses, and flings herself down upon the slabs, crying aloud:

Ah! my friend! my friend!

A MAN

It is just three years to-day since Domitilla died. They stoned her at the further end of the Grove of Proserpine. I gathered her bones, which shone like glowworms in the grass. The earth now covers them!

He casts himself down upon a tomb.

O my betrothed! my betrothed!

AND ALL THE OTHERS

scattered over the plain:

O my sister! O my brother! O my daughter! O my mother!

Some kneel, covering their faces with their hands; others lie down upon the ground with their arms extended; and the sobs they smother shake their breasts with such violence as though their hearts were breaking with grief. Sometimes they look up to heaven, exclaiming:

Have mercy upon her soul, O my God! She languishes in the sojourn of Shades; vouchsafe to admit her to thy Resurrection, that she may enjoy Thy Light!

Or, with eyes fixed upon the gravestones, they murmur to the dead:

Be at peace, beloved! and suffer not! I have brought thee wine and meats!

A WIDOW

Here is pultis, made by my own hands, as he used to like it, with plenty of eggs and a double measure of flour! We are going to eat it together as in other days, are we not?

She lifts a little piece to her lips, and suddenly bursts into an extravagant and frenzied laugh.

The others also nibble a little bit as she does and drink a mouthful of wine.

They recount to each other the stories of their martyrs; grief becomes exalted, libations redouble. Their tear-swimming eyes are fixed upon each other's faces. They stammer with intoxication and grief; gradually hands touch hands, lips join themselves to lips, veils fall open, and they seek each other upon the tombs, between the cups and the torches.

The sky begins to whiten. The fog makes damp their garments; and, without appearing even to know one another, they depart by different ways across the countryside.

———

The sun shines; the weeds and the grass have grown higher; the face of the plain is changed.

And Anthony, looking between tall bamboos, sees distinctly a forest of columns, of bluish-grey color. These are tree-trunks, all originating from one vast trunk. From each branch of the colossal tree descend other branches which may bury themselves in the soil; and the aspect of all these horizontal and perpendicular lines, indefinitely multiplied, would closely resemble a monstrous timberwork, were it not that they have small figs growing upon them here and there, and a blackish foliage, like that of the sycamore.

He perceives, in the forkings of their branches, hanging bunches of yellow flowers, violet flowers also, and ferns that resemble the plumes of splendid birds.

Under the lowest branches the horns of a bubalus gleam at intervals, and the bright eyes of antelopes are visible; there are hosts of parrots; there are butterflies flittering hither and thither; lizards lazily drag themselves up or down; flies buzz and hum; and in the midst of the silence, a sound is audible as of the palpitation of a deep and mighty life.

———

Seated upon a sort of pyre at the entrance of the wood is a strange being—a man—besmeared with cowdung, completely naked, more withered than a mummy; his articulations form knots at the termination of bones that resemble sticks. He has bunches of shells suspended from his ears; his face is very long, and his nose like a vulture's beak. His left arm remains motionlessly erect in air, anchylosed, rigid as a stake; and he has been seated here so long that birds have made themselves a nest in his long hair.

At the four corners of his wooden pyre flame four fires. The sun is directly in front of him. He gazes steadily at it with widely-opened eyes; and, then without looking at Anthony, asks him:

"Brahmin from the shores of the Nile, what hast thou to say regarding these things?"

Flames suddenly burst out on all sides of him, through the intervals between the logs of the pyre; and—

THE GYMNOSOPHIST

continues:

Lo! I have buried myself in solitude, like the rhinoceros. I dwelt in the tree behind me.

The vast fig-tree, indeed, shows in one of its groves a natural excavation about the size of a man.

And I nourished me with flowers and fruits, observing the precepts so rigidly that not even a dog ever beheld me eat.

Inasmuch as existence originates from corruption, corruption from desire, desire from sensation, sensation from contact, I have ever avoided all action, all contact, and perpetually—motionless as the stela of a tomb, exhaling my breath from my two nostrils, fixing my eyes upon my nose, and contemplating the ether in my mind, the world in my members, the moon in my heart—I dreamed of the essence of the great Soul whence continually escape the principles of life, even as sparks escape from fire.

Thus at last I found the supreme Soul in all beings, and all beings in the supreme Soul; and I have been able to make enter in to it mine own soul in which I have enclosed all my senses.

I receive knowledge directly from heaven, like the bird Tchataka, who quenches his thirst from falling rain only.

Even by so much as things are known to me, things no longer exist.

For me now there is no more hope, no more anguish, there is neither happiness nor virtue, nor day nor night, nor Thou nor I—absolutely nothing.

My awful austerities have made me superior to the Powers. A single contraction of my thought would suffice to kill a hundred sons of kings, to dethrone gods, to overturn the world.

He utters all these things in a monotonous voice.
The surrounding leaves shrivel up. Fleeing rats rush over the ground.
He slowly turns his eyes downward toward the rising flames, and then continues:

I have loathed Form, I have loathed Perception, I have loathed even Knowledge itself, for the thought does not survive the transitory fact which caused it; and mind, like all else, is only an illusion.

All that is engendered will perish; all that is dead must live again; the beings that have even now disappeared shall sojurn again in wombs as yet unformed, and shall again return to earth to serve in woe other creatures.

But inasmuch as I have rolled through the revolution of an indefinite multitude of existences, under the envelopes of gods, of men, and of animals, I renounce further wanderings; I will endure this weariness no more! I abandon the filthy hostelry of this body of mine, built with flesh, reddened with blood, covered with a hideous skin, full of uncleanliness; and, for my recompense, I go at last to slumber in the deepest deeps of the Absolute—in Annihilation.

The flames rise to his chest, then envelop him. His head rises through them as through a hole in the wall. His cavernous eyes still remain wide open, gazing.

ANTHONY

rises.

The torch, which had fallen to the ground, has ignited the splinters of wood; and the flames have singed his beard.

With a loud cry, Anthony tramples the fire out; and, when nothing remains but ashes, he exclaims:

Where can Hilarion be? He was here a moment ago.

I saw him!

What! No; it is impossible; I must have been mistaken!

Yet why?... Perhaps my cabin, these stones, this sand, equally have no real existence. I am becoming mad. Let me be calm! Where was I? What was it that happened?

Ah! the gymnosophist!... Such a death is frequent among the sages of India. Kalanos burned himself before Alexander; another did likewise in the time of Augustus. What hatred of life men must have to do thus! Unless, indeed, they are impelled by pride alone?... Yet in any event they have the intrepidity of martyrs!... As for the latter, I can now well believe what has been told me regarding the debauchery they cause.

And before that? Yes: I remember now! the host of the Heresiarchs!... What outcries! What eyes! Yet why so much rebellion of the flesh, so much dissoluteness, so many aberrations of the intellect?

They claim, nevertheless, to seek God through all those ways! What right have I to curse them—I, who stumble so often in mine own path? I was perhaps about to learn more of them at the moment when they disappeared. Too rapid was the whirl; I had no time to answer. Now I feel as though there were more space, more light in my understanding. I am calm. I even feel myself able to ... What is this? I thought I had put out the fire!

A flame flits among the rocks; and soon there comes the sound of a voice—broken, convulsed as by sobs—from afar off, among the mountains.

Can it be the cry of a hyena, or the lamentation of some traveller that has lost his way?

Anthony listens. The flame draws nearer.

And he beholds a weeping woman approach, leaning upon the shoulder of a white-bearded man.

She is covered with a purple robe in rags. He is bareheaded like her, wears a tunic of the same color, and carries in his hands a brazen vase, whence arises a thin blue flame.

Anthony feels a fear come upon him and wishes to know who this woman may be.

THE STRANGER (SIMON)

It is a young girl, a poor child that I lead about with me everywhere.

He uplifts the brazen vase.

Anthony contemplates the girl by the light of its vacillating flame.

There are marks of bites upon her face, traces of blows upon her arms; her dishevelled hair entangles itself in the rents of her rags; her eyes appear to be insensible to light.

SIMON

Sometimes she remains thus for a long, long time without speaking; then all at once she revives,—and discourses of marvellous things.

ANTHONY

In truth?

SIMON

Ennoia; Ennoia! Ennoia!—tell us what thou hast to say!

She rolls her eyes like one awaking from a dream, slowly passes her fingers over her brows, and, in a mournful voice, speaks:

HELENA* (ENNOIA)

I remember a distant land, of the color of emerald. Only one tree grows there.

Anthony starts.

Upon each of its tiers of broad-extending arms, a pair of Spirits dwell in air. All about them the branches intercross, like the veins of a body; and they watch the eternal Life circulating, from the roots deep plunging into darkness even to the leafy summit that rises higher than the sun. I, dwelling upon the second branch, illuminated the nights of Summer with my face.

ANTHONY

tapping his own forehead.
    Ah! ah! I comprehend! her head!

SIMON

placing his finger to his lips:
    Hush! . . .

HELENA

The sail remained well filled by the wind; the keel cleft the foam. He said to me: "What though I afflict my country, though I lose my kingdom! Thou wilt belong to me, in my house!"

How sweet was the lofty chamber of his palace! Lying upon the ivory bed, he caressed my long hair, singing amorously the while.

Even at the close of the day I beheld the two camps, the watchfires being lighted, Ulysses at the entrance of his tent, armed Achilles driving a chariot along the sea-beach.

ANTHONY

Why! she is utterly mad! How came this to pass? . . .

---

* Readers may remember Longfellow's exquisite poem "Helena of Tyre."

SIMON

Hush!... hush!

HELENA

They anointed me with unguents, and sold me to the people that I might amuse them.

One evening I was standing with the sistrum in my hand, making music for some Greek sailors who were dancing. The rain was falling upon the roof of the tavern like a cataract, and the cups of warm wine were smoking.

A man suddenly entered, although the door was not opened to let him pass.

SIMON

It was I! I found thee again!

Behold her, Anthony, she whom they call Sigeh, Ennoia, Barbelo, Prounikos! The Spirits governing the world were jealous of her; and they imprisoned her within the body of a woman.

She was that Helen of Troy whose memory was cursed by the poet Stesichorus. She was Lucretia, the patrician woman violated by kings. She was Delilah, by whom Samson's locks were shorn. She was that daughter of Israel who would give herself to he-goats. She has loved adultery, idolatry, lying and foolishness. She has prostituted herself to all nations. She has sung at the angles of all crossroads. She has kissed the faces of all men.

At Tyre, she, the Syrian, was the mistress of robbers. She caroused with them during the nights; and she concealed assassins amidst the vermin of her tepid bed.

ANTHONY

Ah! what is this to me?...

SIMON

with a furious look:

I tell thee that I have redeemed her, and re-established her in her former splendour; insomuch that Caius Cæsar Caligula became enamoured of her, desiring to sleep with the Moon!

ANTHONY

What then?...

SIMON

Why this, that she herself is the Moon! Has not Pope Clement written how she was imprisoned in a tower? Three hundred persons surrounded the tower to watch it; and the moon was seen at each of the loopholes at the same time, although there is not more than one moon in the world, nor more than one Ennoia!

ANTHONY

Yes ... it seems to me that I remember ...

He falls into a reverie.

SIMON

Innocent as the Christ who died for men, so did she devote herself for women. For the impotence of Jehovah is proven by the transgression of Adam, and we must shake off the yoke of the old law, which is antipathetic to the order of things.*

I have preached the revival in Ephraim and in Issachar by the torrent of Bizor, beyond the Lake of Houleh, in the valley of Maggedo, further than the mountains, at Bostra and at Damascus! Let all come to me who are covered with wine, who are covered with filth, who are covered with blood and I shall take away their uncleanliness with the Holy Spirit, called Minerva by the Greeks! She is Minerva! she is the Holy Spirit! I am Jupiter, Apollo, the Christ, the Paraclete, the great might of God, incarnated in the person of Simon!

---

* See the second part of "Faust," and *Kundry* in "Parsifal."

ANTHONY

Ah! it is thou!... so it is thou! But I know thy crimes!

Thou wast born at Gittoi near Samaria; Dositheus, thy first master, drove thee from him! Thou didst execrate Saint Paul because he converted one of thy wives; and, vanquished by Saint Peter, in thy rage and terror thou didst cast into the waves the bag which contained thy artifices!

SIMON

Dost thou desire them?

Anthony looks at him, and an interior voice whispers in his heart: "Why not?"

SIMON

continues:

He who knows the forces of Nature and the substance of Spirits must be able to perform miracles. It has been the dream of all sages; it is the desire which even now gnaws thee!—confess it!

In the sight of the multitude of the Romans, I flew in the air so high that none could behold me move. Nero ordered that I should be decapitated; but it was the head of a sheep which fell upon the ground in lieu of mine. At last they buried me alive; but I rose again upon the third day. The proof is that thou dost behold me before thee!

He presents his hands to Anthony to smell. They have the stench of corpse-flesh. Anthony recoils with loathing.

I can make serpents of bronze writhe; I can make marble statues laugh; I can make dogs speak. I will show thee vast quantities of gold; I will reestablish kings; thou shalt see nations prostrate themselves in adoration before me! I can walk upon the clouds and upon the waves, I can pass through mountains, I can make myself appear as a youth, as an old man, as a tiger, or as an ant; I can assume thy features; I can give thee mine; I can make the thunder follow after me. Dost hear it?

The thunder rumbles; flashes of lightning succeed.

It is the voice of the Most High! for "the Lord thy God is a fire"; and all creations are accomplished by sparks from the fire-centre of all things.

Thou shalt even now receive the baptism of it—that second baptism announced by Jesus, which fell upon the apostles on a day of tempest when the windows were open!

And stirring up the flame with his hand, slowly, as though preparing to sprinkle Anthony with it, he continues:

Mother of mercies, thou who discoverest all secrets, in order that we may find rest in the eighth mansion ...

ANTHONY

cries out:
Oh! that I had only some holy water!

The flame goes out, producing much smoke.
Ennoia and Simon have disappeared.
An exceedingly cold, opaque and fœtid mist fills the atmosphere.

ANTHONY

groping with his hands like a blind man:
Where am I? ... I fear lest I fall into the abyss! And the cross, surely, is too far from me ... Ah! what a night! what a terrible night!

The mist is parted by a gust of wind; and Anthony sees two men covered with long white tunics.
The first is of lofty stature, with a gentle face, and a grave mien. His blond

hair, parted like that of Christ, falls upon his shoulders. He has cast aside a wand that he had been holding in his hand; his companion takes it up, making a reverence after the fashion of the Orientals.

The latter is small of stature, thick set, flat-nosed, wooly-haired; his neck and shoulders express good-natured simplicity.

Both are barefooted, bareheaded, and dusty, like persons who have made a long journey.

ANTHONY

starting up:
What do ye seek? Speak! Begone from here!

DAMIS

—who is the little man,—
Nay! nay!... be not angered, good hermit! As for that which I seek, I know not myself what it is! Here is the Master.

He sits down. The other stranger remains standing. Silence.

ANTHONY

asks:
Then ye come?...

DAMIS

Oh! from afar off—very far off!

ANTHONY

And ye go?...

DAMIS

pointing to the other:
Whithersoever he shall desire!

ANTHONY

But who may he be?

DAMIS

Look well upon him!

ANTHONY

aside:

He looks like a saint! If I could only dare ...

The mist is all gone. The night is very clear. The moon shines.

DAMIS

Of what art thou dreaming, that thou dost not speak?

ANTHONY

I was thinking ... Oh! nothing!

DAMIS

approaches Apollonius and walks all round him several times, bending himself as he walks, never raising his head.

Master, here is a Galilean hermit who desires to know the beginnings of wisdom.

APOLLONIUS

Let him approach!

Anthony hesitates.

DAMIS

Approach!

APOLLONIUS

in a voice of thunder:

Approach! Thou wouldst know who I am, what I have done, and what I think,—is it not so, child?

ANTHONY

Always supposing that these things can contribute to the salvation of my soul.

APOLLONIUS

Rejoice! I am about to inform thee of them!

DAMIS

in an undertone, to Anthony:

Is it possible? He must surely have at the first glance discerned in thee extraordinary aptitude for philosophy! I shall also strive to profit by his instruction!

APOLLONIUS

First of all, I shall tell thee of the long course which I have followed in order to obtain the doctrine; and if thou canst discover in all my life one evil action, thou shalt bid me pause, for he who hath erred in his actions may well give scandal by his words.

DAMIS

to Anthony:

How just a man! Is he not?

ANTHONY

Indeed I believe him to be sincere.

APOLLONIUS

Upon the night of my birth, my mother imagined that she was gathering flowers by the shore of a great lake. A flash of lightning appeared; and she brought me into the world to the music of the voices of swans singing to her in her dream.

Until I had reached the age of fifteen I was plunged thrice a day into the fountain, Asbadæus, whose waters make perjurers hydropical; and my body was rubbed with the leaves of the cnyza, that I might be chaste.

A Palmyrian princess came one evening to seek me, offering me treasures that she knew to be in the tombs. A hierodule of the temple of Diana slew herself in despair with the sacrificial knife; and the governor of Cilicia, finding all his promises of no avail, cried out in the presence of my family that he would cause my death; but it was he that died only three days after, assassinated by the Romans.

DAMIS

nudging Anthony with his elbow:
Eh? did I not tell thee? What a man!

APOLLONIUS

For the space of four successive years I maintained the unbroken silence of the Pythagorians. The most sudden and unexpected pain never extorted a sigh from me; and when I used to enter the theatre, all drew away from me, as from a phantom.

DAMIS

Wouldst thou have done so much?—thou?

APOLLONIUS

After the period of my trial had been accomplished, I undertook to instruct the priests regarding the tradition they had lost.

ANTHONY

What tradition?

DAMIS

Interrupt him not! Be silent!

APOLLONIUS

I have conversed with the Samaneans of the Ganges, with the astrologers of Chaldea, with the magi of Babylon, with the Gaulish Druids, with the priests of the negroes! I have ascended the four-

teen Olympii; I have sounded the Scythian lakes; I have measured
the breadth of the Desert!

DAMIS

It is all true! I was with him the while!

APOLLONIUS

But first I had visited the Hyrcanian Sea; I made the tour of it;
and descending by way of the country of the Baraomati, where Bu-
cephalus is buried, I approached the city of Nineveh. At the gates
of the city, a man drew near me ...

DAMIS

I—even I, good master! I loved thee from the first! Thou wert
gentler than a girl and more beautiful than a god!

APOLLONIUS

without hearing him:
He asked me to accompany him, that he might serve as inter-
preter.

DAMIS

But thou didst reply that all languages were familiar to thee, and
that thou couldst divine all thoughts. Then I kissed the hem of thy
mantle, and proceeded to walk behind thee.

APOLLONIUS

After Ctesiphon, we entered upon the territory of Babylon.

DAMIS

And the Satrap cried aloud on beholding a man so pale.

ANTHONY

aside:
What signifies this? ...

APOLLONIUS

The king received me standing, near a throne of silver, in a hall constellated with stars; from the cupola hung suspended by invisible threads four great birds of gold, with wings extended.

ANTHONY

dreamily:

Can there be such things in the world?

DAMIS

Ah! that is a city! that Babylon! everybody there is rich! The houses, which are painted blue, have doors of bronze, and flights of steps descending to the river.

Drawing lines upon the ground, with his stick,

Like that, seest thou? And then there are temples, there are squares, there are baths, there are aqueducts! The palaces are roofed with red brass! and the interior ... ah! if thou only knewest!

APOLLONIUS

Upon the north wall rises a tower which supports a second, a third, a fourth, a fifth, and there are also three others! The eighth is a chapel containing a bed. No one enters it save the woman chosen by the priests for the God Belus. I was lodged there by order of the King of Babylon.

DAMIS

As for me, they hardly deigned to give me any attention! So I walked through the streets all by myself. I informed myself regarding the customs of the people; I visited the workshops; I examined the great machines that carry water to the gardens. But I soon wearied of being separated from the Master.

APOLLONIUS

At last we left Babylon; and as we travelled by the light of the moon, we suddenly beheld an Empusa.

DAMIS

Aye, indeed! She leaped upon her iron hoof; she brayed like an ass; she galloped among the rocks. He shouted imprecations at her; she disappeared.

ANTHONY

aside:

What can be their motive?

APOLLONIUS

At Taxilla, the capital of five thousand fortresses, Phraortes, King of the Ganges, showed us his guard of black men, whose stature was five cubits, and under a pavilion of green brocade in his gardens, an enormous elephant, which the queens amused themselves by perfuming. It was the elephant of Porus which had taken flight after the death of Alexander.

DAMIS

And which had been found again in a forest.

ANTHONY

Their speech is superabundant, like that of drunken men.

APOLLONIUS

Phraortes seated us at his own table.

DAMIS

How strange a country that was! During their drinking carousels, the lords used to amuse themselves by shooting arrows under the feet of a dancing child. But I do not approve ...

APOLLONIUS

When I was ready to depart, the king gave me a parasol, and he said to me: "I have a stud of white camels upon the Indus. When thou shalt have no further use for them, blow in their ears. They will come back."

We descended along the river, marching at night by the light of the fire-flies, which glimmered among the bamboos. The slave whistled an air to drive away the serpents; and our camels bent down in passing below the branches of the trees, as if passing under low gates.

One day a black child, who held a golden caduceus in his hand, conducted us to the College of the Sages. Iarchas, their chief, spoke to me of my ancestors, told me of all my thoughts, of all my actions, of all my existences. In former time he had been the River Indus; and he reminded me that I had once been a boatman upon the Nile, in the time of King Sesostris.

DAMIS

As for me, they told me nothing; so that I know not who or what I have been.

ANTHONY

They have a vague look, like shadows!

APOLLONIUS

Upon the shores of the sea we met with the milk-gorged Cynocephali, who were returning from their expedition to the Island Taprobana. The tepid waves rolled blond pearls to our feet. The amber crackled beneath our steps. Whale-skeletons were whitening in the crevasses of the cliffs. At last the land became narrow as a sandal; and after casting drops of ocean water toward the sun, we turned to the right to return.

So we returned through the Region of Aromatics, by way of the country of the Gangarides, the promontory of Comaria, the country of the Sachalites, of the Adramites and of the Homerites; then, across the Cassanian mountains, the Red Sea, and the Island Topazos, we penetrated into Ethiopia through the country of the Pygmies.

ANTHONY

to himself:
How vast the world is!

DAMIS

And after we had returned home, we found that all those whom we used to know were dead.

Anthony lowers his head. Silence.

APOLLONIUS

continues:
Then men began to talk of me the world over.
The plague was ravaging Ephesus; I made them stone an old mendicant there.

DAMIS

And forthwith the plague departed!

ANTHONY

What! Does he drive away pestilence?

APOLLONIUS

At Cnidos, I cured the man that had become enamored of Venus.

DAMIS

Aye! a fool who had even vowed to espouse her.—To love a woman is at least comprehensible; but to love a statue, what madness!—The Master placed his hand upon the young man's heart; and the fire of that love was at once extinguished.

ANTHONY

How! does he also cast out devils?

APOLLONIUS

At Tarentum they were carrying the dead body of a young girl to the funeral pyre.

DAMIS

The Master touched her lips; and she arose and called her mother.

ANTHONY

What! he raises the dead!

APOLLONIUS

I predicted to Vespasian his accession to power.

ANTHONY

What! he foretells the future!

DAMIS

At Corinth there was a . . .

APOLLONIUS

It was when I was at table with him, at the waters of Baia . . .

ANTHONY

Excuse me, strangers—it is very late . . .

DAMIS

At Corinth there was a young man called Menippus . . .

ANTHONY

No! no!—go ye away!

 APOLLONIUS

A dog came in, bearing a severed hand in his mouth.

DAMIS

One evening, in one of the suburbs, he met a woman.

ANTHONY

Do ye not hear me? Begone!

APOLLONIUS

He wandered in a bewildered way around the couches ...

ANTHONY

Enough!

APOLLONIUS

They sought to drive him out.

DAMIS

So Menippus went with her to her house; they loved one another.

APOLLONIUS

And gently beating the mosaic pavement with his tail, he laid the
severed hand upon the knees of Flavius.

DAMIS

But next morning, during the lessons in the school, Menippus
was pale.

ANTHONY

starting up in anger:

Still continuing! Ah! then let them continue till they be weary,
inasmuch as there is no ...

DAMIS

The Master said to him: "O beautiful youth, thou dost caress a serpent; by a serpent thou art caressed! And when shall be the nuptials?" We all went to the wedding.

ANTHONY

Assuredly I am doing wrong, to hearken to such a story!

DAMIS

Servants were hurrying to and fro in the vestibule; doors were opening; nevertheless there was no sound made either by the fall of the footsteps nor the closing of the doors. The Master placed himself beside Menippus. And the bride forthwith became angered against the philosophers. But the vessels of gold, the cupbearers, the cooks, the pantlers disappeared; the roof receded and vanished into air; the walls crumbled down; and Apollonius stood alone with the woman at his feet, all in tears. She was a vampire who satisfied the beautiful young men in order to devour their flesh, for nothing is more desirable for such phantoms than the blood of amorous youths.

APOLLONIUS

If thou shouldst desire to learn the art ...

ANTHONY

I do not wish to learn anything!

APOLLONIUS

The same evening that we arrived at the gates of Rome ...

ANTHONY

Oh! yes!—speak to me rather of the City of Popes!

APOLLONIUS

A drunken man accosted us, who was singing in a low voice.

The song was an epithalamium of Nero; and he had the power to cause the death of whosoever should hear it with indifference. In a box upon his shoulders he carried a string taken from the Emperor's cithara. I shrugged my shoulders. He flung mud in our faces. Then I unfastened my girdle and placed it in this hand.

DAMIS

In sooth, thou wert most imprudent!

APOLLONIUS

During the night the Emperor summoned me to his house. He was playing at osselets with Sporus, supporting his left arm upon a table of agate. He turned and, knitting his brows, demanded: "How comes it that thou dost not fear me?" "Because," I replied, "the God who made thee terrible, also made me intrepid."

ANTHONY

to himself:
There is something inexplicable that terrifies me!

Silence.

DAMIS

breaking the silence with his shrill voice:
Moreover, all Asia can tell thee ...

ANTHONY

starting up:
I am ill! let me be!

DAMIS

But listen. At Ephesus, he beheld them killing Domitian, who was at Rome.

ANTHONY

with a forced laugh:
  Is it possible?

DAMIS

Yes: at the theatre at noon-day, the fourteenth of the Kalenda of October, he suddenly cried out: "Cæsar is being murdered!" and from time to time he would continue to ejaculate: "He rolls upon the pavement. Oh! how he struggles! He rises ... He tries to flee ... The doors are fastened ... Ah! it is all over! He is dead!" And in fact Titus Flavius Domitianus was assassinated upon that very day, as thou knowest.

ANTHONY

Without the aid of the Devil ... certainly ...

APOLLONIUS

He had purposed putting me to death, that same Domitian! Damis had taken flight according to my order, and I remained alone in my prison.

DAMIS

A terrible hardihood on thy part, it must be confessed!

APOLLONIUS

About the fifth hour, the soldiers led me before the tribunal. I had my harangue all ready hidden beneath my mantle.

DAMIS

We others were then upon the shores of Puteoli, we believed thee dead; we were all weeping, when all of a sudden about the sixth hour, thou didst suddenly appear before us, exclaiming: "It is I."

ANTHONY

to himself:
　Even as He ...!

DAMIS

in a very loud voice:
　Precisely!

ANTHONY

Oh! no! ye lie! is it not so?—ye lie!

APOLLONIUS

He descended from heaven. I rise thither, by the power of my virtue that has lifted me up even to the height of the Principle of all things!

DAMIS

Thyana, his natal city, has established in his honor a temple and a priesthood!

APOLLONIUS
draws near Anthony, and shouts in his ear:
　It is because I know all gods, all rites, all prayers, all oracles! I have penetrated into the cave of Trophonius, son of Apollo! I have kneaded for Syracusan women the cakes which they carry to the mountains! I have endured the eighty tests of Mithra! I have pressed to my heart the serpent of Sabasius! I have received the scarf of Cabiri! I have laved Cybele in the waters of the Campanian gulfs, and I have passed three moons in the caverns of Samothracia!

DAMIS

with a stupid laugh:
　Ah! ah! ah! at the mysteries of the good Goddess!

APOLLONIUS

And now we recommence our pilgrimage!

We go to the North to the land of Swans and of snows. Upon the vast white plains, the blind hippopodes break with the tips of their feet the ultramarine plant.

DAMIS

Hasten! it is already dawn. The cock has crowed, the horse has neighed, the sail is hoisted!

ANTHONY

The cock has not crowed! I hear the locusts in the sands, and I see the moon still in her place.

APOLLONIUS

We go to the South, beyond the mountains and the mighty waters, to seek in perfumes the secret source of love. Thou shall inhale the odor of myrrhodion which makes the weak die. Thou shalt bathe thy body in the lake of Rose-oil which is in the Island Junonia. Thou shalt see slumbering upon primroses that Lizard which awakes every hundred years when the carbuncle upon its forehead, arriving at maturity, falls to the ground. The stars palpitate like eyes; the cascades sing like the melody of lyres; strange intoxication is exhaled by blossoming flowers; thy mind shall grow vaster in that air; and thy heart shall change even as thy face.

DAMIS

Master! it is time! The wind has risen, the swallows awaken, the myrtle leaves are blown away!

APOLLONIUS

Yes! let us go!

ANTHONY

Nay! I remain here!

APOLLONIUS

Shall I tell thee where grows the plant Balis, that resurrects the dead?

DAMIS

Nay; ask him rather for the androdamas which attracts silver, iron and brass!

ANTHONY

Oh! how I suffer! how I suffer!

DAMIS

Thou shalt comprehend the voices of all living creatures, the roarings, the cooings!

APOLLONIUS

I shall enable thee to ride upon unicorns and upon dragons, upon hippocentaurs and dolphins!

ANTHONY

weeping:
Oh! oh! oh!

APOLLONIUS

Thou shalt know the demons that dwell in the caverns, the demons that mutter in the woods, the demons that move in the waves, the demons that push the clouds.

DAMIS

Tighten thy girdle! fasten thy sandals!

APOLLONIUS

I shall explain to thee the reason of divine forms—why Apollo stands, why Jupiter is seated, why Venus is black at Corinth, square-shaped at Athens, conical at Paphos.

ANTHONY

clasping his hands:
 Let them begone! let them begone!

APOLLONIUS
 In thy presense I will tear down the panoplies of the Gods; we shall force open the sanctuaries, I will enable thee to violate the Pythoness!

ANTHONY
 Help! O my God!

He rushes to the cross.

APOLLONIUS
 What is thy desire? What is thy dream? Thou needst only devote the moment of time necessary to think of it ...

ANTHONY
 Jesus! Jesus! Help me!

APOLLONIUS
 Dost thou wish me to make him appear, thy Jesus?

ANTHONY
 What? How!

APOLLONIUS
 It shall be He!—no other! He will cast off his crown, and we shall converse face to face!

DAMIS

in an undertone:
 Say thou dost indeed wish it! say thou dost desire it!

Anthony, kneeling before the cross, murmurs prayers. Damis walks around him, with wheedling gestures.

Nay, nay! good hermit, dear Saint Anthony! man so pure, man so illustrious! man who cannot be praised enough! Be not horrified! These are only exaggerated forms of speech, borrowed from the Orientals. That need in no way ...

APOLLONIUS

Let him alone, Damis!

He believes, like a brute, in the reality of things. The terror which he entertains of the Gods prevents him from comprehending them; and he debases his own God to the level of a jealous king!

But thou, my son, do not leave me!

He moves to the edge of the cliff, walking backward, passes beyond the verge of the precipice, and remains suspended in air.

Above all forms, further than the ends of the earth, beyond the heavens themselves, lies the world of Idea, replete with the splendor of the Word! With one bound we shall traverse the impending spaces, and thou shalt behold, in all his infinity, the Eternal, the Absolute, the Being! Come! give me thy hand! Let us thither!

Side by side, both rise up through the air, slowly.
Anthony, clinging to the cross, watches them rise.
They disappear.

V

ANTHONY

walking to and fro, slowly:

That one, indeed, seems in himself equal to all the powers of Hell!

Nebuchadnezzar did not so much dazzle me with his splendours;—the Queen of Sheba herself charmed me less deeply.

His manner of speaking of the gods compels one to feel a desire to know them.

I remember having beheld hundreds of them at one time, in the island of Elephantius, in the time of Diocletian. The emperor had ceded to the Nomads a great tract of country, upon the condition that they should guard the frontiers; and the treaty was concluded in the name of the "Powers Invisible." For the gods of each people were unknown unto the other people.

The Barbarians had brought theirs with them. They occupied the sand-hills bordering the river. We saw them supporting their idols in their arms, like great paralytic children;—others, paddling through the cataracts upon trunks of palm trees, displayed from afar off the amulets hung about their necks, the tattooings upon their breasts; and these things were not more sinful than the religion of the Greeks, the Asiatics, and the Romans!

When I was dwelling in the temple of Heliopolis I would often consider the things I beheld upon the walls:—vultures bearing sceptres, crocodiles playing upon lyres, faces of men with the bodies of serpents, cow-headed women prostrating themselves before ithyphallic gods;—and their supernatural forms attracted my thoughts to other worlds. I longed to know that which drew the gaze of all those calm and mysterious eyes.

If matter can exert such power, it must surely contain a spirit. The souls of the Gods are attached to their images ...

Those possessing the beauty of forms might seduce. But the others ... those of loathsome or terrible aspect ... how can men believe in them?

And he beholds passing over the surface of the ground,—leaves, stones, shells, branches of trees,—then a variety of hydropical dwarfs: these are gods. He bursts into a laugh.

He hears another laugh behind him;—and Hilarion appears, in the garb of a hermit, far taller than before, colossal.

ANTHONY
who feels no surprise at seeing him:
How stupid one must be to worship such things!

HILARION
Aye!—exceedingly stupid!

Then idols of all nations and of all epochs—of wood, of metal, of granite, of feathers, of skins sewn together;—pass before them.

The most ancient of all anterior to the Deluge are hidden under masses of seaweed hanging down over them like manes. Some that are too long for their bases crack in all their joints, and break their own backs in walking. Others have rents torn in their bellies through which sand trickles out.

Anthony and Hilarion are prodigiously amused. They hold their sides for laughter.

Then appear sheep-headed idols. They totter upon their bandy-legs, half-open their eye-lids, and stutter like the dumb,

"Ba! ba! ba!"

The more that the idols commence to resemble the human forms, the more they irritate Anthony. He strikes them with his fist, kicks them, attacks them with fury.

They become frightful,—with lofty plumes, eyes like balls, fingers terminated by claws, the jaws of sharks.

And before these gods men are slaughtered upon altars of stone; others are brayed alive in huge mortars, crushed under chariots, nailed upon trees. There is one all of red-hot iron with the horns of a bull, who devours children.

ANTHONY

Horror!

HILARION

But the gods always demand tortures and suffering. Even thine desired ...

ANTHONY

weeping:

Ah! say no more!—do not speak to me!

The space girdled by the rocks suddenly changes into a valley. A herd of cattle are feeding upon the short grass.

The herdman who leads them observes a cloud;—and in a sharp voice shouts out words of command, as if to heaven.

HILARION

Because he needs rain, he seeks by certain chants to compel the King of heaven to open the fecund cloud.

ANTHONY

laughing:
Verily, such pride is the extreme of foolishness!

HILARION

Why dost thou utter exorcisms?

The valley changes into a sea of milk, motionless and infinite.

In its midst floats a long cradle formed by the coils of a serpent, whose many curving heads shade, like a dais, the god slumbering upon its body.

He is beardless, young, more beautiful than a girl, and covered with diaphanous veils. The pearls of his tiara gleam softly like moons; a chaplet of stars is entwined many times about his breast, and with one hand beneath his head, he slumbers with the look of one who dreams after wine.

A woman, crouching at his feet, awaits the moment of his awaking.

HILARION

Such is the primordial duality of the Brahmans,—the Absolute being inexpressible by any form.

From the navel of the god has grown the stem of a lotus flower; it blossoms, and within its chalice appears another god with three faces.

ANTHONY

How strange an invention!

HILARION

Father, Son, and Holy Spirit are but one and the same Person!

The three faces separate; and three great gods appear.[8]
The first, who is pink, bites the end of his great toe.
The second, who is blue, uplifts his four arms.
The third, who is green, wears a necklace of human skulls.

Before them instantly arise three goddesses[9]—one is enveloped in a net; another offers a cup; the third brandishes a bow.

And these gods, these goddesses, decuple themselves, multiply. Arms grow from their shoulders; at the end of these arms hands appear bearing standards, axes, bucklers, swords, parasols and drums. Fountains gush from their heads, plants grow from their nostrils.

Riding upon birds rocked in palanquins, enthroned upon seats of gold, standing in ivory niches,—they dream, voyage, command, drink wine, respire the breath of flowers. Dancing girls whirl in the dance; giants pursue monsters; at the entrances of grottoes solitaries meditate. Eyes cannot be distinguished from stars; nor clouds from banderoles; peacocks quench their thirst at rivers of gold dust; the embroidery of pavilions seems to blend with the spots of leopards; coloured rays intercross in the blue air, together with flying arrows, and swinging censers.

And all this develops like a lofty frieze, resting its base upon the rocks, and rising to the sky.

ANTHONY

dazzled by the sight:

How vast is their number! What do they seek?

HILARION

The god who rubs his abdomen with his elephant-trunk is the solar Deity, the inspiring spirit of wisdom.[10]

That other whose six heads are crowned with towers, and whose fourteen arms wield javelins,—is the prince of armies,—the Fire-Consumer.[11]

The old man riding the crocodile washes the soul of the dead upon the shore.[12] They will be tormented by that black woman with the putrid teeth, who is the Ruler of Hell.

That chariot drawn by red mares, driven by one who has no

legs, bears the master of the sun[13] through heaven's azure. The Moon-God[14] accompanies him, in a litter drawn by three gazelles.

Kneeling upon the back of a parrot, the Goddess of Beauty[15] presents to Love, her son, her rounded breast. Behold her now, further off, leaping for joy in the meadows. Look! Look! Coiffed with dazzling mitre, she trips lightly over the ears of growing wheat, over the waves; she rises in air, extending her power over all elements!

And among these gods are the Genii of the winds, of the planets, of the months, of the days,—a hundred thousand others;—multiple are their aspects, rapid their transformations. Behold! there is one who changes from a fish into a tortoise: he assumes the form of a boar, the shape of a dwarf.

ANTHONY

Wherefore?

HILARION

That he may preserve the equilibrium of the universe, and combat the works of evil. But life exhausts itself; forms wear away; and they must achieve progression in their metamorphoses.

All upon a sudden appears a

NAKED MAN

seated in the midst of the sand, with legs crossed.

A large halo vibrates, suspended in air behind him. The little ringlets of his black hair in which blueish tints shift symmetrically surround a protuberance upon the summit of his skull. His arms, which are very long, hang down against his sides. His two hands rest flat upon his thighs, with the palms open. The soles of his feet are like the faces of two blazing suns; and he remains completely motionless—before Anthony and Hilarion—with all the gods around him, rising in tiers above the rocks, as if upon the benches of some vast circus. His lips half open; and he speaks in a deep voice:

I am the Master of great charities, the succor of all creatures; and not less to the profane than to believers, do I expound the law.

That I might deliver the world, I resolved to be born among men. The gods wept when I departed from them.

I sought me first a woman worthy to give me birth: a woman of warrior race, the wife of a king, exceedingly good, excessively beautiful, with deep set navel and body firm as adamant;—and at time of the full moon, without the auxiliation of any male, I entered her womb.[16]

I issued from it by the right side. Stars stopped in their courses.

HILARION

murmurs between his teeth:

"And seeing the star, they rejoiced with exceeding great joy!"*

Anthony watches more attentively.

THE BUDDHA†

continuing:

From the furthest recesses of the Himalayas, a holy man one hundred years of age hurried to see me.

HILARION

"A man named Simeon, who should not see death before he had seen the Christ of the Lord!"‡

THE BUDDHA

I was led unto the schools; and it was found that I knew more than the teachers.

---

* Matthew ii: 10.

† "Buddha, or more correctly, the Buddha, for Buddha is an appellative meaning Enlightened."—Max Müller (*Chips*, Vol. I., 206).

‡ Luke ii: 25–26.

HILARION

"...In the midst of the doctors...and all that heard him were astonished at his wisdom!"*

Anthony makes a sign to Hilarion to be silent.

THE BUDDHA

Continually did I meditate in the gardens. The shadows of the trees turned with the turning of the sun; but the shadow of that which sheltered me turned not.

None could equal me in the knowledge of the Scriptures, the enumeration of atoms, the conduct of elephants, the working of wax, astronomy, poetry, pugilism, all the exercises and all the arts!

In accordance with custom, I took to myself a wife; and I passed the days in my kingly palace;—clad in pearls, under a rain of perfumes, fanned by the fly whisks of thirty-three thousand women,— watching my peoples from the height of my terraces adorned with fringes of resonant bells.

But the sight of the miseries of the world turned me away from pleasure. I fled.

I begged my way upon the high roads, clad myself in rags gathered within the sepulchres;—and, hearing of a most learned hermit, I chose to become his slave. I guarded his gate; I washed his feet.

Thus I annihilated all sensation, all joy, all languor.

Then, concentrating my thoughts within vaster meditation, I learned to know the essence of things, the illusion of forms.

Soon I exhausted the science of the Brahmans. They are gnawed by coveteousness and desire under their outward aspect of austerity; they daub themselves with filth, they lie upon thorns,—hoping to arrive at happiness by the path of death!

---

* Ibid ii: 46–47.

HILARION

"Pharisees, hypocrites, whited sepulchres, generation of vipers!"*

THE BUDDHA

I also accomplished wondrous things,—eating but one grain of rice each day (and the grains of rice in those times were no larger than at present)—my hair fell off; my body became black; my eyes receding within their sockets, seemed even as stars beheld at the bottom of a well.

During six years I kept myself motionless, exposed to the flies, the lions and the serpents; and the great summer suns, the torrential rains, lightnings and snows, hails and tempests,—all of these I endured without even the shelter of my lifted hand.

The travellers who passed by, believing me dead, cast clots of earth upon me!

Only the temptation of the Devil remained.

I summoned him.

His sons came,—hideous, scale-covered, nauseous as charnel-houses,—shrieking, hissing, bellowing; interclashing their panoplies, rattling together the bones of dead men. Some belched flame through their nostrils; some made darkness about me with their wings; some wore chaplets of severed fingers; some drank serpent-venom from the hollows of their hands;—they were swine-headed; they were rhinoceros-headed or toad-headed; they assumed all forms that inspire loathing or affright.

ANTHONY

to himself:

I also endured all that in other days!

THE BUDDHA

Then did he send me his daughters—beautiful with daintily-painted faces, and wearing girdles of gold. Their teeth were whiter

---

* Matthew xxiii: 27, 33.

than the jasmine-flower; their thighs round as the trunk of an elephant. Some extended their arms and yawned, that they might so display the dimples of their elbows; some winked their eyes; some laughed; some half-opened their garments. There were blushing virgins, matrons replete with dignity, queens who came with great trains of baggage and of slaves.

ANTHONY

aside:

Ah! he too?

THE BUDDHA

Having vanquished the Demon, I nourished myself for twelve years with perfumes only;—and as I had acquired the five virtues, the five faculties, the ten forces, the eighteen substances, and had entered into the four spheres of the invisible world, Intelligence became mine! I became the Buddha!

All the gods bow themselves down. Those having several heads bend them all simultaneously.

He lifts his mighty hand aloft and resumes:

That I might effect the deliverance of beings, I have made hundreds of thousands of sacrifices! To the poor I gave robes of silk, beds, chariots, houses, heaps of gold and of diamonds. I gave my hands to the one-handed, my legs to the lame, my eyes to the blind;—even my head I severed for the sake of the decapitated. In the day that I was King, I gave away provinces;—when I was a Brahman I despised no one. When I was a solitary, I spake kindly words to the robber who slew me. When I was a tiger I allowed myself to die of hunger.

And having, in this last existence, preached the law, nothing now remains for me to do. The great period is accomplished! Men, animals, the gods, the bamboos, the oceans, the mountains, the sand-grains of the Ganges, together with the myriad myriads of the stars,—all shall die;—and until the time of the new births, a flame shall dance upon the wrecks of worlds destroyed!

Then a great dizziness comes upon the gods. They stagger, fall into convulsions, and vomit forth their existences. Their crowns burst apart; their banners fly away. They tear off their attributes, their sexes, fling over their shoulders the cups from which they quaffed immortality, strangle themselves with their serpents, vanish in smoke;—and when all have disappeared . . .

HILARION

solemnly exclaims:

Thou hast even now beheld the belief of many hundreds of millions of men.

Anthony is prostrate upon the ground, covering his face with his hands. Hilarion, with his back turned to the cross, stands near him and watches him. A considerable time elapses.

———

Then a singular being appears—having the head of a man upon the body of a fish. He approaches through the air, upright, beating the sand from time to time with his tail; and the patriarchal aspect of his face, by contrast with his puny little arms, causes Anthony to laugh.

OANNES

in a plaintive voice:

Respect me! I am the contemporary of beginnings.

I dwelt in that formless world where hermaphroditic creatures slumbered, under the weight of an opaque atmosphere, in the deeps of dark waters—when fingers, fins, and wings were blended, and eyes without heads were floating like mollusks, among human-faced bulls, and dog-footed serpents.

Above the whole of these beings, Omoroca, bent like a hoop, extended her woman-body. But Belus cleft her in two halves; with one he made the earth; with the other, heaven;—and the two equal worlds do mutually contemplate each other.

I, the first consciousness of Chaos, arose from the abyss that I might harden matter, and give a law unto forms:—also I taught men to fish and to sow: I gave them knowledge of writing, and of the history of the gods.

Since then I have dwelt in the deep pools left by the Deluge. But the desert grows vaster about them; the winds cast sand into them; the sun devours them;—and I die upon my couch of slime, gazing at the stars through the water. Thither I return.

He leaps and disappears in the Nile.

HILARION

That is an ancient God of the Chaldeans!

ANTHONY

ironically:
What, then, were those of Babylon?

HILARION

Thou canst behold them!

And they find themselves upon the platform of a lofty quadrangular tower dominating six other towers, which, narrowing as they rise, form one monstrous pyramid. Far below a great black mass is visible—the city, doubtless—extending over the plains. The air is cold; the sky darkly blue; multitudes of stars palpitate above.

In the midst of the platform rises a column of white stone. Priests in linen robes pass and repass around it, so as to describe by their evolutions a moving circle; and with faces uplifted, they gaze upon the stars.

HILARION

pointing out several of these stars to Anthony:
There are thirty principal stars. Fifteen look upon the upper side of the earth; fifteen below. At regular intervals one shoots from the upper regions to those below; while another abandons the inferior deeps to rise to sublime altitudes.

Of the seven planets, two are beneficent; two evil; three ambiguous:—all things in the world depend upon the influence of these eternal fires. According to their position or movement presages may be drawn;—and here thou dost tread the most venerable place upon earth. Here Pythagoras and Zoroaster have met;—here for twelve thousand years these men have observed the skies that they might better learn to know the gods.

ANTHONY

The stars are not gods.

HILARION

Aye, they say the stars are gods; for all things about us pass away;—the heavens only remain immutable as eternity!

ANTHONY

Yet there is a master.

HILARION

pointing to the column:

He! Belus!—the first ray, the Sun, the Male!—The Other, whom he fecundates, is beneath him!

Anthony beholds a garden, illuminated by lamps.

He finds himself in the midst of the crowd, in an avenue of cypress-trees. To right and left are little pathways leading to huts constructed within a wood of pomegranate trees, and enclosed by treillages of reeds.

Most of the men wear pointed caps, and garments bedizened like the plumage of a peacock. But there are also people from the North clad in bearskins, nomads wearing mantles of brown wool, pallid Gangarides with long earrings;—and there seems to be as much confusion of rank as there is confusion of nations; for sailors and stone-cutters elbow the princes who wear tiaras blazing with carbuncles and who carry long canes with carven knobs. All proceed upon their way with dilated nostrils, absorbed by the same desire.

From time to time, they draw aside to make way for some long covered

*wagon drawn by oxen, or some ass jolting upon his back a woman bundled up
in thick veils, who finally disappears in the direction of the cabins.*

*Anthony feels afraid; he half-resolves to turn back. But an unutterable cu-
riosity takes possession of him and draws him on.*

*At the foot of the cypress-trees there are ranks of women squatting upon
deerskins, all wearing in lieu of diadem a plaited fillet of ropes. Some, mag-
nificently attired, loudly call upon the passers-by. Others, more timid, seek to
veil their faces with their arms, while some matron standing behind them,
their mother doubtless, exhorts them. Others, their heads veiled with a black
shawl, and their bodies entirely nude, seem from afar off to be statues of flesh.
As soon as a man has thrown some money upon their knees, they arise.*

*And the sound of kisses is heard under the foliage,—sometimes a great
sharp cry.*

HILARION

These are the virgins of Babylon, who prostitute themselves to
the goddess.

ANTHONY

What goddess?

HILARION

Behold her!

*And he shows him at the further end of the avenue, upon the threshold of
an illuminated grotto, a block of stone representing the sexual organ of a
woman.*

ANTHONY

Ignominy!—how abominable to give a sex to God!

HILARION

Thou thyself dost figure him in thy mind as a living person!

Anthony again finds himself in darkness.

———

He beholds in the air a luminous circle, poised upon horizontal wings.

This ring of light girdles, like a loose belt, the waist of a little man wearing a mitre upon his head and carrying a wreath in his hand. The lower part of his figure is completely concealed by immense feathers outspreading about him like a petticoat.

It is—

ORMUZD

—the God of the Persians. He hovers in the air above, crying aloud:

I fear! I can see his monstrous jaws.

I did vanquish thee, O Ahriman! But again thou dost war against me.

First revolting against me, thou didst destroy the eldest of creatures, Kaiomortz, the Man-Bull. Then didst thou seduce the first human couple, Meschia and Meschiané; and thou didst fill all hearts with darkness, thou didst urge thy battalions against heaven!

I also had mine own, the people of the stars; and from the height of my throne I contemplated the marshalling of the astral hosts.

Mithra, my son, dwelt in heavens inaccessible. There he received souls, from thence did he send them forth; and he arose each morning to pour forth the abundance of his riches.

The earth reflected the splendour of the firmament. Fire blazed upon the crests of the mountains,—symbolizing that other fire of which I had created all creatures. And that the holy flame might not be polluted, the bodies of the dead were not burned; the beaks of birds carried them aloft toward heaven.

I gave to men the laws regulating pastures, labour, the choice of wood for the sacrifices, the form of cups, the words to be uttered in hours of sleeplessness;—and my priests unceasingly offered up prayers, so that worship might be as the eternity of God in its endlessness. Men purified themselves with water, loaves were offered upon the altars, sins were confessed aloud.

Homa* gave himself to men to be drunk, that they might have his strength communicated to them.

While the Genii of heaven were combatting the demons, the children of Iran were pursuing the serpents. The King, whom an innumerable host of courtiers served upon their knees, represented me in his person, and wore my coiffure. His gardens had the magnificence of a heaven upon earth; and his tomb represented him in the act of slaying a monster,—emblem of Good destroying Evil.

For it was destined that I should one day definitely conquer Ahriman, by the aid of Time-without-limits.

But the interval between us disappears;—the deep night rises! To me! ye Amschaspands, ye Izeds, ye Ferouers! Succor me, Mithra! seize thy sword! And thou, Kaosyac, who shall return for the universal deliverance, defend me! What!—none to aid!

Ah! I die! Thou art the victor, Ahriman!

Hilarion, standing behind Anthony, restrains a cry of joy;—and Ormuzd is swallowed up in the darkness.

Then appears:

THE GREAT DIANA OF EPHESUS
black with enamelled eyes, her elbows pressed to her side, her forearms extended, with hands open.

Lions crawl upon her shoulders; fruits, flowers, and stars intercross upon her bosom; further down three rows of breasts appear; and from her belly to her feet she is covered with a tightly fitting sheath from which bulls, stags, griffins, and bees seem about to spring, their bodies half-protruding from it. She is illuminated by the white light emanating from a disk of silver, round as the full moon, placed behind her head.

---

* Or, Haoma, also Hom, the sacred plant, whose fermented juice occupied an important place in the practical rites of Iran. Supposed to be the same plant known in botany as *Sarcostemma viminalis*. Deified in Iranian worship, like the sacred drink *Soma* in the Vedic hymns. The *Soma* was the fermented extract of the *Asclepias acida* or *Sarcostemma ritalis*. See Marius Fontane, "L'Inde Védique," "Les Iraniens."

Where is my temple?
Where are my Amazons?
What is this I feel?—I, the Incorruptible!—a strange faintness comes upon me!

Her flowers wither, her over-ripe fruits become detached and fall. The lions and the bulls hang their heads; the stags foam at the mouth, as though exhausted; the buzzing bees die upon the ground.

She presses her breasts, one after the other. All are empty! But under a desperate effort her sheath bursts. She seizes it by the bottom, like the skirt of a robe, throws her animals, her fruits, her flowers, into it,—then withdraws into the darkness.

And afar off there are voices, murmuring, growling, roaring, bellowing, belling. The density of the night is augmented by breaths. Drops of warm rain fall.

ANTHONY

How sweet the odour of the palm trees, the trembling of leaves, the transparency of springs! I feel the desire to lie flat upon the Earth that I might feel her against my heart; and my life would be reinvigorated by her eternal youth!

He hears the sound of castanets and of cymbals; and men appear, clad in white tunics with red stripes,—leading through the midst of a rustic crowd an ass, richly harnessed, its tail decorated with knots of ribbons, and its hoofs painted.

A box covered with a saddle-cloth* of yellow material shakes to and fro upon its back, between two baskets,—one receives the offerings contributed,— eggs, grapes, pears, cheeses, fowls, little coins; and the other basket is full of roses, which the leaders of the ass pluck to pieces as they walk before the animal, shedding the leaves upon the ground.

They wear earrings and large mantles; their locks are plaited, their cheeks

---

* Apuleius says, "a silken mantle."

painted; olive-wreaths are fastened upon their foreheads by medallions bear-
ing figurines;—all wear poniards in their belts, and brandish ebony-handled
whips, having three thongs to which osselets are attached. *

Those who form the rear of the procession place upon the soil,—so as to
remain upright as a candelabrum,—a tall pine, which burns at its summit,
and shades under its lower branches a lamb.

The ass halts. The saddle-cloth is removed. Underneath appears a second
covering of black felt. Then one of the men in white tunics begins to dance,
rattling his crotali;—another, kneeling before the box, beats a tambourine and

THE OLDEST OF THE BAND

begins:

Here is the Good Goddess, the Idean of the mountains, the
Great Mother of Syria! Come ye hither, good people all!

She gives joy to men, she heals the sick; she sends inheritances;
she satisfies the hunger of love.

We bear her through the land, rain or shine, in fair weather, or in
foul.

Oft times we lie in the open air, and our table is not always well
served. Robbers dwell in the woods. Wild beasts rush from their
caverns. Slippery paths border the precipices. Behold her! behold
her!

They lift off the covering; and a box is seen, inlaid with little pebbles.

Loftier than the cedars, she looks down from the blue ether.
Vaster than the wind she encircles the world. Her breath is exhaled
by the nostrils of tigers; the rumbling of her voice is heard beneath
the volcanoes; her wrath is the tempest; the pallor of her face has
whitened the moon. She ripens the harvest; by her the tree-bark
swells with sap; she makes the beard to grow. Give her something;
for she hates the avaricious!

---

* Apuleius says, "strung with knuckle-bones of sheep."

The box opens; and under a little pavilion of blue silk appears a small image of Cybele—glittering with spangles, crowned with towers, and seated in a chariot of red stone, drawn by two lions, with uplifted paws.

The crowd presses forward to see.

THE ARCHIGALLUS

continues:

She loves the sound of resounding tympanums, the echo of dancing feet, the howling of wolves, the sonorous mountains and the deep gorges, the flower of the almond tree, the pomegranate and the green fig, the whirling dance, the snoring flute, the sugary sap, the salty tear,—blood! To thee, to thee!—Mother of the mountains!

They scourge themselves with their whips; and their chests resound with the blows;—the skins of the tambourines vibrate almost to bursting. They seize their knives; they gash their arms.

She is sorrowful; let us be sorrowful! Our suffering is necessary in order to please her! Thereby your sins will be remitted. Blood purifies all—fling its red drops abroad like blossoms! She, the Great Mother, demands the blood of another creature—of a pure being!

The Archigallus raises his knife above the head of a lamb.

ANTHONY

seized with horror:

Do not slay the lamb!

There is a gush of purple blood.

The priest sprinkles the crowd with it; and all—including Anthony and Hilarion—standing around the burning tree, silently watch the last palpitations of the victim.

A Woman comes forth from the midst of the priests; she resembles exactly the image within the little box.

She pauses, perceiving before her a Young Man wearing a Phrygian cap.

His thighs are covered with a pair of narrow trousers, with lozenge-shaped openings here and there at regular intervals, closed by bow knots of coloured material. He stands in an attitude of langour, resting his elbow against a branch of the tree, holding a flute in his hand.

CYBELE

flinging her arms about his waist:

I have traversed all regions of the earth to join thee—and famine ravaged the fields. Thou hast deceived me! It matters not! I love thee! Warm my body in thine embrace! Let us be united!

ATYS

The springtime will never again return, O eternal Mother! Despite my love, it is no longer possible for me to penetrate thy essence. Would that I might cover myself with a painted robe like thine. I envy thy breasts, swelling with milk, the length of thy tresses, thy vast flanks that have borne and brought forth all creatures. Why am I not thou?—Why am I not a woman?—No, never! depart from me! My virility fills me with horror!

With a sharp stone he emasculates himself and runs furiously from her, holding his severed member aloft.

The priests imitate the god; the faithful do even as the priests. Men and women exchange garments, embrace;—and the tumult of bleeding flesh passes away, while the sound of voices remaining becomes even more strident,—like the shrieking of mourners, like the voices heard at funerals.

———

A huge catafalque, hung with purple, supports upon its summit an ebony bed, surrounded by torches and baskets of silver filagree, in which are verdant leaves of lettuce, mallow and fennel. Upon the steps of the construction, from summit to base, sit women all clad in black, with loosened girdles and bare feet, holding in their hands, with a melancholy air, great bouquets of flowers.

At each corner of the estrade urns of alabaster, filled with myrrh, slowly send up their smoke.

Upon the bed can be perceived the corpse of a man. Blood flows from his thigh. One of his arms hangs down lifelessly;—and a dog licks his finger-nails and howls.

The row of torches placed closely together prevents his face from being seen; and Anthony feels a strange anguish within him. He fears lest he should recognize some one.

The sobs of the women cease; and after an interval of silence,

ALL

psalmody together:

Fair! fair!—all fair he is! Thou hast slept enough!—lift thy head!—arise!

Inhale the perfume of our flowers—narcissus—blossoms and anemones, gathered in thine own gardens to please thee. Arouse thee! thou dost make us fear for thee!

Speak to us! What dost thou desire? Wilt thou drink wine?—wilt thou lie in our beds?—dost wish to eat the honeycakes which have the form of little birds?

Let us press his hips,—kiss his breast! Now!—now!—dost thou not feel our ring-laden fingers passing over thy body?—and our lips that seek thy mouth?—and our tresses that sweep thy thighs? O faint God, deaf to our prayers!

They cry aloud, and rend their faces with their nails; then all hush,—and the howling of the dog continues in the silence.

Alas! alas! Woe!—the black blood trickles over his snowy flesh! See! his knees writhe!—his sides sink in! The bloom of his face hath damp-ened the purple. He is dead, dead! O weep for him! Lament for him!

In long procession they ascend to lay between the torches the offerings of their several tresses, that seem from afar off like serpents, black or blond;—and the catafalque is lowered gently to the level of a grotto,—the opening of a shadowy sepulchre that yawns behind it.

Then

A WOMAN

bends over the corpse.

Her long hair, uncut, envelops her from head to feet. She sheds tears so abundantly that her grief cannot be as that of the others, but more than human—infinite.

Anthony dreams of the Mother of Jesus. She speaks:

Thou didst emerge from the Orient, and didst take me, all trembling with the dew, into thy arms, O Sun! Doves fluttered upon the azure of thy mantle; our kisses evoked low breezes among the foliage; and I abandoned myself wholly to thy love, delighting in the pleasure of my weakness.

Alas! alas—Why didst thou depart, to run upon the mountains?

A boar did wound thee at the time of the autumnal equinox!

Thou art dead; and the fountains weep,—the trees bend down. The wind of winter whistles through the naked brushwood.

My eyes are about to close, seeing that darkness covers thee! Now thou dwellest in the underworld near the mightiest of my rivals.

O Persephone, all that is beautiful descends to thee, never to return!

Even while she speaks, her companions lift the dead, to place him within the sepulchre. He remains in their hands. It was only a waxen corpse.

Wherefore Anthony feels something resembling relief.

All vanish;—and the hut, the rocks, and the cross reappear.

———

But upon the other side of the Nile, Anthony beholds a Woman, standing in the midst of the desert.

She retains in her hand the lower part of a long black veil that hides all her face; supporting with her left arm a little child to whom she is giving suck. A great ape crouches down in the sand beside her.

She uplifts her head toward heaven; and in spite of the great distance, her voice is distinctly heard.

ISIS

O Neith, Beginning of all things! Ammon, Lord of Eternity; Pthah, demiurgos; Thoth, his intelligence; gods of the Amenthi, particular triads of the Nomes,—falcons in the azure of heaven, sphinxes before the temples, ibises perched between the horns of oxen, planets, constellations, shore, murmurs of the wind, gleams of the light,—tell me where I may find Osiris!

I have sought him in all the canals and all the lakes—aye, further yet, even to Phœnician Byblos. Anubis, with ears pricked up, leaped about me, and yelped, and thrust his muzzle searchingly into the tufts of the tamarinds. Thanks, good Cynocephalos—thanks to thee!

She gives the ape two or three friendly little taps upon the head.

Hideous Typhon the red-haired slew him, tore him in pieces! We have found all his members. But I have not that which rendered me fecund!

She utters wild lamentations.

ANTHONY
is filled with fury. He casts stones at her, reviles her.
Begone! thou shameless one!—Begone!

HILARION
Nay! respect her! Her religion was the faith of thy fathers!—thou didst wear her amulets when thou wert a child in the cradle.

ISIS
In the summers of long ago, the inundation drove the impure beasts into the desert. The dykes were opened, the boats dashed against each other; the panting earth drank the river with the intoxication of joy. Then, O God, with the horns of the bull, thou

didst lie upon my breast, and then was heard the lowings of the
Eternal Cow!

The seasons of sowing and reaping, of threshing and of vintage, followed each other in regular order with the years. In the
eternal purity of the nights, broad stars beamed and glowed. The
days were bathed in never-varying splendour. Like a royal couple
the Sun and the Moon appeared simultaneously, at either end of
the horizon.

Then did we both reign above a sublimer world, twin-monarchs,
wedded within the womb of eternity—he bearing a coucoupha-
headed sceptre; I, the sceptre that is tipped with a lotus-flower;
both of us erect with hands joined; and the crumblings of empires
affected not our attitude.

Egypt extended, below us, monumental and awful, long-shaped
like the corridor of a temple; with obelisks on the right, pyramids
on the left, and its labyrinth in the midst. And everywhere were
avenues of monsters, forests of columns, massive pylons flanking
gates summit-crowned with the mysterious globe—the globe of
the world, between two wings.

The animals of her Zodiac also existed in her pasture lands; and
filled her mysterious writing with their forms and colours. Divided
into twelve regions as the year is divided into twelve months—each
month, each day also having its own god—she reproduced the immutable order of heaven. And man even in dying changed not his
face; but saturated with perfumes, invulnerable to decay, he lay
down to sleep for three thousand years in another and silent Egypt.

And that Egypt, vaster than the Egypt of the living, extended beneath the earth.

Thither one descended by dark stairways leading into halls
where were represented the joys of the good, the tortures of the
wicked, all that passes in the third and invisible world. Ranged
along the wall the dead in their painted coffins awaited their turn;
and the soul, exempted from migrations, continued its heavy slumber until the awakening into a new life.

Nevertheless, Osiris sometimes came to see me. And by his ghost I became the mother of Harpocrates.

She contemplates the child.

Aye! it is he. Those are his eyes; those are his locks, plaited into ram horns! Thou shalt recommence his works. We shall bloom again like the lotus. I am still the Great Isis!—none has yet lifted my veil! My fruit is the Sun!

Sun of Springtime, clouds now obscure thy face! The breath of Typhon devours the pyramids. But a little while ago I beheld the Sphinx flee away. He was galloping like a jackal.

I look for my priests,—my priests clad in mantles of linen, with their great harps, and bearing a sacred bark, adorned with silver pateras. There are no more festivals upon the lakes!—no more illuminations in my delta!—no more cups of milk at Philæ! Apis has long ceased to reappear.

Egypt! Egypt! thy great motionless gods have their shoulders already whitened by the dung of birds; and the wind that passes over the desert rolls with it and the ashes of thy dead!—Anubis, guardian of ghosts, abandon me not!

The Cynocephalos has vanished.
She shakes her child.

But ... what ails thee ... thy hands are cold, thy head droops!

Harpocrates expires. Then she cries aloud with a cry so piercing, funereal, heart-rending, that Anthony answers it with another cry, extending his arms as to support her.
She is no longer there. He lowers his face, overwhelmed by shame.

———

All that he has seen becomes confused within his mind. It is like the bewilderment of travel, the illness of drunkenness. He wishes to hate; and yet a vague pity softens his heart. He begins to weep, and weeps abundantly.

HILARION

What makes thee sorrowful?

ANTHONY

after having long sought within himself for a reply:

I think of all the souls that have been lost through these false gods!

HILARION

Dost thou not think that they ... sometimes ... bear much resemblance to the True?

ANTHONY

That is but a device of the Devil to seduce the faithful more easily. He attacks the strong through the mind, the weak through the flesh.

HILARION

But luxury, in its greatest fury, has all the disinterestedness of penitence. The frenzied love of the body accelerates the destruction thereof,—and proclaims the extent of the impossible by the exposition of the body's weakness.

ANTHONY

What signifies that to me? My heart sickens with disgust of these bestial gods, forever busied with carnages and incests!

HILARION

Yet recollect all those things in the Scripture which scandalize thee because thou art unable to comprehend them! So also may these Gods conceal under their sinful forms some mighty truth.

There are more of them yet to be seen. Look around!

ANTHONY

No, no!—it is dangerous!

Hilarion

But a little while ago thou didst desire to know them. Is it because thy faith might vacillate in the presence of lies? What fearest thou?

The rocks fronting Anthony have become as a mountain.

A line of clouds obscures the mountain half way between summit and base; and above the clouds appears another mountain, enormous, all green, unequally hollowed by valleys nestling in its slopes, and supporting at its summit, in the midst of laurel-groves, a palace of bronze, roofed with tiles of gold, and supported by columns having capitals of ivory.

In the centre of the peristyle

Jupiter

—colossal, with torso nude,—holds Victory in one hand, his thunderbolts in the other; and his eagle, perched between his feet, rears its head.

Juno

seated near him, rolls her large eyes, beneath a diadem whence her windblown veil escapes like a vapour.

Behind them,

Minerva

standing upon a pedestal, leans on her spear. The skin of the Gorgon covers her breast, and a linen peplos falls in regular folds to the nails of her toes. Her glaucous eyes, which gleam beneath her vizor, gaze afar off, attentively.

On the right of the palace, the aged

Neptune

bestrides a dolphin beating with its fins a vast azure expanse which may be sea or sky, for the perspective of the Ocean seems a continuation of the blue ether: the two elements are interblended.

On the other side weird

PLUTO

in night-black mantle, crowned with diamond tiara and bearing a sceptre of ebony, sits in the midst of an islet surrounded by the circumvolutions of the Styx;—and this river of shadow empties itself into the darknesses, which form a vast black gulf below the cliff,—a bottomless abyss.

MARS

clad in brass, brandishes as in wrath his broad shield and his sword.

HERCULES

leaning upon his club, gazes at him from below.

APOLLO

his face ablaze with light, grasps with outstretched right arm the reins of four white horses urged to a gallop; and

CERES

in her ox-drawn chariot advances toward him with a sickle in her hand. Behind her comes

BACCHUS

riding in a very low chariot, gently drawn by lynxes. Plump and beardless, with vine leaves garlanding his brow, he passes by holding in his hand an overflowing cup of wine. Silenus riding beside him reels upon his ass. Pan of the pointed ears blows upon his syrinx; the Mimallonides beat drums; the Mænads strew flowers; the Bacchantes turn in the dance with heads thrown back and hair dishevelled.

DIANA

with tunic tucked up, issues from the wood together with her nymphs. At the further end of a cavern,

VULCAN

among his Cabiri, hammers the heated iron; here and there the aged Rivers

*leaning recumbent upon green rocks pour water from their urns; the Muses
stand singing in the valleys.*

The Hours, all of equal stature, link hands; and

MERCURY

*poses obliquely upon a rainbow, with his caduceus, winged sandals, and
winged petasus.*

*But at the summit of the stairway of the Gods,—among clouds soft as
down, from whose turning volutes a rain of roses falls,—*

VENUS ANADYOMENE

*stands gazing at herself in a mirror.—her eyes move languorously beneath
their slumbrous lids.*

*She has masses of rich blond hair rolling down over her shoulders; her
breasts are small; her waist is slender; her hips curve out like the sweeping
curves of a lyre; her thighs are perfectly rounded; there are dimples about her
knees; her feet are delicate; a butterfly hovers near her mouth. The splendour
of her body makes a nacreous-tinted halo of bright light about her; while all
the rest of Olympus is bathed in a pink dawn, rising gradually to the heights
of the blue sky.*

ANTHONY

Ah! my heart swells! A joy never known before thrills me to the
depths of my soul! How beautiful, how beautiful it is!

HILARION

They leaned from the heights of cloud to direct the way of
swords; one used to meet them upon the high roads; men had them
in their houses—and this familiarity divinized life.

Life's aim was only to be free and beautiful. Nobility of attitude
was facilitated by the looseness of garments. The voice of the ora-
tor, trained by the sea, rolled its sonorous waves against the porticoes of marble. The ephebus, anointed with oil, wrestled all naked
in the full light of the sun. The holiest of actions was to expose perfection of forms to all.

And these men respected wives, aged men, suppliants. Behind the temple of Hercules there was an altar erected to Pity.

Victims were immolated with flowers wreathed about the fingers of the sacrificer. Even memory was exempted from thoughts of the rottenness of death. Nothing remained but a little pile of ashes. And the Soul, mingling with the boundless ether, rose up to the gods.

Bending to whisper in Anthony's ear:

And they still live! The Emperor Constantine adores Apollo. Thou wilt find the Trinity in Samothracian mysteries,—baptism in the religion of Isis,—redemption in the faith of Mithra,—the martyrom of a God in the festivals of Bacchus. Prosperpine is the Virgin!... Aristæus is Jesus!

ANTHONY

remains awhile with downcast eyes, as if in deep thought; then suddenly re-peats aloud the Symbol of Jerusalem,[17] as he remembers it, uttering a long sigh between each phrase:

I believe in one only God, the Father,—and in one only Lord, Jesus Christ,—the first born son of God,—who was incarnated and made man,—who was crucified,—and buried,—who ascended into Heaven,—who will come to judge the living and the dead,—of whose Kingdom there shall be no end;—and in one Holy Spirit,—and in one baptism of repentance,—and in one Holy Catholic Church,—and in the resurrection of the flesh,—and in the life everlasting!

Immediately the cross becomes loftier and loftier; it pierces the clouds, and casts its shadow upon the heaven of the Gods.

All grow pale. Olympus shudders.

And at its base Anthony beholds vast bodies enchained, sustaining the rocks upon their shoulders,—giant figures half buried in the deeps of caverns. These are the Titans, the Giants, the Hecatonchires, the Cyclops.

A VOICE

rises, indistinct and awful, like the far roar of waves, like the din of forests in time of tempest, like the mighty moaning of the wind among the precipices:

We knew these things!—we knew them! There must come an end even for the Gods! Uranus was mutilated by Saturn,—Saturn by Jupiter. And Jupiter himself shall be annihilated. Each in his turn;—it is Destiny!

And little by little they sink into the mountain, and disappear. Meanwhile the golden tiles of the palace rise and fly away.

JUPITER

has descended from his throne. At his feet the thunderbolts lie, smoking like burning coals about to expire;—and the great eagle bends its neck to pick up its falling feathers.

Then I am no longer the master of all things,—most holy, most mighty, god of the phratrias and Greek peoples,—ancestor of all the Kings,—Agamemnon of heaven!

Eagle of apotheoses, what wind from Erebus has wafted thee to me? or, fleeing from the Campus Martius, dost thou bear me the soul of the last of the Emperors?

I no longer desire to receive those of men! Let the Earth keep them; and let them move upon the level of its baseness. Their hearts are now the hearts of slaves;—they forget injuries, forget their ancestors, forget their oaths,—and everywhere the folly of crowds, the mediocrity of individuals, the hideousness of races, hold sway!

He pants with such violence that his sides seem ready to burst asunder; he clenches his hands. Weeping, Hebe offers him a cup. He seizes it.

No, no! So long as there shall be a brain enclosing a thought, in whatsoever part of the world;—so long as there shall exist a mind hating disorder, creating Law,—so long will the spirit of Jupiter live!

But the cup is empty.
He turns its edge down over his thumbnail.

Not one drop left! When the ambrosia fails, the Immortals must indeed depart!

The cup drops from his hands; and he leans against a column, feeling himself about to die.

JUNO

Thou shouldst not have had so many amours! Eagle, bull, swan, rain of gold, cloud and flame, thou didst assume all forms,— dissipate thy light in all elements,—lose thy hair upon all beds! This time the divorce is irrevocable; and our domination, our very existence, dissolved!

She passes away in air.

MINERVA

has no longer her spear; and the ravens nesting among the sculptures of the freizes, wheel about her, pecking at her helmet.

Let me see whether my vessels cleave the bright sea, returning to my three ports,—let me discover why the fields are deserted, and learn what the daughters of Athens are now doing.

In the month of Hecatombeon my whole people came to worship me, under the guidance of their magistrates and priests. Then, all in white robes and wearing chitons of gold, they advanced the long line of virgins bearing cups, baskets, parasols; then the three hundred sacrificial oxen, and the old men having green boughs, the soldiers with clashing of armour, the ephebi singing hymns, flute players, lyre players, rhapsodists, dancing women;—and lastly attached to the mast of a trireme mounted upon wheel, my great veil embroidered by virgins who had been nourished in a particular way for a whole year. And when it had been displayed in all the streets, in all the squares, and before the temples, in the midst of the ever-chanting procession, it was borne step by step up the hill of the Acropolis, grazed the Propylæa, and entered the Parthenon.

But a strange feebleness comes upon me,—me the Industrious One! What! what! not one idea comes to me! Lo! I am trembling more than a woman.

She turns, beholds a ruin behind her, utters a cry, and stricken by a fallen fragment, falls backward upon the ground.

HERCULES
has flung away his lion-skin; and with feet firmly braced, back arched, teeth clenched, he exhausts himself in immeasurable efforts to bear up the mass of crumbling Olympus.

I vanquished the Cercopes, the Amazons, and the Centaurs. Many were the kings I slew. I broke the horn of the great river, Achelous. I cut the mountains asunder, I joined oceans; I freed nations from slavery; and I peopled lands that were desolate. I travelled through the countries of Gaul; I traversed the deserts where thirst prevails. I defended the gods from their enemies; and I freed myself from Omphale. But the weight of Olympus is too great for me. My arms grow feebler:—I die!

He is crushed beneath the ruins.

PLUTO
It is thy fault, Amphytrionad! Wherefore didst thou descend into my empire?

The vulture that gnaws the entrails of Tityus lifted its head;—

the lips of Tantalus were moistened;—the wheel of Ixion stopped.

Meanwhile the Kæres extended their claws to snatch back the escaping ghosts; the Furies tore the serpents of their locks; and Cerberus, fettered by thee with a chain, sounded the death rattle in his throat, and foamed at all his three mouths.

Thou didst leave the gate ajar; others have come. The daylight of men has entered into Tartarus!

He sinks into the darkness.

NEPTUNE

My trident can no longer call up the tempests. The monsters that terrified of old lie rotting at the bottom of the sea.

Amphitrite whose white feet tripped lightly over the foam, the green Nereids seen afar off in the horizon, the scaly Sirens who stopped the passing vessels to tell stories, and the ancient Tritons mightily blowing upon their shells, all have passed away. All is desolate and dead; the gaiety of the great Sea is no more!

I shall not survive it! Let the vast Ocean engulf me!

He vanishes beneath the azure.

DIANA

clad in black and surrounded by her dogs, which have been changed into wolves:

The freedom of the deep forests once intoxicated me; the odours of the wild beasts and the exhalations of the marshes made me as one drunk with joy. But the women whose maternity I protected now bring dead children into the world. The moon trembles with the incantations of witches. Desires of violence, of immensity, seize me, fill me. I wish to drink poisons,—to lose myself in vapours, in dreams!

And a passing cloud carries her away.

MARS

unhelmed and covered with blood:

At first I fought alone;—singlehanded I would provoke a whole army by my insults,—caring nothing for countries or nations, demanding battle for the pleasure of carnage alone.

Afterward I had comrades. They marched to the sound of flutes, in good order, with equal step, respiring above their bucklers, with plumes loftily nodding, lances oblique. Then on we rushed to battle with mighty eagle cries. War was joyous as a banquet. Three hundred men strove against all Asia.[18]

But the Barbarians are returning! and by myriads they come, by millions! Ah! since numbers, and engines, and cunning are stronger than valour, it were better that I die the death of the brave!

He kills himself.

VULCAN

sponging the sweat from his limbs:

The world is growing cold. The source of heat must be nourished, the volcanoes and rivers of flowing metal underground! Strike harder!—with full swing of the arms,—with might and main!

The Cabiri wound themselves with their hammers, blind themselves with sparks, and, groping, lose themselves in the darkness.

CERES

standing in her chariot, impelled by wheels having wings at their hubs:

Stop! Stop!

Ah! it was with good reason that the exclusion of strangers, atheists, Epicureans, and Christians was commended! Now the mystery of the basket has been unveiled; the sanctuary profaned: all is lost!

She descends a precipitous slope—shrieking, despairing, tearing her hair.

Ah! lies, lies! Daira has not been restored to me! The voice of brass calls me to the dead. This is another Tartarus, whence there is no return! Horror!

The abyss engulfs her.

BACCHUS

with a frenzied laugh:

What matters it? The Archon's wife is my spouse! The law itself reels in drunkenness. To me the new song, the multiplied forms!

The fire by which my mother was devoured flows in my veins. Let it burn yet more fiercely, even though I perish!

Male and female, complaisant to all, I abandon myself to you, Bacchantes! I abandon myself to you, Bacchanalians!—and the vine shall twine herself about the tree-trunks! Howl! dance! writhe! Loosen the tiger and the slave!—rend flesh with ferocious bitings!

And Pan, Silenus, the Bacchantes, the Mimallonides and the Mænads,— with their serpents, torches, sable masks,—cast flowers at each other, unveil a phallic effigy, kiss it,—shake their tympanums, strike their thyrsi, pelt each other with shells, devour grapes, strangle a goat, and tear Bacchus asunder.

APOLLO

furiously whipping his coursers, while his blanching locks are falling from his head:

I have left far behind me stony Delos, so pure that all now there seems dead; and I must strive to reach Delphi ere its inspiring vapour be wholly lost. The mules browse in its laurel groves. The Pythoness has wandered away, and cannot be found.

By a stronger concentration of my power, I will obtain sublime hymns, eternal monuments; and all matter will be penetrated by the vibrations of my cithara!

He strikes the strings of the instrument. They burst, lashing his face with their broken ends. He flings the cithara away; and furiously whipping his quadriga, cries:

No! enough of forms! Further, higher!—to the very summit!—to the realm of pure thought!

But the horses back, rear, dash the chariot to pieces. Entangled by the harness, caught by the fragments of the broken pole, he falls head foremost into the abyss.
The sky is darkened.

VENUS

blue with cold, shivering:
Once with my girdle I made all the horizon of Hellas.

Her fields glowed with the roses of my cheeks; her shores were outlined after the fashion of my lips; and her mountains, whiter than my doves, palpitated beneath the hands of the statuaries. My spirit's manifestation was found in the ordinances of the festivals, in the arrangement of coiffures, in the dialogues of philosophers, in the constitution of republics. But I have doted too much upon men! It is Love that has dishonoured me!

She casts herself back weeping:

This world is abominable. There is no air for me to breathe!
O Mercury, inventor of the lyre, conductor of souls, take me away!

She places one finger upon her lips, and describing an immense parabola, falls into the abyss.
Nothing is now visible. The darkness is complete.
Only, that from the eyes of Hilarion escape two flashes, two rays of lurid light.

ANTHONY

begins at last to notice his immense stature.

Already several times, while thou wert speaking, it seemed to me thou wert growing taller; and it was no illusion. How? Explain to me ... Thy aspect terrifies me!

Footsteps are heard approaching.

What is that?

HILARION

extending his arm:
Look!

Then, under a pale beam of moonlight, Anthony distinguishes an interminable caravan defiling over the summit of the rocks;—and each voyager, one after the other, falls from the cliff into the gulf below.

First comes the three great gods of Samothrace,—Axieros, Axiokeros, Axiokersa,—united together as in a fascia, purple-masked, all with hands uplifted.

Æsculapius advances with a melancholy air, not even perceiving Samos and Telesphorus, who question him with gestures of anguish. Elean Sosipolis, of python-form, rolls his coils toward the abyss. Dosipœna, becomes dizzy, leaps in of her own accord. Britomartis, shrieking with fear, clutches fast the meshes of her net. The Centaurs come at a wild gallop, and roll pell-mell into the black gulf.

Behind them, all limping, advance the bands of the mourning Nymphs. Those of the meadows are covered with dust; those of the woods moan and bleed, wounded by the axes of the woodcutters.

The Gelludes, the Strygii, the Empusæ, all the infernal goddesses, form one pyramid of blended fangs, vipers, and torches;—and seated upon a vulture-skin at its summit, Eurynome, blue as the flies that corrupt meat, devours her own arms.

Then in one great whirl simultaneously disappear the bloody Orthia,

Hymina of Orchomenus, the Laphria of the Patræns, Aphia of Agina, Bendis of Thrace, Stymphalia with thighs like a bird's. Triopas, in lieu of three eyes, has now but three empty orbits. Erichthonius, his legs paralysed, crawls upon his hands like a cripple.

HILARION

What a pleasure, is it not?—to see them all in the abjection of their death-agony! Climb up here beside me, on this rock; and thou shalt be even as Xerxes, reviewing his army.

Beyond there, very far, dost thou behold that fair-bearded giant, who even now lets fall his sword crimsoned with blood?—that is the Scythian Zalmoxis between two planets,—Artimpasa, Venus, and Orsiloche, the Moon.

Still further away, now emerging from pallid clouds, are the gods whom the Cimmerians adore, even beyond Thule!

Their huge halls were warm, and by the gleam of swords that tapestried the vault, they drank their hydromel from horns of ivory. They ate the liver of the whale in dishes of brass wrought by the hammers of demons; or, betimes, they listened to captive sorcerers whose fingers played upon harps of stone.

They are feeble! They are cold! The snow makes heavy their bearskins; and their feet show through the rents in their sandals.

They weep for the vast fields upon whose grassy knolls they were wont to draw breath in pauses of battle; they weep for the long ships whose prows forced a way through the mountains of ice;—and the skates wherewith they followed the orb of the poles, upbearing at the length of their mighty arms all the firmament that turned with them.

A gust of frosty wind carries them off.
Anthony turns his eyes another way.
And he perceives—outlined in black against a red background—certain strange personages, with chinbands and gauntlets, who throw balls at one another, leap over each other's heads, make grimaces, dance a frenzied dance.

HILARION

Those are the divinities of Etruria, the innumerable Æsars.

There is Tages, by whom augury was invented. With one hand he seeks to augment the divisions of the sky; with the other he supports himself upon the earth: let him sink therein!

Nortia gazes at the wall into which she drove nails to mark the number of the passing years. Its whole surface is now covered; and the period is accomplished.

Like two travellers overtaken by a storm, Kastur and Pulutuk, trembling, seek to shelter themselves beneath the same mantle.

ANTHONY

closes his eyes:
Enough! Enough!

But with a mighty noise of wings, all the Victories of the Capitol pass through the air,—hiding their faces with their hands, dropping the trophies hanging upon their arms.

Janus,—lord of crepuscules,—flees upon a black ram; and one of his two faces is already putrified; the other slumbers with fatigue.

Summanus, now headless, the god of the dark heavens, presses against his heart an old cake shaped like a wheel.

Vesta, beneath a ruined cupola, tries to relight her extinguished lamp.

Bellona gashes her cheeks,—without being able to make that blood flow by which her devotees were purified.

ANTHONY

Mercy!—they weary me!

HILARION

Before, they amused thee!

And he shows him in a grove of bean trees, a Woman, completely naked,—on all fours like an animal and covered by a black man holding in each hand a torch.

It is the goddess of Aricia, with the demon Virbius. Her sacerdote, the King of the grove, had to be an assassin;* and the fugitive slaves, the despoilers of corpses, the brigands of the Via Salaria, the cripples of the Pons Sublicius, all the human vermin of the Suburra worshipped no deities so fervently!

In the time of Marcus Antonius the patrician women preferred Libitina.

And he shows him under the shadow of cypresses and rose-trees, another Woman, clad in gauze. Around her lie spades, litters, black hangings, all the paraphernalia of funerals. She smiles. Her diamonds shine afar off through spiders' webs. The Larvæ, like skeletons, show their bones through the branches; and the Lemures, who are phantoms, extend their bat-like wings.

At the end of a field lies the god Terminus, uprooted, and covered with ordures.

In the centre of a furrow, the great corpse of Vertumnus is being devoured by red dogs.

The rustic deities all depart, weeping:—Sartor, Sarrator, Vervactor, Collina, Vallona, Hostilinus—all wearing little hooded mantles, and carrying either a hoe, a pitchfork, a hurdle, or a boar-spear.

HILARION

Their spirits made prosperous the villa,—with its dovecots, its parks of dormice and snails, its poultry-yards protected by nets, its warm stables fragrant with odours of cedar.

Also they protected all the wretched population who dragged the irons upon their legs over the flinty ways of the Sabine country,—those who called the swine together by sound of horn,—

---

* Readers will recollect the lines in Macaulay's *Lays of Ancient Rome:*
  "Beneath Aricia's trees,
    Those trees in whose dim shadow
  A ghastly priest doth reign,
    The priest who slew the slayer,
  And must himself be slain."

those who were wont to gather the bunches at the very summits of the elms,—those who drove the asses, laden with manure, over the winding bypaths. The panting labourer, leaning over the handle of his plough, prayed them to give strength to his arms; and under the shade of the lindens, beside calabashes filled with milk, the cowherds were wont, in turn, to sound their praises upon flutes of reed.

Anthony sighs.
And in the centre of a chamber, upon a lofty estrade, an ivory bed is visible, surrounded by persons bearing torches of pine.

Those are the deities of marriage. They await the coming of the bride!

Domiduca should lead her in,—Virgo unfasten her girdle,—Subigo place her in the bed,—and Præma open her arms, and whisper sweet words into her ear.

But she will not come!—and they dismiss the others:—Nona and Decima who watch by sick-beds; the three Nixii who preside over child-birth; the two nurses, Educa and Potina; and Carna, guardian of the cradle, whose bouquet of hawthorne keeps evil dreams from the child.

Afterwards, Ossipago should strengthen his knees;—Barbatus give him his first beard; Stimula inspire his first desires; Volupia grant him his first enjoyment; Fabulinus should have taught him to speak, Numera to count, Camœna to sing, Consus to reflect.

This chamber is empty; and there remains only the centenarian Nænia beside the bed,—muttering to herself the dirge she was wont to howl at the funerals of aged men.
But her voice is soon drowned by sharp cries. These are uttered by:

THE LARES DOMESTICI
crouching at the further end of the atrium, clad in dog-skins, with flowers wreathed about their bodies,—pressing their clenched hands against their cheeks, and weeping as loudly as they can.

Where is the portion of food we received at each repast, the kindly care of the maid-servant, the smile of the matron, the merriment of the little boys playing at knucklebones on the mosaic pavement of the court-yard? When grown up, they used to hang about our necks their bullæ of gold or leather.

What happiness it was, when on the evening of a triumph, the master, entering, turned his humid eyes upon us! He would recount his combats; and the little house would be prouder than a palace; sacred as a temple.

How sweet were the family repasts, above all on the morrow of the Feralia! Tenderness for the dead appeased all discords; all kissed each other, while drinking to the glories of the past, and the hopes of the future.

But the ancestors, of painted wax, locked up behind us, are slowly becoming covered with mold. The new races, visiting their own deceptions upon us, have shattered our jaws; our wooden bodies are disappearing piecemeal under the teeth of rats.

And the innumerable gods, watching over doors, kitchens, cellars, baths, disperse in every direction—under the form of enormous ants running over the pavement, or great butterflies soaring away.

CREPITUS

makes himself heard:

I, too, was honored once! Libations were made to me. I was a God!

The Athenian saluted me as a presage of good-fortune, whilst the devout Roman cursed me with raised fists, and the Egyptian pontiff, abstaining from beans, trembled at the sound of my voice and paled at my odor.

When the vinegar of armies ran down unshaven beards, and soldiers feasted upon acorns, peas, and raw onions, and when the butchered he-goat was cooking in the rancid butter taken from shepherds, without a thought for his companions, no man held back. Solid nourishment made for resounding digestions. In the broad day of the countryside, the men were accustomed to relieving themselves with earnest application.

And so it was that I passed without scandal, like the other of life's needs: like Mena the torment of virgins, and like the gentle Rumina who protects the nurse's breast when it is swollen with bluish veins. I was joyful. I made merry. And expanding easily under my sway, the dinner guest exhaled his gaiety through the openings of his body.

I had days of which to be proud. Good Aristophanes trotted me across the stage; and the emperor Claudius Drusus bade me sit at his table. In the laticlavi of the patricians, I moved about majestically! Golden vessels, like tympani, resonated beneath me;—and, when filled with eels, with truffles, and with pies, the Master's bowel moved with a blast, the attentive universe knew that Cæsar had dined!

But now, I am relegated to the populace; and a cry goes up even at my name!

And Crepitus goes off, uttering a groan.

Then a roll of thunder is heard;

A VOICE

I was the God of Armies, the Lord, the Lord God!

I pitched the tents of Jacob on the hills; and in the midst of the sands I nourished my chosen people in their flight.

It was I who consumed the city of Sodom with fire! It was I who overwhelmed the world with the waters of the Deluge! It was I that drowned Pharaoh, with all the princes, sons of Kings,—making the sea to swallow up his chariots of war, and his charioteers.

I, the Jealous God, held all other gods in abomination. I brayed the impure in my anger; the mighty I cast down; and swiftly the desolation of my wrath ran to the right and to the left, like a dromedary loosened in a field of maize.

I chose the humble to deliver Israel. Angels, flame-winged, spake to them from out the bushes.

Perfumed with spikenard, with cinnamon and myrrh, clad in transparent robes, and shod with high-heeled sandals,—women of valiant heart went forth to slay captains.[19] The passing wind carried my prophets with it.

My law I graved upon tables of stone. Within that law my people were enclosed, as within a strong citadel. They were my people. I was their God! The land was mine; the men also belonged to me, together with their every thought, and all their works, and the tools they wrought with, and their posterity.

My ark reposed within a triple sanctuary,—surrounded by curtains of purple and lighted candelabra. I had a whole tribe to serve me as servants, swinging censers; and the high-priest, robed in robes of hyacinth, wore upon his breast precious stones disposed in symmetrical order.

Woe! Woe! the Holy of Holies is open, the veil is rent, the perfumes of the holocaust are dissipated by all the winds of heaven. The jackal whines in the sepulchres; my temple is destroyed; my people dispersed!

The priests have been strangled with the girdles of their robes. The women languish in captivity; the holy vessels have all been melted!

The voice, becoming more distant:

I was the God of Armies, the Lord, the Lord God!

An enormous silence follows,—and deepest night.

ANTHONY

All have passed away.

SOME ONE

replies:

I remain!

And Hilarion stands before him—but transfigured wholly,—beautiful as an archangel, luminous as a sun, and so lofty that in order to behold his face

ANTHONY

is compelled to throw back his head, to look up as though gazing at a star.
Who art thou?

HILARION

My kingdom is vast as the universe; and my desire knows no limits. I go on forever,—freeing minds, weighing worlds,—without hatred, without fear, without pity, without love, and without God. Men call me Science!

ANTHONY

recoiling from him:
Say, rather, that thou art ... the Devil!

HILARION

fixing his eyes upon him:
Wouldst thou behold him?

ANTHONY

cannot detach his eyes from that mighty gaze:—the curiosity of the Devil comes upon him. His terror augments; yet his wish grows even to boundlessness.
Yet if I should see him ... if I were to see him! ...

Then in a sudden spasm of wrath:

The horror that I have of him will free me from his presence forever.... Yes!

A cloven foot appears.
Anthony regrets his wish.
But the Devil has flung him upon his horns and bears him away.

VI

He flies beneath him, outstretched like a swimmer; his vast-spreading wings, wholly concealing him, seem like one huge cloud.

ANTHONY

Whither do I go?

But a little while ago I beheld in a glimpse the form of the Accurst. Nay!—'tis a cloud that upbears me! Perhaps I am dead, and am ascending to God. . . .

How freely I respire! The immaculate air seems to vivify my soul. No sense of weight!—no more suffering!

Far below me the lightning breaks,—the horizon broadens, widens,—the rivers cross each other. That blond-bright spot is the desert; that pool of water the ocean.

And other oceans appear,—vast regions of which I knew nothing. There are the countries of the blacks, which seem to smoke like brasiers,—then is the zone of snows always made dim by fog. Would I might behold those mountains where the sun, each evening, sinks to rest.

THE DEVIL

The sun never sinks to rest!

Anthony is not surprised at this voice. It seems to him an echo of his own thought—a response made by his own memory.

Meanwhile the earth gradually assumes the shape of a ball; and he beholds it in the midst of the azure, turning upon its poles, and revolving about the sun.

THE DEVIL

So it does not form the centre of the universe? Pride of man! humiliate thyself!

ANTHONY

Now I can scarcely distinguish it. It mingles confusedly with other glowing worlds. The firmament itself is but one tissue of stars.

And they still rise.

No sound!—not even the hoarse cry of eagles! Nothing!... I listen for the harmony of the spheres.

THE DEVIL

Thou wilt not hear them! Nor wilt thou behold the antichthonus of Plato,—or the central furnace of Philolaus,—or the spheres of Aristotle,[20] or the seven heavens of the Jews, with the great waters above the vault of crystal!

ANTHONY

Yet from below the vault seemed solid as a wall!—on the contrary I penetrate it, I lose myself in it!

And he beholds the moon,—like a rounded fragment of ice filled with motionless light.

THE DEVIL

Formerly it was the sojourn of souls. Even the good Pythagoras adorned it with magnificent flowers, populated it with birds.

ANTHONY

I can see only desolate plains there, with extinct craters yawning under a black sky.

Let us go towards those milder-beaming stars, that we may contemplate the angels who uphold them at arms' length, like torches!

THE DEVIL

bears him into the midst of the stars.

They attract at the same time that they repel each other. The action of each one results from that of others, and contributes thereunto,—without the aid of any auxiliary, by the force of a law, the virtue of order alone.

ANTHONY

Yes!... yes! My intelligence grasps the great truth! It is a joy greater than all tender pleasures! Breathless I find myself with astonishment at the enormity of God!

THE DEVIL

Even as the firmament ever rises as thou dost ascend, so with the expansion of thy thought will He become greater to thee; and after this discovery of the universe thou wilt feel thy joy augment with the broadening and deepening of the infinite.

ANTHONY

Ah! higher!—higher still!—forever higher!

Then the stars multiply, scintillate. The Milky Way develops in the zenith like a monstrous belt, with holes at intervals; through these rents in its brightness stretches of prolonged darkness are visible. There are rains of stars, long trains of golden dust, luminous vapours that float and dissolve.

At times a comet suddenly passes by; then the tranquillity of innumerable lights recommences.

Anthony, with outstretched arms, supports himself upon the Devil's horns, and thus occupies all the space between them.

He remembers with disdain the ignorance of other days, the mediocrity of his dreams. And now those luminous globes he was wont to gaze upon from below are close to him! He distinguishes the intercrossing of the lines of their orbits, the complexity of their courses. He beholds them coming from afar,— and, like stones suspended in a sling, describe their circles, form their hyperbolas.

He perceives, all within the field of his vision at once, the Southern Cross and the Great Bear, the Lynx and the Centaur, the nebula of Dorado, the six suns in the constellation of Orion, Jupiter with his four satellites, and the triple ring of the monstrous Saturn!—all the planets, all the stars that men will discover in the future! He fills his eyes with their light; he overburthens his mind with calculation of their distances: then, bowing his head, he murmurs.

What is the purpose of all that?

THE DEVIL

There is no purpose!

How could God have a purpose? What experience could have instructed him?—what reflection determined him?

Before the beginning he could not have acted;—and now his action would be useless.

ANTHONY

Yet he created the world, at one time, by his word only!

THE DEVIL

But the beings that people the earth come upon it successively. So also, in heaven, new stars arise—different effects of varying causes.

ANTHONY

The varying of causes is the will of God!

THE DEVIL

But to admit several acts of will in God is to admit various causes, and therefore to deny his unity!

His will is inseparable from his essence. He can have but one will, having but one essence; and inasmuch as he eternally exists, he acts eternally.

Contemplate the sun! From its surface leap vast jets of flame, casting forth sparks that disperse beyond to become worlds here-after;—and further than the last, far beyond those deeps where thou seest only night, whirl other suns,—and behind them others again, and beyond those yet others, without end . . .

ANTHONY

Enough! Enough! I fear!—I will fall into the abyss.

THE DEVIL

pauses, and rocks Anthony gently in the midst of space:

Nothingness is not—there is no void! Everywhere and forever bodies move upon the immovable deeps of space. Were there boundaries to space, it would not be space, but a body only: it is limitless!

ANTHONY

stupefied by wonder:

Limitless!

THE DEVIL

Ascend skyward forever and forever,—yet thou wilt not attain the summit. Descend below the earth for billions of billions of centuries: never wilt thou reach the bottom. For there is no summit, there is no bottom; there is no Above, no Below—there is no end.

And Space itself is comprised in God, who is not a portion thereof of such or such a size,—but is Immensity itself!

ANTHONY

slowly:
Matter ... then, ... must be a part of God?

THE DEVIL

Why not? Canst thou know the end of God?

ANTHONY

Nay: on the contrary, I prostrate, I crush myself beneath his mightiness!

THE DEVIL

And yet thou dost pretend to move him! Thou dost speak to him,—thou dost even adorn him with virtues,—with goodness, justice, mercy,—in lieu of recognising that all perfections are his!

To conceive aught beyond him is to conceive God above God, the Being above the Being. For He is the only being, the only substance.

If the Substance could be divided, it would not be the Substance, it would lose its nature: God could not exist. He is therefore indivisible as infinite;—and if he had a body, he would be composed of parts, he would not be One—he would not be infinite. Therefore he is not a Person!

ANTHONY

What! my prayers, my sobs, my groans, the sufferings of my flesh, the transports of my love,—have all these things gone out to a lie ... to emptiness ... unavailingly—like the cry of a bird, like a whirl of dead leaves?

He weeps.

Oh, no!—there is Some One above all things,—a great Soul, a Lord, a Father whom my heart adores and who must love me!

THE DEVIL

Thou dost desire that God were not God;—for did he feel love, or anger, or pity, he would abandon his perfection for a greater or a lesser perfection. He can stoop to no sentiment, nor be contained in any form.

ANTHONY

One day, nevertheless, I shall see him!

THE DEVIL

With the blessed, is it not?—when the finite shall enjoy the infinite in some restricted place, containing the Absolute!

ANTHONY

Matters not!—there must be a paradise for the good, as there is a hell for the wicked!

THE DEVIL

Can the desire of thy mind create the law of the universe? Without doubt evil is indifferent to God,—forasmuch as the Earth is covered with it!

Is it through impotence that he endures it, or through cruelty that he maintains it?

Dost thou fancy that he is eternally readjusting the world, like an imperfect machine?—that he is forever watching the movements of all beings, from the flight of a butterfly to the thought of a man?

If he have created the universe, his providence is superfluous. If Providence exists, then creation is defective.

But evil and good concern only thee—even like night and day, pleasure and pain, death and birth, which are relative only to one corner of space, to a special centre, to a particular interest. Since the Infinite is permanent, the Infinite is;—and that is all!

The Devil's wings have been gradually expanding: now they cover all space.

ANTHONY
now perceives nothing: a great faintness comes upon him.

A hideous cold freezes me, even to the depths of my soul! This is beyond the extreme of pain! It is like a death that is deeper than death. I roll in the immensity of darkness; and the darkness itself enters within me. My consciousness bursts beneath this dilation of nothingness!

THE DEVIL

Yet the knowledge of things comes to thee only through the medium of thy mind. Even as a concave mirror, it deforms the objects it reflects; and thou hast no means whatever of verifying their exactitude.

Never canst thou know the universe in all its vastness; consequently it will never be possible for thee to obtain an idea of its cause, to have a just notion of God, nor even to say that the universe is infinite,—for thou must first be able to know what the Infinite is!

May not Form be, perhaps, an error of thy senses,—Substance a figment of thy imagination?

Unless, indeed, that the world being a perpetual flux* of things, appearance, on the contrary, be wholly true; illusion the only reality.

But art thou sure thou dost see?—art thou even sure thou dost live? Perhaps nothing exists!

---

* The original text seems to me slightly obscure. The idea of the universe being a perpetual ebb and flow of shapes, a flood of forms passing away to reappear like waves, is that of the Nidana-Sutris: "Individuality is only a form ... *Everything is only a flux of aggregates,* interminably uniting and disuniting," as Barth observes in his "Religions of India."

The Devil has seized Anthony, and, holding him at arms' length, glares at him with mouth yawning as though to devour him.

Adore me, then!—and curse the phantom thou callest God!

Anthony lifts his eyes with a last effort of hope.
The Devil abandons him.

VII

ANTHONY
finds himself lying upon his back, at the verge of the cliff.
The sky commences to blanch.

Is it the glow of dawn, or only an effect of moonlight?

He tries to rise, falls back,—his teeth chattering:

I feel such a helplessness of weakness … as though all my bones
were broken!

Why?

Ah! the Devil!—I remember;—he even repeated to me all that I
learned from the aged Didymus respecting the opinions of Xenophanes, Heraclitus, of Melissus, of Anaxagoras,—concerning the
infinite, the creation, the impossibility of knowing anything!

And yet I believed that I could unite myself to God!

Laughing bitterly:

Ah! madness! madness! Is the fault mine? Prayer has become intolerable to me! My heart is dry as a rock! Once, it was wont to overflow with love!...

The sand used to smoke of mornings like the odourous dust of a censer;—at sunset flowers of fire used to bloom upon the cross; and in the middle of the night, it often seemed as though all beings and all things, lying under the same awful silence, were adoring the Lord with me. O charms of prayer, felicities of ecstasy, gifts of heaven,—what have become of you?

I remember a voyage I made with Ammon in search of a solitary place suited for the establishment of a monastery. It was the last evening; we hastened our steps, walked side by side, murmuring hymns, without conversing. As the sun sank, the shadows of our bodies lengthened like two obelisks, continually growing taller, and moving before us. Here and there we planted crosses, made with fragments of our sticks, to mark the site of a future cell. Night was tardy in her coming; and waves of darkness overspread the earth, even while a vast rose-coloured light still glowed in heaven.

When I was a child, I used to amuse myself by building hermitages with pebbles. My mother sitting beside me would watch attentively.

Will she not have cursed me for having abandoned her?—will she not have plucked out her white hair by handfuls in the despair of her grief? And her corpse remains lying on the floor of the hut, under the roof of reeds, between the crumbling walls. Through an orifice a hyena, snuffing, thrusts his head, advances his maw!... horror! horror!

He sobs.

No: Ammonaria will not have abandoned her!
Where is she now,—Ammonaria?
Perhaps at the further end of a bathroom, she removes her garments one after the other: first the mantle, then the girdle, then

the first tunic, the second lighter tunic, all her necklaces,—and the vapour of cinnamon envelops her naked limbs. At last she lies down upon the tepid mosaic. Her long hair, spreading below the curve of her hips, seems like a sable fleece; and the oppressiveness of the heated air causes her to pant; her waist arched, her breasts standing out ... What! ... my flesh rebels again! Even in the midst of grief am I tortured by concupiscence. To be subjected thus unto two tortures at once is beyond endurance! I can no longer bear myself!

He leans over, and gazes into the abyss.

The man who should fall would be killed. Nothing easier: it were only necessary to roll over upon my left side:—only one movement!—one!

Then suddenly appears—

An Aged Woman

Anthony starts to his feet in affright. It seems to him that he beholds his mother arisen.

But this woman is far older, and prodigiously thin.

A shroud, knotted about her head, hangs down, together with her white hair, the full length of her legs, slender as crutches. The brilliancy of her ivory-coloured teeth make her earthy skin darker still. The orbits of her eyes are full of shadow; and far back within them two flames vacillate, like the lamps of sepulchres.

She says:

Advance. What hinders thee?

Anthony

stammering:

I fear ... to commit a sin!

SHE

replies:

But King Saul killed himself! Razias, a just man, killed himself! Saint Pelagia of Antioch killed herself! Dommina of Aleppo and her two daughters—all three saints—killed themselves; and remember also how many confessors delivered themselves up to the executioner in their impatient longing for death. That they might enjoy death more speedily, the virgins of Miletus strangled themselves with their girdles. At Syracuse the philosopher Hegesias preached so eloquently upon death that men deserted the lupanars to go hang themselves in the fields. The patricians of Rome sought for death as a new form of debauch.

ANTHONY

Aye! the love of death is strong. Many an anchorite has succumbed to it.

THE OLD WOMAN

To do that which will make thee equal unto God—think! He created thee: thou wilt destroy his work—thou! and by thy courage,—of thy own free will! The enjoyment that Erostratus knew was not greater than this. And moreover thy body has so long mocked thy soul that it is full time thou shouldst take vengeance upon it. Thou wilt not suffer. It will soon be over. Of what art thou afraid?—a wide, black hole! Perhaps it is a void!

Anthony hearkens without replying; and upon the other side appears:

ANOTHER WOMAN

—young and marvellously beautiful. At first he takes her to be Ammonaria.

But she is taller, blond as honey, very plump, with paint upon her cheeks and roses upon her head. Her long robe, weighty with spangles, gleams with metallic lustre;—her fleshy lips are sanguinolent; and her somewhat heavy eyelids are so drowned with languor that one would almost take her to be blind.

She murmurs:

Nay, live! enjoy! Solomon counsels joy! Follow the guiding of thy heart and the desire of thine eyes!

ANTHONY

What joy is there for me? My heart is weary; my eyes are dim!

SHE

answers:

Seek the suburb of Racotis; push open a door that is painted blue;—and when thou shalt be in the atrium where a fountain jet murmurs unceasingly, a woman will present herself before thee—in peplos of white silk striped with gold; her hair is unloosed, her laugh like the clatter of crotali. She is skilful. In her caress thou wilt taste the pride of initiation and the appeasement of desire.

Nor dost thou know the fever of adulteries; the house-breaking, the abductions, the joy of seeing in all her nakedness the very one that inspired respect when clothed.

Hast ever pressed to thy bosom a virgin who loved thee? Dost remember the surrenders of her modesty,—the passing away of her remorse in a sweet flow of tears?

Thou canst even now imagine thyself walking with her—canst thou not?—in the wood by the light of the moon? At each pressure of your joined hands, a sweet shuddering passes through you both,—looking closely into each other your eyes seem to outpour into one another something like immaterial fluid;—and thy heart fills; it bursts; it is a suave whirl of eddying passion, an overflowing of intoxication ...

THE OLD WOMAN

One need not possess joys in order to taste their bitterness! Even to view them from afar off begets loathing of them. Thou must be fatigued by the monotony of the same actions, the length of the days, the hideousness of the world, the stupidity of the sun?

ANTHONY

Aye, indeed!—I loathe all that he shines upon!

THE YOUNG WOMAN

Hermit! hermit! thou wilt find diamonds among the flints, fountains beneath the sand, a delectation in all the hazards thou dost despise; and there are even upon earth places of such beauty that the sight of them would make thee desire to press the whole world against thy heart with love.

THE OLD WOMAN

Each evening that thou liest down upon the earth to slumber, thou dost hope that it may soon lie upon thee and cover thee!

THE YOUNG WOMAN

Yet thou dost believe in the resurrection of the flesh—which is but the translation of life into eternity!

Even as she speaks, the Old Woman becomes still more fleshless; and above her skull, from which the white hair has disappeared, a bat circles in the air.

The Young Woman has become fatter. Her robe gleams with shifting colours; her nostrils palpitate, her eyes roll softly.

THE FORMER

opening her arms, exclaiming:

Come to me!—I am Consolation, repose, oblivion, eternal calm! *and*

THE OTHER

offering her breasts.

I am the sleep-giver, life, happiness inexhaustible!

Anthony turns to flee from them. Each lays a hand on his shoulder. The Shroud parts, exposes the Skeleton of Death.

The robe splits asunder, and leaves the whole body of Lust exposed:—her waist is slender, her rear enormous; her long and undulating hair flutters in the wind.

Anthony stands motionless between the two, considering them.

DEATH

says to him:

What matters it, whether now or at another time! Thou art mine,—like suns, nations, cities, kings, mountain-snows, and the grasses of the fields. I fly higher than the hawks of heaven. I run more swiftly than the gazelle; I overtake even Hope; I vanquished the Son of God!

LUST

Resist not. I am the Omnipotent! The forests re-echo with my sighs; the waters tremble with my agitations. Virtue, courage, piety, dissolve in the perfume of my mouth. Man I accompany in every step that he makes; and even from the threshold of the tomb he turns to me!

DEATH

I will find for thee that which thou hast vainly sought for, by the gleam of torches, upon the faces of the dead,—or among those awful sands that are formed of human remains, where thou wast wont to wander beyond the Pyramids. From time to time, the fragment of a skull rolled under thy sandal. Thou didst take up the dust: thou didst let it trickle through thy fingers; and thy thought, blending with it, sank into nothingness.

LUST

My gulf is deeper! Statues of marble have inspired obscene loves. Men rush to conjunctures that terrify. Fetters are riveted that the fettered curse. Whence the bewitchment of courtesans, the extravagance of dreams, the immensity of my sadness?

DEATH

Mine irony depasseth all others! There are convulsions of delight at the funerals of kings, at the extermination of a whole people; and war is made with music, with plumes, with banners, with harness of gold,—with vast display of ceremony that my due of homage may be greater.

LUST

My rage equals thine. I also yell; I bite. I, too, have sweats of agony, and aspects cadaverous.

DEATH

It is I that make thee awful! Let us intertwine!

Death laughs mockingly; Lust roars. They clasp each other about the waist, and chant alternately:

—I hasten the dissolution of matter!
—I facilitate the dispersion of germs!
—Thou dost destroy for my renovations!
—Thou dost engender for my destructions!
—Ever-active my power!
—Fecund, my putrefaction!

And their voices, whose rolling echoes fill the horizon, deepen and become so mighty that Anthony falls backward as if thunder-stricken.
A shock from time to time causes him to reopen his eyes; and he perceives in the midst of the darkness a manner of monster before him.
It is a skull, crowned with roses, dominating the torso of a woman nacreously white. Below, a shroud starred with specks of gold forms something like a tail; and the whole body undulates, after the fashion of a gigantic worm erect on end.

———

The vision attenuates,—disappears.

ANTHONY

rising to his feet:

The Devil yet again, and under his twofold aspect: the spirit of fornication, and the spirit of destruction.

Neither affrights me. I repel happiness; and I know myself to be eternal.

Thus death is only an illusion, a veil, masking betimes the continuity of life.

But Substance being unique, wherefore should forms be varied?

Somewhere there must be primordial figures, whose bodily forms are only symbols. Could I but see them, I would know the link between matter and thought; I would know in what Being consists!

Such were the figures painted at Babylon upon the walls of the temple of Belus; and others like them covered a mosaic in the port of Carthage. I myself have sometime beheld in the sky, as it were, forms of spirits. Those who cross the desert meet with animals surpassing all conception....

*And opposite, upon the further side of the Nile, suddenly appears the Sphinx.**

He stretches his paws, shakes the bandelets upon his forehead, and crouches upon his belly.

Leaping, flying, spitting fire through her nostrils, lashing her winged sides with her dragon-tail, the green-eyed Chimera circles, barks.

The thick curls of her head tossed back upon one side mingle with the hair of her loins; on the other side they hang down to the sand, quivering with the swinging of her body, to and fro.

---

* Winkelmann claims to have been the first to discover that the Egyptian sphinxes were bisexual—females before—males otherwise. (See Book II, chap. I, § 25.) Flaubert speaks of the Sphinx in the masculine like Philemon. (See also Signor Carlo Fea's note upon the paragraph in Winkelmann, old French edition. An II, R. F.)

THE SPHINX
remaining motionless, and gazing at the Chimera:
Hither, Chimera! rest awhile!

THE CHIMERA
No! never!

THE SPHINX
Do not run so fast, do not fly so high, do not bark so loudly!

THE CHIMERA
Do not call me!—call me no more; since thou must remain forever dumb!

THE SPHINX
Cease casting thy flames in my face, and uttering thy yells in my ear: thou canst not melt my granite!

THE CHIMERA
Thou shalt not seize me, terrible sphinx!

THE SPHINX
Thou art too mad to dwell with me!

THE CHIMERA
Thou art too heavy to follow me!

THE SPHINX
Yet whither goest thou, that thou shouldst run so fast?

THE CHIMERA
I gallop in the corridors of the Labyrinth—I hover above the mountains—I graze the waves in my flight—I yelp at the bottom of precipices—I suspend myself with my mouth from the skirts of clouds—I sweep the shores with my dragging tail; and the curves

of the hills have taken their form from the shape of my shoulders! But thee I find perpetually immobile, or perhaps making strange designs with thy claws upon the sand.

THE SPHINX

It is because I keep my secret!—I dream and calculate.

The sea returns to its bed; the wheat bends back and forth in the wind; the caravans pass by; the dust flies; cities crumble; and yet my gaze, which naught can deviate, remains fixed, gazing through all intervening things, upon a horizon that none may reach.

THE CHIMERA

I am light and joyous! I offer to the eyes of men dazzling perspectives with Paradise in the clouds above, and unspeakable felicity afar off. Into their souls I pour the eternal madnesses; projects of happiness, plans for the future, dreams of glory and vows of love, and all virtuous resolutions.

I urge men to perilous voyages and great enterprises. I have chiselled with my claws the wonders of architecture. It was I who suspended the little bells above the tomb of Porsenna, and surrounded the quays of Atlantis with a wall of orichalcum.

I seek for new perfumes, for vaster flowers, for pleasures never felt before. If I perceive in any place a man whose mind reposes in wisdom, I fall upon him, and strangle him.

THE SPHINX

All those tormented by the desire of God, I have devoured.

In order to climb up to my royal brow, the strongest ascend upon the flutings of my bandelets as upon the steps of a stairway. Then a great lassitude comes upon them, and they fall backward.

Anthony begins to tremble.

He is no longer before his cabin, but in the desert itself, with those two monsters beside him, whose breath is hot upon his shoulders.

THE SPHINX

O thou Fantasy, bear me away upon thy wings that my sadness may be lightened!

THE CHIMERA

O thou Unknown, I am enamoured of thine eyes! Like a hyena in heat I turn about thee, soliciting those fecundations whereof the desires devour me!

Ope thy mouth, lift thy feet—mount upon my back!

THE SPHINX

My feet, since they have been outstretched, can move no more. Like a scurf, lichen has formed upon my jaws. By dint of long dreaming I have no longer aught to say.

THE CHIMERA

Thou liest, hypocrite Sphinx! Wherefore dost thou always call me and always disown me?

THE SPHINX

It is thou, indomitable caprice, that dost forever pass and repass, whirling in thy course!

THE CHIMERA

Is the fault mine? What? Let me be!

She barks.

THE SPHINX

Thou movest away! thou dost escape me!

He growls.

THE CHIMERA

Essay!—thou crushest me!

THE SPHINX

Nay!—impossible!

And gradually sinking down he disappears in the sand; while the Chimera, ramping with tongue protruding, departs, describing circles on her way.

The breath of her mouth has produced a fog.

Through this mist Anthony perceives wreathings of clouds, undecided curves.

At last he can distinguish something like the appearance of human bodies. And first:

THE ASTOMI

approach, like bubbles of air traversed by sunlight.

Do not breathe too hard! The drops of rain bruise us, false notes excoriate us, darknesses blind us! Composed wholly of breezes and of perfumes, we float along, we roll along:—a little more than Dreams, yet not quite beings....

THE NISNAS

have only one eye, one cheek, one hand, one leg, half a body, half a heart. They say:

We live quite in our halves of houses, with our halves of wives and our halves of children.

THE BLEMMYES

who have no head at all:

Our shoulders are all the broader;—and there is no ox, rhinoceros, or elephant able to carry what we carry.

Something dimly resembling features—as it were a vague face—imprinted upon our breasts: that is all! We think digestions; we subtleize secretions. God, in our belief, floats peacefully within the interior chyles.

We go straight upon our way, through all mires, crossing all morasses, skirting the edges of all abysses: and we are the most laborious, the most happy, the most virtuous of all peoples!

THE PYGMIES

We, good little men, swarm upon the world like vermin upon the hump of a dromedary.

We are burned, drowned, crushed; and we always reappear, more vivacious and countless than before—terrible by reason of our numbers!

THE SCIAPODS

Fettered to the earth by our hair, long as lianas, we vegetate beneath the shelter of our feet, broad as parasols; and the light comes to us through the thickness of our heels. No annoyances for us, no work! The head as low as possible—that is the secret of happiness!

Their lifted thighs,—resembling the trunks of trees,—multiply.

And a forest appears. Great apes clamber through it on all fours:—these are men with the heads of dogs.

THE CYNOCEPHALI

We leap from branch to branch in search of eggs to gulp down; and we pluck the little fledglings alive; then we put their nests upon our heads in lieu of caps.

We tear off the teats of cows; and we put out the eyes of lynxes: we let fall our dung from the heights of the trees—we parade our turpitude in the full light of the sun.

Lacerating the flowers, crushing the fruits, befouling the springs, violating women, we are the masters of all,—by the strength of our arms, and the ferocity of our hearts.

Ho! companions!—gnash with your jaws!

Blood and milk pour down their chops. The rain streams over their hairy backs.

Anthony inhales the freshness of the green leaves.

—

There is a movement among them, a clashing of branches; and all of a sudden appears a huge black stag, with the head of a bull, having between his ears a thicket of white horns.

THE SADHUZAG

My seventy-four antlers are hollow like flutes.

When I turn me toward the wind of the South, there issue from them sounds that draw all the ravished animals around me. The serpents twine about my legs; the wasps cluster in my nostrils; and the parrots, the doves, the ibises, alight upon the branches of my horns.

—Listen!

He throws back his horns, whence issues a music of sweetness ineffable.
Anthony presses both hands upon his heart. It seems to him as though his soul were being borne away by the melody.

THE SADHUZAG

But when I turn me toward the wind of the North, my antlers, more thickly bristling than a battalion of lances, give forth a sound of howlings: the forests are startled with fear; the rivers remount toward their sources; the husks of fruits burst open; and the bending grasses stand erect on end, like the hair of a coward.

—Listen!

He bends his branching antlers forward: hideous and discordant cries proceed from them. Anthony feels as though his heart were torn asunder.
And his horror augments upon beholding:

THE MARTICHORAS

a gigantic red lion, with human face, and three rows of teeth.

The gleam of my scarlet hair mingles with the reflection of the great sands. I breathe through my nostrils the terror of solitudes. I spit forth plague. I devour armies when they venture into the desert.

My claws are twisted like screws, my teeth shaped like saws; and my curving tail bristles with darts which I cast to right and left, before and behind!

—See! see!

The Martichoras shoots forth the keen bristles of his tail, which irradiate in all directions like a volley of arrows. Drops of blood rain down, spattering upon the foliage.

THE CATOBLEPAS
a black buffalo with a pig's head, falling to the ground, and attached to his shoulders by a neck long, thin, and flaccid as an empty gut.

He wallows flat upon the ground, and his feet entirely disappear beneath the enormous mane of coarse hair which covers his face.

Fat, melancholy, fierce—thus I continually remain, feeling against my belly the warmth of the mud. So heavy is my skull that it is impossible for me to lift it. I roll it slowly all around me, open-mouthed; and with my tongue I tear up the venomous plants bedewed with my breath. Once, I even devoured my own feet without knowing it.

No one, Anthony, has ever beheld mine eyes,—or at least, those who have beheld them are dead. Were I to lift my eyelids—my pink and swollen eyelids, thou wouldst forthwith die.

ANTHONY
Oh, that one! Ugh! As though I could desire it?... Yet his stupidity fascinates me. No, no! I will not!

He gazes fixedly upon the ground.

—

But the weeds take fire; and amidst the contortions of the flames, arises

THE BASILISK
a great violet serpent, with trilobate crest, and two fangs, one above, one below.

Beware, lest thou fall into my jaws! I drink fire. I am fire—and I inhale it from all things: from clouds, from flints, from dead trees, the fur of animals, the surface of marshes. My temperature maintains the volcanoes: I lend glitter to jewels: I give colours to metals.

THE GRIFFIN
a lion with a vulture's beak, and white wings, red paws and blue neck.

I am the master of deep splendours. I know the secrets of the tombs wherein the Kings of old do slumber.

A chain, issuing from the wall, maintains their heads upright. Near them, in basins of porphyry, the women they loved float upon the surfaces of black liquids. Their treasures are all arrayed in halls, in lozenge-shaped designs, in little heaps, in pyramids;—and down below, far below the tombs, and to be reached only after long travelling through stifling darkness, there are rivers of gold bordered by forests of diamonds, there are fields of carbuncles and lakes of mercury.

Addossed against the subterranean gate I remain with claws uplifted; and my flaming eyes spy out those who seek to approach. The vast and naked plain that stretches away to the end of the horizon is whitened with the bones of travellers. But for thee the gates of bronze shall open; and thou shalt inhale the vapour of the mines, thou shalt descend into the caverns.... Quick! quick!

He burrows into the earth with his paws, and crows like a cock.
A thousand voices answer him. The forest trembles.
And all manner of frightful creatures arise:—The Tragelaphus, half deer, half ox; the Myrmecoles, lion before and ant behind, whose genitals are set reversely; the python Askar, sixty cubits long, that terrified Moses; the huge weasel Pastinaca, that kills the trees with her odour; the Presteros, that makes those who touch it imbecile; the Mirag, a horned hare, that dwells in the islands of the sea. The leopard Phalmant bursts his belly by roaring; the triple-headed bear Senad tears her young by licking them with her tongue; the dog Cepus pours out the blue milk of her teats upon the rocks. Mosquitoes begin to hum, toads commence to leap; serpents hiss. Lightnings flicker. Hail falls.

Then come gusts, bearing with them marvellous anatomies:—Heads of alligators with hoofs of deer; owls with serpent tails; swine with tiger-muzzles; goats with the crupper of an ass; frogs hairy as bears; chameleons huge as hippopotami; calves with two heads, one bellowing, the other weeping; fœtuses of quadruplets holding one another by the navel and spinning like tops; winged bellies flitting hither and thither like gnats.

They rain from the sky, they rise from the earth, they pour from the rocks; everywhere eyes flame, mouths roar, breasts bulge, claws are extended, teeth gnash, flesh clacks against flesh. Some of them give birth; others copulate, or devour each other at a mouthful.

Suffocating under their own numbers, multiplying by their own contact, they climb over one another; and move about Anthony with a surging motion as though the ground were the deck of a ship. He feels the trail of snails upon the calves of his legs, the chilliness of vipers upon his hands:—and spiders spinning about him enclose him within their network.

But the monstrous circle breaks, parts; the sky suddenly becomes blue; and

THE UNICORN

appears.

Gallop! Gallop!

I have hoofs of ivory, teeth of steel; my head is the colour of purple, my body the colour of snow; and the horn of my forehead is bestreaked with the tints of the rainbow.

I travel from Chaldea to the Tartar desert,—upon the shores of the Ganges and in Mesopotamia. I overtake the ostriches. I run so swiftly that I draw the wind after me. I rub my back against the palm-trees. I roll among the bamboos. I leap rivers with a single bound. Doves fly above me. Only a virgin can bridle me.

Gallop! Gallop!

Anthony watches him depart.

And as he gazes upward, he beholds all the birds that nourish themselves with wind: the Gouith, the Ahuti, the Alphalim, the Iukneth, of the mountains of Kaf, the homai of the Arabs—which are the souls of murdered men. He hears the parrots that utter human speech; and the great Pelasgian palmipeds that sob like children or chuckle like old women.

A saline air strikes his nostrils. Now a vast beach stretches before him.

———

In the distance jets of water arise, spouted by whales; and from the very end of the horizon come

THE BEASTS OF THE SEA

round as wineskins, flat as blades, denticulated like saws, dragging themselves over the sand as they approach.

Thou wilt accompany us to our immensities, whither as yet no one has descended!

Divers peoples inhabit the countries of the Ocean. Some dwell in the sojourn of tempests; others swim freely amid the transparency of chill waves;—or, like oxen, graze upon the coral plains, or suck in through their trunks the reflux of the tides,—or bear upon their shoulders the vast weight of the sources of the sea.

Phosphorences gleam in the moustaches of the seals, shift in the scales of fish. Echini whirl like wheels; ammonites uncoil like cables; oysters make their shell hinges squeak; polypi unfold their tentacles; medusæ quiver like balls of crystal suspended; sponges float hither and thither; anemones ejaculate water; wrack and sea-mosses have grown all about.

And all sorts of plants extend themselves into branches, twist themselves into screws, lengthen into points, round themselves out like fans. Gourds take the appearance of breasts; lianas interlace like serpents.

The Dedaims of Babylon, which are trees, bear human heads for fruit; Mandragoras sing;—the root Baaras runs through the grass.

———

And now the vegetables are no longer distinguishable from the animals. Polyparies that seem like trees have arms upon their branches. Anthony thinks he sees a caterpillar between two leaves: it is a butterfly that takes flight. He is about to step on a pebble: a grey locust leaps away. One shrub is bedecked with insects that look like petals of roses; fragments of ephemerides form a snowy layer upon the soil.

———

And then the plants become confounded with the stones.

*Flints assume the likeness of brains; stalactites of breasts; the flower of iron resembles a figured tapestry.**

He sees efflorescences in fragments of ice, imprints of shrubs and shells— yet so that one cannot detect whether they be imprints only, or the things themselves. Diamonds gleam like eyes; metals palpitate.

And all fear has departed from him!

He throws himself down upon the ground, and leaning upon his elbows, watches breathlessly.

———

Insects that have no stomachs persistently eat; withered ferns bloom again and reflower; absent members grow again.

At last he perceives tiny globular masses, no larger than pinheads, with cilia all round them. They are agitated with a vibratite motion.

ANTHONY

deliriously:

O joy! O bliss! I have beheld the birth of life. I have seen the beginning of motion! My pulses throb even to the point of bursting. I long to fly, to swim, to bark, to bellow, to howl. Would that I had wings, a carapace, a shell,—that I could breathe out smoke, wield a trunk,—make my body writhe,—divide myself everywhere,— be in everything,—emanate with all the odours,—develop myself like the plants,—flow like water,—vibrate like sound—shine like light,—assume all forms—penetrate each atom—descend to the very bottom of matter,—be matter itself!

———

* Fleurs de fer, "flowers of iron." In mineralogy *flos ferri,* a form of Aragonite.

Day at last appears;—and, like tabernacle curtains uplifted, clouds of gold uprolling in broad volutes unveil the sky.

Even in the midst thereof, and in the very disk of the sun, beams the face of Jesus Christ.

Anthony makes the sign of the cross, and resumes his devotions.

FINIS

APPENDIX

THE DEATH OF CHRIST IN A MODERN CITY

(This passage is found in the penultimate manuscript draft of Flaubert's *Temptation*. The author intended it to follow Jehovah's soliloquy in the fourth tableau and finally decided against including it. As with the vision in the sixth tableau of modern science, a knowledge of future occurrences could be justified by the powers attributed to Anthony as a thaumaturge.)

—

Anthony can now hear nothing. As he listens, the silence seems to augment and the shadows are so dark that he is astonished not to feel their resistance as he opens his arms. Yet, they suffocate him as would a black marble casing moulded about his person.

Then the darkness opens, making as if two high and parallel walls; at their end, in the far-off distance, a city appears.

Smoke escapes from the houses, tongues of fire twist upwards in the dense air. Iron bridges span rivers of filth; carriages, sealed as tightly as coffins, encumber the long, straight streets; here and there, women's faces appear in the glow of lights coming from the taverns wherein one can see large, brightly shining mirrors. Men dressed in hideous suits of clothes, grotesquely either thin or obese, run as if pursued, with chin lowered and gaze averted, as if they all had something to hide.

And lo! in their midst, Saint Anthony beholds JESUS.

As he walks, his back has become hunched, his hair has whitened,—and his cross, which he carries on one shoulder, is bent and describes an immense arc.

The cross is too heavy. He calls out; no one comes to his side. He knocks at the doors of houses. They remain closed.

On he goes, beseeching those around him to look, to remember. No one has the time to listen. His voice is drowned out by the noise of the city. He staggers and falls to his knees.

The sound of his fall brings men of all nations, from Germans to Negroes,—and in the delirium of their vengeance, they shout in his ear:

"For thee we have spilt oceans of human blood, fashioned gags with the wood of thy cross, hidden every hypocrisy beneath thy robe, absolved every crime in the name of thy mercy!—Moloch in a lamb's garb, lo! thy agony has lasted too long; Die at last!—and arise not!"

And then others, those that loved him, still bearing on their cheeks the stain of their tears, say unto him: "Therefore have we prayed enough, wept enough, hoped enough!—Cursed be thou for our long waiting, by our unfulfilled hearts!"

A king strikes him with his sceptre, accusing him of having exalted the weak; and the people tear at him with their fingernails, reproaching him for having sustained the monarchies.

Some bow down before him, in derision. Others spit in his face, not in anger but from habit. Merchants wish to have him sit in their shops. Pharisees claim that he is obstructing the way; doctors who have examined his wounds claim that there is nothing miraculous there in which to believe; and philosophers add: "He was nothing but a phantom."

No one gives him so much as a glance; no one knows him.

And so he lies in the filth, and the light from a winter sun strikes his dying eyes.

Life continues about him. Carts splatter him. Whores brush against him. The passing idiot throws him his laughter, the assassin his crime, the drunken man his vomit, the poet his song. The multitudes trample him underfoot, grinding him asunder,—and finally,—when on the pavement there remains only his large heart, beating ever more slowly—there is not, as on Calvary, a formidable cry heard by all—but barely a sigh, a whisper of expiring breath.

The shadows close.

ANTHONY

The horror! I saw nothing! were it so, my God, then what would remain?

GLOSSARY

The creation of this glossary owes much to Claudine Gothot-Mersch's edition of *La Tentation de saint Antoine* (Gallimard, 1983). Entries have been modified and supplemented as needed. My warmest expression of thanks is reserved for Louisa and Nanne, whose assistance was invaluable. *M.O.*

A

ABRAXAS: a word in Greek letters expressing the number 365, which corresponds, in the doctrine of the Basilidians, to the number of aeons or of created heavens; by extension, the stone on which this word is engraved.

ABYSS: the first of the aeons; the supreme deity in the doctrine of Valentinus.

ACHARAMOTH, OR ACHAMOTH: in the doctrine of Valentinus, a feminine aeon, daughter of Sophia (mother of the Demiurge), and predestined to be the companion of the aeon Jesus.

ACHELOUS: a river of Epirus and the god of this river. Achelous took the form of a bull to fight with Hercules over Deianira. Hercules won and tore off one of the bull's horns, which the Naiades used for the Horn of Plenty (cornucopia).

ADAMITES: a Gnostic sect of Egypt who worshiped nude, like Adam and Eve in the Garden of Eden.

ADONAI: "my lord," in Hebrew; one of the names in the Scriptures designating God.

ADRAMITES: an ancient people of southern Arabia.

ÆONS, OR AEONS: for the Gnostics, beings that emanated from the supreme principle of all things. Some commentators have likened them to the Platonic Ideas, but they are more personal and subjective. The word derives from the Greek term for "time" and seems to mean "eternal."

ÆSAR: Etruscan name for the divinity.

ÆSCULAPIUS: the Roman god of medicine and of healing, identified with the Greek god Asclepius. Often represented in the form of a serpent.

ÆTIUS: fourth-century heresiarch, disciple of Arius, and leader of the Aetian sect.

AGAMEMNON: Greek king and head of the Argive force at Troy.

AHRIMAN: in the ancient religion of Iran, the divinity of evil, opposed to Ormuzd.

AHUTI: a sort of monkey (and not a bird) that "lived off the wind."

AKSAR: Flaubert would have read about this python in the work of Samuel Bochart, the French theologian.

ALEP: city in Syria.

ALEXANDER: Alexander III of Macedon, 356–323 BCE, called "the Great." Conqueror of the civilized world.

ALEXANDER, SAINT: bishop of Alexandria, opponent of Arius, member of the Nicene Council, died 328.

ALEXANDRIA: city in Egypt founded by Alexander the Great in 331. The crossroads of religions and melting pot of Gnostic sects in the early Christian era.

ALPHALIM, THE HULPALIM: a sort of monkey. See Ahuti.

AMAZONS: in Greek mythology, an ancient race of women warriors.

AMENTHI, OR AMENTHES: Hades in the early Egyptian religion. The souls of the dead descend there to be judged.

AMMON: Egyptian deity, identified with Zeus; represented by a ram's head.

AMMON, SAINT: monk and founder of the monasteries of Nitria, died ca.

345–50. Athanasius relates that Anthony was miraculously apprised of his death.

AMMONARIA: A virgin Ammonaria who suffered martyrdom in Alexandria in 250 was perhaps the origin of Flaubert's character.

AMPHITRIONAD, OR AMPHITRYONIAD, DESCENDANT OF AMPHITRYON: Zeus took the form of Amphitryon to seduce his wife, Alcmene, who became the mother of Heracles.

AMPHITRITE: in Greek mythology, the queen of the sea and wife of Poseidon.

AMSCHASPANDS: the first order of spirits of good in the ancient religion of Iran. Ormuzd is the creator and first of the Amschaspands.

ANAXAGORUS: Greek philosopher, born 500 BCE. Teacher of Pericles and Euripides, and perhaps of Socrates.

ANCHORITE: one who lives alone and apart from society for religious meditation, a religious hermit, a solitary; to be distinguished from a cenobite, or a monk living in a religious community.

ANCYRA: today, Ankara.

ANDRODAMAS: a stone that supposedly calms anger.

ANGELS: in the Judeo-Christian religion, spiritual beings superior to mankind but inferior to God. The hierarchy of angels can vary, but the most detailed system is that of Pseudo-Dionysius: nine choirs forming three ascending hierarchies: angels, archangels, principalities—powers, virtues, dominations—thrones, cherubim, seraphim.

ANTHONY, SAINT: Egyptian anchorite, 251–356. See Foreword.

ANTIOCH: the capital city of ancient Syria. Council of Antioch: There were ten councils at Antioch, the most noteworthy of which were the three of 264–69, leading to the excommunication of the bishop Paul of Samostata.

APELLES: disciple of Marcion. Like his teacher, he rejected the entire Old Testament, but unlike him, and in the manner of the Christians, recognized but a single divine principle.

APHIA, OR APHAIA: goddess to whom the temple at Aegina is dedicated. Identifies with Artemis (Diana) and with Britomartis.

APIS: sacred ox worshiped at Memphis, "living symbol of Osiris in all his aspects."

APOLLINARISTS: followers of Apollinaris the Younger, died ca. 381–90, who held that the divine Word fulfilled in Jesus the functions of the human soul (which he did not possess), and that his impassable body suffered the tortures of the Passion in appearance only.

APOLLO: Greek and Roman god of poetry, music, prophecy, and medicine. He is associated with the sun and with reason.

APOLLONIUS OF TYANA: Greek philosopher of the Neo-Pythagorean school, born a few years before the Christian era, died in Ephesus in 97, at the age of a hundred years. An ascetic, he traveled throughout Asia and became interested in Oriental mysticism. The narrative of his travels, given by his disciple Damis, and later by Philostratus, is full of miraculous events, including one incident of raising a woman from the dead. By the third century and the time of Hierocles, his reputation rivaled that of Jesus. Flaubert's sources for this long section were varied and probably included Voltaire (for whom Flaubert had lasting admiration), who would have been far more interested in Apollonius's practical ethics than in questions of divinity.

ARCHIGALLUS: high priest in the cult of Cybele.

ARCHON: title given to the nine magistrates who ruled Athens in the Classical Age. One of them, the king, was responsible for religious worship; his wife played a role in the festival to Dionysus.

ARCHONTICS: a Gnostic sect of the second half of the fourth century, based on writings interpreting the life of Seth, last son of Adam and Eve.

ARICIA: city of Latium. Virbius had a place of honor there in the temple of Diana.

ARIANS: disciples of Arius.

ARISTÆUS: a benevolent deity whose worship was widespread throughout ancient Greece. Son of Apollo and the nymph Cyrene, he introduced the cultivation of bees and of the vine and olive. Often identified with Zeus, Apollo, and Dionysus. Creuzer, Flaubert's probable source, says that Aristæus is "immortal, at once god and man."

ARIUS: heresiarch from Alexandria. He contested the doctrine of the Trinity, maintaining that the Son was but the first of creatures, and that he was subordinate to the Father. His doctrine, which he wrote in verse to be learned by "the simplest of believers," was condemned by the Nicene Council.

AROMATICS, REGION OF THE: the north coast of Somalia.

ARSENIUS: The Melecians accused Athanasius of having him killed and, when it was shown that he was still alive, of having attempted to burn him alive in his own house.

ARTIMPASA: Scythian goddess of the moon.

ASBADÆUS, OR ASBAMÆUS: name of a spring dedicated to Zeus Asbamæus (keeper of oaths), near Tyana.

ASCITES: second-century heretics. Among their rites was to dance before a filled wineskin, symbolizing that they were themselves these new wineskins filled with the new wine mentioned by Jesus in Matthew ix: 17.

ASCLEPIUS: Greek god of medicine. See Æsculapius.

ASTOMI: a fabulous people, mentioned by Pliny. Having no mouth, the Astomi live on the air and the odors that they breathe.

ASTOPHAÏOS, OR ASTAPHAÏOS: water spirit of the Ophites. Its name might be derived from a biblical designation for the divinity.

ATHANASIUS, SAINT: Church Father (ca. 296–373). A disciple of Anthony, he became counselor to Alexander, bishop of Alexandria, whom he accompanied to the Nicene Council, where he stood firmly against the Arians. Having succeeded Alexander in 328, he was variously exiled, condemned, even deposed, and then restored to his functions, according to the vicissitudes of the struggle between orthodoxy and Arianism. Among his many writings was *The Life of Antony*, the sole contemporary biographical source concerning the hermit. See Foreword.

ATYS: mythical shepherd of Anatolia, beloved of Cybele. As he resisted her advances, she struck him with madness, and he castrated himself. Atys was associated with the festivals of Cybele, which coincided with the return of spring.

AUDIANS: disciples of Audius, or Audi. Born in Mesopotamia, Audius was rigidly austere in his conduct and severely reproached bishops and priests for the smallest lapse in their own. This attitude was responsible for a schism after the Nicene Council.

AXIEROS, AXIOKEROS, AXIOKERSA: the three principal Cabiri in the religion of Samothrace. They may be seen as Love, the Male Principal, and the Female Principal; or as Demeter, Hades, and Persephone.

B

BAARAS: a marvelous plant that was supposedly useful against enchantments.

BAASA: city in Ethopia.

BABEL: Hebrew name for Babylon. Tower of Babel: a tower that Noah's descendants undertook to build, the summit of which would "penetrate the heavens." Yahweh was angered and sowed confusion in the language of the workers (Genesis ix: 1–9).

BABYLON: an ancient city on the Euphrates, capital of Babylonia and, later, of Chaldea. Known for its wealth, luxury, and debauchery.

BACCHANALIANS, BACCHANTES: men and women who participated in bacchanals, or the orgiastic festivals of the god Bacchus, god of wine and revelry. Women bacchantes were also called mænads, or "possessed women." These terms could designate ritual participants or divine beings associated with the god. The tyrsus was the symbol of the god: a staff surmounted by a pinecone and clad with intertwined ivy and vine shoots.

BACTRIA, BACTRIANA: ancient name for the country in central Asia east of Persia (Iran).

BAIA: city with thermal baths, near Naples, much frequented in ancient times.

BALAAM: Mesopotamian sorcerer. Called by the king of Moab to curse the Hebrews, he mistreated his she-ass, who was stopped by the angel of Yahweh, and she reproached him for his cruelty. The angel inspired Balaam to give benedictions and prophecies, in the place of curses (Numbers xxii).

BALACIUS: prefect to the emperor Constantine. Having scorned the letters that Anthony sent to him about the persecution of Athanasius, he is said to have died five days later, after being bitten by an enraged horse.

BALIS: according to Pliny, a plant that could heal serpent bites and, according to others, could resuscitate the dead.

BARAOMATI: ancient term for the people of India.

BARBATUS: one of the local patron deities of the Romans, presiding over growth.

BARBELO: female aeon whose name means "daughter of the Lord," and specially honored by a series of sects called "barbelognostic": the Barbelites, the Ophites, the Nicolaitans, the Simonians.

BARKOUF: fictive prophet to whom Basilides attributed certain revelations.

BARDESANES: founder of a Gnostic school in Syria. Born 154 in Edessa, died 222. A philospher versed in astrology, he combated Marcionism and other heresies and proclaimed, at peril to his life, his Christian faith. His system is related to that of Valentinus: It is comprised of seven couples of aeons, emanations of the supreme deity, and of the creative powers of the world. The world is governed by other, inferior powers residing in the seven planets and twelve constellations of the Zodiac. Bardesanes wrote some 150 Gnostic hymns.

BASILISK: a mythical serpent whose gaze had the power to kill.

BASILIDES: a Gnostic philosopher from Alexandria (first half of the second century). He claimed to teach the true Christian doctrine that he received from Glaucias, a translator of Saint Peter. In his system, there are 365 emanations of the supreme God (whence the numerical name of Abraxas to designate the Pleroma). His successors gave the Redeemer the name of Kaulakau; they considered that "by redemption, human souls are elevated or transported to the intellectual realm, despite their chains to the material realm." Affirming that Jesus escaped death by changing places with Simon of Cyrene (who was crucified in his stead), they avoided martyrdom, reasoning that perfect beings were held to obey no moral law.

BEAR, THE GREAT: Ursa Major, the constellation.

BELLEROPHON: a legendary Greek hero. In Homer's account of his life (*Iliad* 6: 178–245), he was the son of Glaucus; he tamed the winged horse, Pegasus; and he slew the Chimaera. He prospered. The gods came to hate him, perhaps because of hubris, and killed his daughter and one of two sons. He then wandered all alone, tormented, "across the Alean plain."

BELUS: the supreme deity of the Chaldeans (homologous to Zeus).

BENDIS: the Thracian goddess of the moon. She was identified with Artemis (Diana), and her festivals were orgiastic in nature.

BIZOR: a river in southern Palestine.

BLEMMYES: in Pliny, headless monsters with mouth and eyes fixed in their chest. They are of southern Egyptian or Ethiopian origin. "Blemmyes" is also used to refer to a real people.

BOSTRA, OR BOSTA: Syrian city, capital of Roman Arabia.

BUDDHA, THE: Shakyamuni, Indian sage, prophet, and founder of Buddhism (ca. 560–480 BCE). The word "buddha" designates those who possess perfect knowledge and supreme reason, but it is applied particularly to Shakyamuni. Buddhism began as a reaction to Brahmanism and became progressively separated from it. The original practice died out, but Buddhism came back in Tantric practice.

BRAHMAN: a priest of Brahma, or Brahmanism.

BRITOMARTIS: a divinity of Crete, companion of Artemis (Diana). She is said to have invented fishing nets (or, in another version of her legend, was saved from drowning by the nets of fishermen).

BUBALUS, OR BUBALIS: a large African antelope with recurved horns.

BYBLOS: Phoenician port. Legend has it that Isis went there for the coffin of Osiris, buried in a wooden column that supported the palace roof.

BYSSUS: a material used in the preparation of fine cloth.

C

CABIRI: deities of Phoenician origin, also worshiped in Egypt and in parts of Greece (Samothrace, Thebes). Herodotus calls them the sons of Hephæstus (Vulcan).

CADUCEUS: laurel or olive branch surmounted by two wings and enveloped by two serpents; a symbol of peace.

CÆSAREUM: temple to Caesar in Alexandria.

CAFF: according to the Zend-Avesta, the ancient text of the Zoroastrians, a mountain that emerged from the Albordj, the mythic aboriginal mountain.

CAINITES: a Gnostic sect of the second century honoring those who were persecuted by the god of the Jews: Cain, Esau, the citizens of Sodom and Gomorrah, etc. Their holy book was a Gospel attributed to Judas (a benefactor of humanity who betrayed Jesus in order to allow the Redemption). They were similar to the Ophites, named for the geni-serpent Ophis.

CALIXTUS, OR CALLISTUS, SAINT: Pope from 217 to 222, he died a martyr (though perhaps the victim of a riot, he was considered a martyr). The *Philosophoumena* accused him (wrongly) of heresy on the question of the Trinity.

CAMŒNA: Latin term for the Muses; here, a secondary goddess responsible for instruction in song.

CANOPUS, RIVER: a branch of the Nile, on which was situated the city of Canope (perhaps Aboukir).

CAPE OF GARDEFUI, OR GARDAFUI: on the coast of Somalia, at the entrance to the Gulf of Aden.

CAPPADOCIA: ancient country of Asia Minor. False Prophetess of Cappadocia: a woman who, in the third century, traveled throughout the land announcing the end of the world.

CARNA: Roman goddess of the flesh. Her mission was to keep vampires away from newborn infants.

CARPOCRATES: leader of a Gnostic school in Alexandria, ca. 120.

CARPOCRATIANS: followers of Carpocrates. Characterized by their eclecticism, they esteemed Pythagoras, Plato, Moses, and Jesus as great men, each having access to the truth. They rejected all moral law, believing that the soul must experience everything before death if it is not to be reincarnated. Perhaps in order to conquer evil through evil, they established the community of women in total debauchery.

CASSANIAN MOUNTAINS: mountains in western Arabia.

CASSITERIA: cassiterite, the chief ore of tin.

CATOBLEPAS: a mythic beast resembling a wild bull, mentioned by Pliny and Elianos.

CELEPHUS: a leper.

CENTAUR: here, a constellation.

CEPUS: a mythic animal described by Elianos as resembling a cynocephalous, or dog-faced baboon.

CERBERUS: in Greek mythology, the three-headed dog that guarded the gates to Hades.

CERCOPES: legendary inhabitants of an island near Africa or Sicily. Zeus changed them into monkeys, and Heracles put them in chains.

CERDO: a Syrian Gnostic of the second century who went to Rome around 140. He held that the law of Moses and the teachings of the prophets were not the fruit of divine inspiration.

CERES: in Roman mythology, the goddess of agriculture; identified with the Greek Demeter. The mysteries of Eleusis were associated with Ceres and her cult of agrarian worship.

CERINTHUS: one of the first Gnostics, born in Judea. For him and his disciples, Jesus was a man with more power and virtues than other men;

the Christ descended in Jesus and then returned to the Pleroma. Jesus was not resurrected from the dead, but would be resurrected.

CERINTHIANS: followers of Cerinthus. Like the Ebionites, they adopted the Gospel of the Hebrews.

CHAOS: in Greek mythology, the original void.

CHARITY: one of the three theological virtues for the Christians; one of the aeons in the doctrine of Valentinus.

CHIMERA, OR CHIMAERA: a fabulous monster, represented as having a lion's head, a goat's body, and a serpent's tail.

CHITON: a kind of tunic.

CHRIST: a word meaning "the anointed one." It was first used to designate anyone marked by the divine for an important mission on earth. Applied to Jesus by the early faithful (Christians), the title came to refer to him alone. Several Gnostic sects distinguished the man Jesus from the Christ, however, who in their doctrines was one of the aeons of the Pleroma, a divine principle related to Jesus variously, according to the different systems of belief.

CHURCH: in the doctrine of Valentinus, the aeon of the ogdoad (first series of eight aeons). The aeon Church is an emanation of Mongenes (Intelligence, only son of the supreme deity), as the Christian Church is an emanation of Jesus Christ.

CILICIA: an ancient country of Asia Minor.

CIMMERIANS: a ancient nomadic people from the far north or west of Europe, who by the seventh century were in Asia Minor. The first mention of them is by Homer, in the *Odyssey.*

CIRCUMCELLIONITES: in the fourth century, sectarians of North Africa whose revolt was at once social, religious, and perhaps nationalistic. Joined in anarchistic groups, they gave themselves over to pillage. They shared with the Donatists the doctrine that required a politically independent Church, proclaimed that the validity of the sacraments depended on that of the priest who administered them, and required that all Christians seek martyrdom.

CLAUDIUS DRUSUS: the Roman emperor Nero.

CLEMENT, SAINT: Church Father, ca. 150–216. Greek philosopher and moralist, head of the Catechetical school in Alexandria. In his writings, he positioned himself as a champion of Christian faith and orthodoxy in the face of pagan religions and of Gnosticism. In his *Stromates,* he defends the right of theological reflection and of the study of Greek philosophy. In the *Hypotyposes* (the text of which is lost), he supposedly affirmed that matter was eternal.

CLEMENT, POPE: Clement I, bishop of Rome, ca. 89–97. Numerous apocryphal writings have been attributed to him, notably the *Recognitiones.*

CNIDOS: an ancient city of Caria, in Asia Minor, known for its temple to Aphrodite and statue of the goddess made by Praxiteles.

CNYZA: an herb.

COLLINA: Roman goddess of hillsides.

COLLYRIDIANS: fourth-century heretics who worshiped the Virgin as a goddess. Their name came from the cakes (in Greek: *collyra*) offered to her in sacrifice.

COLZIM: a mountain several hours distant from the Red Sea, in Lower Egypt. Anthony's final refuge, where a monastery bears his name. See Foreword.

COMARIA: probably Cape Comorin, a headland forming the extreme southern point of the peninsula of India.

CONSTANTINE: Roman emperor (born ca. 280, died 337). A convert to Christianity, he officially recognized its practice. He defended orthodox Christians against the heretics and, in 325, convened at Nicæa the first ecumenical council, in which he was an active participant. He later recalled the Arians, however, whose doctrine had been condemned by the Council, and he exiled their adversary, Athanasius. His conversion served political ends, allowing the State rapidly to establish authority over the Church.

CONSUS: Roman deity of good advice.

COUCOUPHA: a jackal's head, often atop an Egyptian scepter.

COUNT: a title given to certain dignitaries in the late Roman Empire.

CREPITUS: one of the household deities and the Roman god of flatulence, though most probably a modern invention. His speech was first written by Flaubert in 1848–49 and remained unchanged into the published version of the work in 1874. It is the longest of the passages expunged from Hearn's translation by his previous editors (see the Foreword).

CRISPUS: Emperor Constantine's son, executed on the order of his father after his stepmother, Fausta, accused him of incestuous desires.

CROTALS: a sort of castanet or bell played for the worship of the goddess Cybele.

CTESIPHON: a Babylonian city on the left bank of the Tigris and the capital of Persia under the Parthian kings.

CUBRICUS, OR CORBICIUS: the first name of Manes, according to early Greek theologians.

CUMÆ: a town of Campania, in southern Italy.

CYBELE: a Phrygian goddess known to the Romans as the Great Goddess, also as the Mountain Mother. She personified earthly abundance. At the festivals in her name, for the return of Atys, a savage rite was performed whereby celebrants wounded themselves with knives. All priests of Cybele may have undergone castration, and the high priest, or Archigallus, definitely did.

CYNOCEPHALOS: dog-headed baboon, sacred to the Egyptians. Flaubert uses the term in reference to Anubis, whom he portrays as a monkey, and also for a species of mythical animal having a human body and a dog's head, which he read of in Elianos.

CYPRIAN, SAINT: Church Father, born around 210 in Carthage, where he was made bishop in 249. During the persecution led by Decius in 250, he hid for a year, an action that brought him criticism. Positioning himself as head of the Church in Africa, he tried vainly to gain acceptance in Rome for his ideas concerning heretics and *lapsi,* or those who had abjured their faith. He was martyred in Rome in 258.

D

DAIRA: probably one of the names for Persephone.

DAMIS: a historical figure, disciple of Apollonius of Tyana, whose memoirs served Philostratus as the basis for his *Life of Apollonius.*

DANIEL: Hebrew prophet of the royal house of David. Led into captivity in Babylon, he interpreted the dreams of Nebuchadnezzar, who, prostrating himself, recognized that the god of Daniel was the god of gods (Daniel ii).

DECIMA: Roman local patron deity who looked after the tenth month of a prolonged pregnancy.

DEDAIMS, OR DUDAÏM: a Hebrew word for a kind of mandrake.

DEEP, THE: in the doctrine of Valentinus, the invisible, unthinkable sojourn of the supreme God.

DEMETRIUS: Demetrius I, king of Macedonia, died 284 BCE.

DEMIURGOS, OR DEMIURGE: the creator of the world. Term used by Plato

(*Timeon*), then by Plotinus and by the Gnostics. Several Gnostic sects assimilated the Demiurge with the god of the Jews, Yahweh. See Sabaoth.

DGIAN-BEN-DGIAN: hero of an Oriental legend, mythic builder of the pyramids. His shield, or buckler, was also legendary.

DIOCLETIAN: Caius Aurelius Valerius Diocletianus; Roman emperor 284–305. Persecutor of early Christians.

DIONYSIUS: bishop of Alexandria in 247. During the Decian persecution, he escaped death but was forced to leave Egypt. He asked Novatianus for clemency on behalf of those who had abjured during the persecution. An intellectual, he was a disciple of Origen.

DIANA: Roman goddess of virginity and of the moon (Greek name: Artemis). The Diana of Epheses: A pantheistic figure, uniting the attributes of different deities, she symbolized nature and fecundity.

DIDYMUS: ecclesiastical writer of Alexandria, born about 309. Though blind from the age of four, he became well versed in many branches of learning and was head of the Catechetical school, where he had as a pupil Saint Jerome, but not Anthony, who was some sixty years Didymus's senior.

DOSIPŒNA: goddess of the Arcadians, assimilated with Ceres.

DOMIDUCA: Roman local patron deity. According to Saint Augustine, she watched over Romans returning home. For Flaubert, she was under the denomination of Juno.

DOMITIAN: Titus Flavius Domitianus; Roman emperor (81–96) and persecutor of early Christians.

DOMITILLA: early Christian woman from the family of Flavius, exiled by Domitian. She is thought to have been martyred.

DOMMINA, OR DOMNINA, OF ALEPPO: Denounced by her husband as being a Christian, she fled with her two daughters to avoid the Domitian persecutions. Arrested in Edessa, all three jumped to their death in the river. They are honored as martyrs.

DOSITHEUS: first-century Samaritan, one of the first authors of Gnosticism, teacher of Simon Magus.

E

EBIONITES: a sect founded by a Judeo-Christian group that took refuge in Pella after the sack of Jerusalem by the Romans. They affirmed the necessity of passing through Judaic revelation, its rites and symbols, to enter into Christian revelation. An important tenet of their belief was in the humanity of Jesus.

EDUCA, ALSO EDUSA: Roman local patron deity who presided over the feeding of children.

ELEPHANTINE ISLAND: an island of the Nile, facing the present Aswan. Many temples were built there.

ELISA: the name Elisa designated the founder of Carthage and, by extension, the city itself.

ELKESAITES: disciples of Elkesai (literally, the Hidden Power of God). Their heretical beliefs were similar to those of the Ebionites, with whom they shared respect for the old Law. They affirmed that Jesus was a simple prophet, and that the Holy Spirit was the sister of the Christ. As a young man, Manes joined them.

ELOI: one of the Bible's names for God.

ELVIRA: a city in Spain (the present Granada) where, in about 300, a Council was held. It is the earliest council of the Catholic Church of which there have survived disciplinary canons.

EMATH: city in Syria, on the Orontes River.

EMMAUS: the town in Palestine where Jesus is said to have appeared to his disciples after his crucifixion.

EMPUSA: a mythical specter associated with Hecate; she possessed the power to change her shape and coupled with her victims before devouring them.

ENCRATITES: a sect whose name means "the abstemious." They exalted virginity and based their beliefs on apocrypha attributed to Saint Paul or Saint Thomas.

ENNOIA: a Greed word meaning "Thought." In the belief system of Simon Magus, it was the first thought of God, mother of all that exists. Subject to metempsychosis and tied to the laws and forms of the material world, Thought was the object of ignominies forever renewed on the part of rebel spirits. Simon claimed to have rediscovered this first thought of God in the slave Helena, whom he purchased in Tyre.

EPHESUS: ancient city in Asia Minor.

EPHRAIM: a tribe of Israel.

ERGASTULA: a prison for slaves, often underground.

ERICHTHONIUS: an agricultural deity, in the form of a serpent or of a man-serpent.

EROSTRATUS: the Ephesian who set fire to the temple of Artemis in 365, on the birthday of Alexander the Great, in order to become famous. The Ephesians forbade mention of his name.

ESAU: son of Isaac and Rebekah, who sold his birthright to his younger brother, Jacob (Genesis xxv: 21–34, xxvii).

ESQUILINE: one of the seven hills of Rome; one of the city gates in Rome where the road to Tibur (Tivoli) begins.

EUCRATITES: a heretical group that ridiculed pagans and subscribed to one of the many competing gospels.

EUNOSTUS: one of the two ports of Alexandria.

EURYNOME: in Greek mythology, the daughter of Ocean and Thetis, and mother of the three Graces.

EUSEBIUS: more than twenty-five saints of the early Church bear this name, and it is difficult at best to say which one Flaubert had in mind as the holy man who gave Anthony the example of mortification. The most renowned was Esubius of Cæsarea (ca. 260–340), Church Father, bishop of Cæsarea, and a voluminous writer: His *Church History* is especially important. He defended the doctrines of Origen and was sympathetic toward Arius. He contributed to the deposing of Athanasius.

EUSTATES: according to Flaubert's notes, among "the principal officers of the court."

EUSTOLIA: the woman beloved by Leontius, bishop of Antioch.

F

FABULINUS: Roman local patron deity who taught children to speak.

FAITH: one of the three theological virtues for the Christians; one of the aeons in the doctrine of Valentinus.

FATHER: the first person of the Trinity for the Christians; one of the aeons in the doctrine of Valentinus.

FERALIA: literally, "day of offerings"; in Rome, festivals in honor of the gods of the dead or of the souls of ancestors.

FEROUERS: in the ancient religion of Iran, the third class of spirits of the realm of Ormuzd. They are the model for all beings, combat evil spirits, and protect the pious.

FLAVIUS: Titus Flavius Vespasianus, the emperor Vespasian (9–79, emperor from 69).

FURIES: in Greek and Roman mythology, three terrible female spirits with serpent hair who pursued the perpetrators of unavenged crimes.

G

GANGARIDES: people living along the Ganges River.

GELLUDES: a type of vampire.

GITTOI: in Samaria; the birthplace of Simon Magus.

GLAUCOS: in Greek mythology, the son of Minos and Pasiphaë. Having fallen to his death in a vat of honey, he was resuscitated with the aid of a miraculous plant brought by a serpent, perhaps the god Asclepius (Latin, Æsculapius).

GNOSIS: from the Greek, meaning "knowledge." Religious knowledge superior to that of mere believers, it refers to the various mystical doctrines of the Gnostics that combined, in the early centuries of the Common Era, Christianity with elements of Greek and Oriental philosophical and religious traditions, and that were denounced as heretical.

GORGON: serpent-haired Medusa, slain by Perseus, who offered her head to Athena; the goddess affixed it to her shield.

GOUITH: a fabulous bird that spent its entire life aloft, never descending even to eat or drink.

GREAT PORT, THE: one of the two ports of Alexandria.

GREGORY: probably Gregory the Thaumaturge (ca. 210–70), disciple of Origen and bishop of Neocæsarea. He evangelized the interior of western Asia Minor.

GRIFFIN: a fabulous beast whose duty was to watch over treasures, especially those of Apollo.

GYMNOSOPHIST: literally, a naked sage. A name given to Indian philosophers who lived in the wilds in a condition of extreme austerity. Often identified with Brahmans.

H

HARPOCRATES: second son, after Horus, of Isis and Osiris, born after the death of his father.

HEBE: in Greek mythology, the goddess of youth and cupbearer of the gods.

HEBREWS: a Semitic people of the ancient Middle East, a group of whom settled in Palestine calling themselves the People of Israel—Israel being the name given by the Lord to Jacob (Genesis xxxii: 29), who was, according to the tradition, the father of this people.

HECATOMBEON: the first month of the Athenian year (July to August).

HECATONCHIRES: in Greek, "having one hundred hands." In mythology, giants having a hundred arms, children of heaven and earth. Zeus kept them in Hades, at first as prisoners and then as jailers.

HEGESIAS: philosopher of the school of Cyrene (ca. 300 BCE) who taught that death was preferable to life, given that pleasure—the only desirable good—was out of reach.

HELENA OF TYRE: the companion of Simon Magus and a slave prostitute whom he purchased at Tyre. He considered her to be the first thought of God (Ennoia), and himself to be the first God. Her cult prospered in part by association with that of Helen of Troy, who was still worshiped in the early centuries of the Common Era.

HELIOPOLIS: one of the oldest cities of Egypt whose ancient significance was entirely religious.

HELLAS: region of the Hellenes in northern Greece; hence Greece, the Greeks.

HELVIDIANS: disciples of Helvidius who believed that Mary had children with Joseph and that virginity was not superior to marriage (contrary to the dominant doctrine of early orthodox Christians).

HERCULES: in Greek and Roman mythology (Greek name: Herakles), the demigod son of Zeus and Alcmene, known for his strength. He was often represented with a club.

HERESIARCHS: a heresiarch is the author of a heresy; a heretic is one who professes a heresy.

HERMAS: a Christian prophet of Rome and author of *The Shepherd,* a work of apocalyptic visions published in 140. He had been the slave of a woman named Rhoda, for whom, though he was married, he felt an unrequited love. She reproached him for his feeling by appearing to him in a celestial vision. An old woman representing the Church also appeared to him.

HERMES: the god of travelers and, earlier, of fertility. Statues to the god were erected along the roads and consisted of block pillars, surmounted by a head and ornamented with a phallus.

HERMOGENES: second-century heresiarch who tried to reconcile Stoicism with Christian dogma. He affirmed that matter was eternal and that Jesus ascended to the sun, rather than to heaven.

HERMIANS: followers of Hermias, a fifth-century Christian apologist who attacked paganism for its lack of logic in understanding the soul.

HIERODULE: a temple attendant; also, name given to sacred courtesans who prostituted themselves to strangers and pilgrims.

HOLY GHOST, HOLY SPIRIT: the third person of the Trinity in Christian doctrine. It was manifest at the baptism of Jesus as a dove; at the Pentecost as tongues of fire. It is also called the Paraclete. For some Gnostics, the Holy Spirit is a woman, and the disciples of Simon Magus believe that it was incarnate in the person of Helena.

HOURS: in mythology, the daughters of Zeus and Themis; they presided over the seasons and are associated with Ceres.

HILARION, SAINT: (ca. 290–371) an abbot and anchorite who is at the origin of monasticism in Palestine. Born in Gaza, he went to Alexandria for his education, where he converted to Christianity; about 306 he visited Saint Anthony and became his disciple. He returned to Gaza to live an eremitic life and had many disciples of his own. In Flaubert's *Temptation,* Satan assumes Hilarion's form in order to tempt the hermit. Athanasius, in his *Life of Anthony,* recounts similar instances of transformations whereby the devil took on the shape of holy men to beguile Anthony with misleading speech. See Foreword.

HIPPOPODS: a mythical people with horses' hooves for feet.

HOMAI: according to Bochart, one of Flaubert's sources, the Arabs believed that the soul of a murdered man whose assassin had not been found became a *hama,* causing a song of ill portent to be heard on the victim's grave.

HOMERITES, OR HIMYARITES: an ancient people of southern Arabia.

HOSTILINUS: a deity in Latium invoked to assure a good wheat harvest; the feminine form, Hostilina, is more common.

HOULEH: a lake in Palestine, crossed by the Jordan River.

HYMNIA: a name for Artemis (Diana) in Orknomenos, an ancient city in Greece.

HYRCANIA: an ancient district of Asia; the sea of Hyrcania: the Caspian Sea.

I

IAARAB: an ancient king of Sheba.

IABDALAOTH, OR IALDABAOTH: the Demiurge (see Demiurgos), or the Creator, in the doctrine of the Ophites and in many other Gnostic sects. Taken from the Hebrew, his name means Son of Darkness. He is at once Satan and Yahweh.

IAKHSCHAB: an ancient king of Sheba, son of Iaarab.

IAO: another form of the name Yahweh or Jehovah.

IARCHAS: Hindu sage who instructed Apollonius in the occult sciences, particularly divination.

INTELLIGENCE: the name of Monogenes, or the only son of the supreme deity; one of the first aeons in the doctrine of Valentinus.

IDEAN: one from Mount Ida, in Asia Minor, near the ancient city of Troy.

ISIS: Egyptian deity, sister-wife of Osiris, mother of Horus and Harpocrates, universal mother and healer. Isis worship was among the most successful of the pagan cults competing with Christianity, continuing in Greece until the sixth century.

ISSACHAR: one of the twelve tribes of Israel, named for one of the sons of Jacob.

ISSEDONIA: an ancient region of Scythia.

ITHYPHALLIC: having an erect phallus.

IUKNETH, OR IUKNEH: a monstrous bird mentioned in the Talmud.

IXION: in Greek mythology, the king of the Lapithæ in Thessaly. Finally pardoned for the murder of his father-in-law, he was admitted to Olympus, where he tried to seduce Hera. Zeus condemned him to be tied to a blazing wheel that rolls unceasingly through the air. Often associated with the sun.

IZEDS: the second series of genii created by Ormuzd in the ancient religion of Iran. They govern the world.

J

JANUS: Roman god of beginnings and endings. He is represented by a head with two faces, front and back.

JERUSALEM, THE CELESTIAL: the City of God that some early Christians believed would come from heaven.

JESUS: founding figure of the Christian religion. Christians see in him the

Messiah announced in the Scriptures and call him the Christ (the one anointed by the Lord), recognizing in him two natures: the one divine (the Son of God and the second person of the Trinity), and the other human. Many of the heretical sects diverge from orthodoxy on the question of the dual nature of Jesus, refusing him either the one or the other. In the doctrine of Valentinus, the Monogenes or Only Son of God (called *Nous,* or Intelligence) engendered the Christ to reestablish order in the Pleroma that had been troubled by the errors of Sophia. That done, the aeons created the aeon Jesus, the redeemer of the lower world, as the Christ had been that of the Pleroma.

JOANNA: wife of Khouza, Herod's intendant. She is mentioned in Luke xxiv: 10 as one of the women who informed the apostles of the empty tomb.

JOHN: Nestorian bishop of the Church of Persia; participated in the Nicene Council.

JUDAS: one of twelve apostles of Jesus who betrayed him to his enemies. The Cainites revered him as the one who, by this treasonous act, made possible the Redemption.

JUNO: the Roman name for Hera, queen of the gods and wife of Jupiter.

JUNONIA: first in mythology, and then in ancient geography, one of the Islands of the Blessed (today the Canaries).

JUPITER: the Roman name for Zeus, king of the gods.

K

KAIOMORTZ: the first man in the ancient religion of Iran. He leaped from the side of the bull Aboudad, in which Ormuzd had placed the seed of all life.

KALANOS: Indian sage; Cicero relates that he immolated himself before Alexander.

KAOSYAC, PERHAPS FOR SAOSHYANT: the "ultimate Savior" or "Savior of the end of time" in the ancient religion of Iran.

KASTAN, PERHAPS FOR CAHTAN: king of Sheba, patriarch of the dynasty.

KASTUR: Etruscan form of Castor, brother of Polydeuces or Pollux (here Polutuk), mythical sons of Zeus and Leda, called the Dioscuri. They sailed with the Argonauts. Their cult was very popular in Rome.

KAULAKAU: the Basilidians' name for the Savior. Related to the expression "qav la qav" in Isaiah xxviii: 10, "here a little, and there a little." The repetitive form is associated with perfection.

KERES: for the Greeks, female genii of death who, in the *Iliad,* dragged the dead and dying off to Hades with their sharpened fingernails.

KNOUPHUS, OR KNOUPHIS: for the Egyptian Gnostics, one of the manifestations of the supreme deity and the benign creator of the world. He is represented as a snake- or wormlike form, often with a human head or face. He corresponds to the Egyptian god-serpent Kneph.

L

LABDANUM: an aromatic resin.

LAPHRIA: the name by which Artemis (Diana) was worshiped in the Peloponnesian seaport of Patras.

LARES DOMESTICI: Roman house gods, or local patron deities, who presided over the daily life of families and households.

LARVAE: in Rome, evil spirits, souls of the unburied dead.

LATICLAVI: plural of the Latin *laticlavus,* the purple bands sewn to the togas worn by Roman senators; hence, as here, the togas themselves. They were a sign of prestige and power.

LEMURES: in Rome, ghosts of the dead that inhabit the wall panels of houses.

LEONTIUS: a priest of Antioch. Forbidden cohabitation with a girl named Eustolia, he castrated himself. He became a bishop in about 348 and adhered to some of the heretical beliefs of the Arians.

LIBITINA: a Latium goddess who presided over funerals; assimilated with Persephone. Also confused with Venus through association with the word "libido."

LIFE: one of the aeons, in the doctrine of Valentinus.

LUCIUS: several martyrs were known by this name.

M

MACARIUS THE ELDER: Egyptian anchorite (ca. 300–91) who went to live in the desert at the age of thirty. Numerous mystical and erotic texts are attributed to him.

MAGEDDO: a valley of Palestine (today, Israel) between Mount Tabor and Mount Carmel.

MAN: one of the aeons in the doctrine of Valentinus.

MANDRAGORAS, OR MANDRAKE: a plant that, for the Ancients, had secret properties. Because its roots resemble the form of the human body, it was said that the mandrake moaned when pulled from the ground.

MANES: (ca. 215–77) Babylonian founder of Manichaeism, a Gnostic religion that became very widespread; its basis was in the literal opposition between light (good) and darkness (evil). Christ and salvation were of the light; all things of darkness and of the night were to be eschewed. Judeo-Christian as well as Zoroastrian elements influenced the religion. Manes is said to have written a gospel that he illustrated with allegorical drawings. He led the life of an ascetic missionary and preached throughout Asia, traveling even into China. A conspiracy of the Magian fanatics brought about his condemnation in Persia, where he was crucified. His corpse was flayed and, some say, the skin stuffed.

MANIPLE: a silk band worn hanging over the left forearm as a Eucharistic vestment.

MARCEL OF ANCYRA, OR AGKURA: bishop of Agkura (Ankara) in the third century. He opposed the Arians but was accused of Sabellianism (see Sabellius).

MARCELLINA: disciple of Carpocrates; Saint Augustin reported that she worshiped and burned incense to images of Jesus, Paul, Homer, and Pythagoras.

MARCION: second-century schismatic and heresiarch, founder of the Marcionite Church. He was excommunicated by Rome and affiliated himself with Cerdo. Marcion represented Christianity as a belief with no antecedents, pitting the good God against the god of the Jews, who was guilty of having submitted man to the law of Moses. He based much of his teaching on the Pauline epistles and reduced the New Testament to a reading of the Gospel of Luke.

MARCIONITES: disciples of Marcion; their schismatic church survived long after the death of the heresiarch and has been traced to the seventh century.

MARCOSIANS: disciples of Marcos "the Magus," or seer, who was affiliated with the school of Valentinus. From Saint Irenæus, we learn of certain of their unorthodox rites, including the "spiritual nuptials," which may have been licentious.

MAREOTIS, LAKE: a lagoon of the delta of the Nile, south of Alexandria.

MARS: Roman name for Ares, god of war.

MARTICHORAS: a mythical animal. In Iranian mythology, the martichoras presided over the reign of impure animals, as the unicorn did over that of the pure.

MAXIMILLA: a prophetess of Montanism (see Montanus).

MELCHISEDECH: Hebrew for "king of righteousness." The sect of the Melchisedechians placed their leader above the terrestrial Savior, claiming that he helped the angels in their work of self-perfection as Jesus had helped mankind. Melchisedech considered himself the celestial Savior. The sect was founded in Rome by Theodosius "the banker," disciple of Theodosius "the tanner," head of the Theodosian sect.

MELETIANS: sectarians also known as the Church of Martyrs, followers of Meletius, fourth-century bishop of Lycopolis. Their church was schismatic: After Meletius's death around 325, his followers sided with the Arians in the controversy with Athanasius.

MELISSUS: Greek philosopher of the Eleatic School, fifth century BCE.

MENA: deity of Latium, daughter of Jupiter, under whom Mena presides over the monthly purification of women.

MENIPPUS: not the third-century satirist of the same name but a young Corinthian, beloved of an empusa who had taken the form of a woman and whom Apollonius unmasked the day of the wedding.

MERINTHIANS: heretics who refused to recognize a divine nature in Jesus.

MESCHIA AND MESCHIANÉ: Adam and Eve in the mythology of ancient Iran. At the death of Kaiomortz, his seed fell to the ground; a tree sprang up which carried, instead of fruit, ten human couples, among whom were Meschia and Meschiané, the parents of the human race. They were seduced by Ahriman, who presented them with fruits that caused the loss of their beatitudes.

MESSALINES: Gnostic sect holding prayer above all else and condemning work as a sin. They refused all liturgy and had neither altar nor sacraments.

METHODIUS: Greek bishop, theologian, and writer, a disciple and then adversary of Origen. Died ca. 311. He held that the Word was originally with Adam and, after the fall, was with Christ.

MILETUS: city in Asia Minor. The virgins of Miletus: Weary with life, they sought death but were dissuaded by the threat of their naked cadavers being exposed.

MIMALLONIDES: Bacchantes.

MINERVA: in Roman mythology, daughter of Jupiter; identified with the Greek goddess Pallas Athena.

MINOS: in Greek mythology, the son of Zeus and king of Crete. By his wife, Pasiphaë, he fathered numerous children, including Deucalion, Glaucus, Ariadne, and Phaedra. After his death, he became the judge of the newly arrived in Hades.

MIRAG: a fabulous animal: a hare with horns.

MITHRA: Persian god of light, whose worship, the last one of importance to be brought from the Orient to Rome, spread throughout the empire and became the greatest antagonist to Christianity. Initiation into the mysteries of Mithra was accompanied by severe trials.

MOLOCH: a god of the Phoenicians and of the Carthaginians, unto whom children were sacrificed. Moloch figures prominently, and horrifically, in Flaubert's 1862 Carthaginian novel, *Salammbô*.

MONTANISTS: disciples of Montanus.

MONTANUS: probably from Mysia, near the Phrygian border, Montanus began prophesying the end of the world and the coming of the celestial Jerusalem around 156. He presented himself as the Paraclete announced by Christ. The movement that he started, which was then continued by Maximilla and Priscilla, perturbed the Church of Asia Minor, and the Montanists were declared heretics. Montanism preached absolute continence and the seeking of martyrdom, and women were given important functions.

MOST HIGH, THE: God.

MUSES: any of the nine divinities who presided over literature, the arts, and sciences.

MUSEUM: a palace in Alexandria dedicated to the Muses.

MYRMECOLES, OR MYRMECOLEO: a fabulous animal about which Flaubert would have read in Bochart.

MYRRHODION: resinous gum drawn from myrrh.

N

NAENIA: the Roman goddess of funereal songs or lamentation (*nenia*).

NEITH: an Egyptian goddess, divine mother of all things.

NEPTUNE: the Roman name for Poseidon, god of the seas.

NICÆA: an ancient city in Bithynia, in Asia Minor, site of the first ecumenical council, convened by the emperor Constantine in 325. Between 250 and 300 bishops attended, and the emperor himself participated. The heresiarch Arius was condemned; after much debate, the consubstantiality of the Father and the Son was declared, and the Nicene Creed was formulated.

NICOLAITANS: followers of the second-century heresiarch Nicholas of Antioch. The sect professed moral libertinism, believing that giving the body over to pleasure was the only way to free the soul from the flesh. It is said that they ate of the animals sacrificed to pagan gods and prostituted themselves.

NINEVEH: a city in ancient Assyria, on the Tigris River.

NISNAS: fantastic beings, described by Bochart, one of Flaubert's sources.

NITIRA: a marshy country of Lower Egypt where the first anchorites sought refuge.

NIXII: in Rome, the three deities who oversaw childbirth. Their kneeling statues were on the Capitol.

NOMES: administrative divisions in ancient Egypt.

NONA: for the Romans, the local patron deity who protected the ninth month of pregnancy.

NORTIA: the Etruscan goddess of destiny, luck, and time.

NOVATIANS: sectarian followers of Novatianus, Roman presbyter and one of the first antipopes. He opposed the reintegration into the Church of those Christians who had sacrificed to idols. He had himself been elected bishop of Rome by certain priests, against Cornelius, who was elected according to form. The Nicene Council encouraged the return to the Church of the Novatians, but the schism lasted in some places until the seventh century.

NUMBERS: the calculations of the Babylonians and Chaldeans; also, the lists, genealogies, and census-taking of the Hebrews in the Book of Numbers.

NUMERA: the Roman goddess of numbers.

O

OANNES: a fish god of the Chaldeans who emerged from the water to liberate the first humans from their savage state. He is the author of all civilization and of all knowledge.

OLYMPUS: a mountain mass in Greece; on one of the summits, the Greeks placed the sojourn of the gods. The "fourteen Olympii" refer to the various peaks of the chain.

OMOPHORUS: for the western Manicheans (see Manes), the corresponding figure for Atlas. He bore upon his shoulders the eight earths and the ten firmaments that made up the universe.

OMOROCA: in the story of the Genesis attributed to Oannes, Omoroca incarnated the primitive water in the form of the first woman. Cutting her in two, the god Belus divided chaos into the heaven and the earth.

OMPHALE: in Greek mythology, a queen of Lydia in whose service Hercules had to spin wool and perform other womanly duties, dressed as a woman.

ONAGER: wild ass.

OPHITES: a Gnostic sect of the second century, similar to the Valentinians. They held that Sophia gave birth to the Demiurge Iabdalaoth, who created man in an imperfect state, without a soul and crawling. Thanks to Sophia, a ray of light animated this imperfect creature, who became the image of the supreme God, and the jealous Iabdalaoth became Satan, the spirit of evil who forbade mankind all knowledge. Sophia, on the contrary, sent to man the geni-serpent Ophis, who led man to taste the fruit of the tree of knowledge, giving man knowledge of heavenly things. Both man and Ophis were thrown down into matter, where Ophis became either evil or good; this latter belief was held by the sectarians evoked by Flaubert. As with most Gnostics, the Ophites made a distinction between the Christ (one of the aeons) and Jesus, upon whom the Christ descended after the baptism in the Jordan.

ORAIOS: one of the seven angels created by the Demiurge.

ORCHOMENUS: a city in the ancient Arcadia.

ORICHALCUM: a metal with fabulous properties, mentioned by ancient writers.

ORIGEN: Greek theologian (185–254) and Church Father who, after Clement, taught at the school in Alexandria. His reputation as a teacher of diverse fields was widespread throughout the East. Wary of temptation, he followed the Bible literally and castrated himself. Ordained and then divested, he finally established himself in Cæsarea. He was tortured during the Decian persecutions and may have died from wounds suffered then. A very erudite and powerfully original philosopher, he is the founder of biblical exegesis, for which he borrowed from

Gnosticism and Neoplatonism. He was among the most prolific writers of the ancient church, the number of his works being estimated by some at six thousand. For Origen, Christianity is a practical and saving principle that has revealed itself historically in a series of facts, and that simple faith is sufficient for the renewal and salvation of mankind.

ORMUZD: for the ancient Persians, the god of goodness and light.

ORSILOCHE: in the region of the Taurus Mountains (Turkey), Artemis (Diana) was worshiped as the moon under this name.

ORTHIA: literally, rigid. Epithet for Artemis (Diana) in Sparta, where, each year, youths underwent severe flagellation that they were to tolerate without complaint.

OSSIPAGO, OR OSSIPAGINA: deity responsible for the formation of the skeleton of a fetus.

P

PABENA, OR MORE PLAUSIBLY TABENNISI: the Egyptian village near Dendera, where Saint Pachomius established his first monastery.

PACHOMUS, OR PACHOMIUS, SAINT: (292–346) Egyptian monk who founded Christian cenobitical life (monks living in a community), which, according to legend, he was called to do by an angel. At his death, the order that he had established, the Tabennesiots, had nine monasteries, with some three thousand monks, and a nunnery. Saint Athanasius was his friend and protector during periods of difficulty with neighboring bishops.

PALÆSIMONDUS: the ancient Greek name for Sri Lanka.

PAN: in Greek mythology, the deity of all nature. He is represented as a satyr. See Syrinx.

PANDIO: southern Hindustan.

PANEADES, OR PANEAS: city of Palestine, near the headwaters of the Jordan River.

PANEUM: an artificial hill in the center of Alexandria.

PANTHERUS: Origen wrote in *Contra Celsum* that Celsus had portrayed Jesus' birth as resulting from adulterous congress between Mary and a Roman soldier of this name.

PAPHNUTIUS: bishop of Upper Egypt who was martyred under Diocletian, his right eye having been torn out, and his left leg hamstrung; he participated in the Nicene Council.

PAPHOS: an ancient city and sanctuary on the west coast of Cyprus. The ancient Greeks worshiped Aphrodite here in the form of a giant conical stone (see Venus).

PARACLETE: "the consoler," a name that Christians give to the Holy Ghost. In the doctrine of Valentinus, it is one of the aeons. Montanus claimed to be the Paraclete, as did Manes.

PARTHENON: temple of Pallas Athena, on the Acropolis in Athens. In Greek, *parthenos* refers to a virgin; the temple is so named because of the goddess's virginity (see Diana).

PASTINACA: Flaubert found the description of this animal in Elianos.

PATERNIANS: fourth-century heretics who believed that the flesh was the work of the devil and so indulged in all manner of debauchery.

PATREANS: inhabitants of Patras, in Greece.

PATRICIAN: under Constantine, an honorific title conferred for distinguished services; its holder ranked next after the emperor and the consul.

PAUL: according to tradition, the first Christian hermit. A wealthy and cultured resident of Thebaid, he fled into the mountain wilderness to escape the Decian persecution and thereafter maintained a life of solitude.

PAUL, SAINT: Apostle of the Gentiles (ca. 5–67), he converted to Christianity when Christ appeared to him on the way to Damascus, where he was going to oppose the Christians. He preached the Gospel in Arabia, Syria, and Cilicia, then in Antioch, and all around the Aegean Sea. He wrote fourteen Epistles, which form part of the New Testament. His influence as a Christian thinker has been pervasive. In the early days of Christianity, he was able to bridge the gap between the ultra-conservative Judeo-Christians and the Gnostics.

PAUL OF SAMOSATA: patriarch bishop of Antioch (260–72) whose heresy lay in his insistence on the humanity of Jesus.

PELAGIA OF ANTIOCH, SAINT: a virgin of Antioch who threw herself from a rooftop during the Diocletian persecution in order to escape a soldier with violent intent.

PEPLOS: a woman's cloak, often draped on statues of goddesses.

PEPUZZA: town in Phrygia, holy site for the Montanists.

PERFECTION: one of the aeons in the doctrine of Valentinus.

PERSEPHONE: in Greek mythology, the daughter of Zeus and Demeter

(Ceres); called Proserpina by the Romans (in English, Proserpine). Hades abducted her and took her to the underworld. Demeter bargained with Zeus so her daughter might return to earth for six months out of the year, remaining in Hades for the other six months. Persephone symbolizes the changing of the seasons.

PETASUS: a broad-brimmed hat, typical of representations of Mercury.

PETRUS, OR PETER, OF ALEXANDRIA: bishop of Alexandria (300–11); martyred in 311. He advised persecuted Christians to buy their lives with money.

PHAROS: an isle closing the port of Alexandria. A tower of white marble, called by the same name, was built on it, upon which fires were maintained to guide ships. The lighthouse was one of the Seven Wonders of the World.

PHILÆ: an island of the Nile, sacred to Isis, in Upper Egypt.

PHILOLAUS: (born ca. 480) Greek philosopher of the Pythagorean school. He was the first to propound the movement of the earth, which, along with the sun, moon, stars, and five planets, moved around a central hearth, or the house of Zeus.

PHRAORTES: a philosopher king of India who received Apollonius and sent him to study with the sage Iarchas.

PHRATRIA: an Athenian tribal division.

PIONIUS: a priest from Smyrna, martyred in 250.

PISPERI, PISPIR: today Dayr al-Maymun, a mountain in Lower Egypt where Anthony sojourned from 286 to 305 in an abandoned fort and where he founded a monastery. See Foreword.

PLEROMA: for the Gnostics, the divine spiritual world made up of the aeons.

PLUTO: in Greek and Roman mythology, the god ruling over Hades.

POLYCARP, SAINT: (ca. 69–155) bishop of Smyrna and one of the Apostolic Fathers; disciple of Saint John and teacher of Saint Irenæus. He was martyred at the stake in Smyrna.

PONS SUBLICIUS: a bridge in ancient Rome that connected two of Rome's seven hills, the Aventinus and the Janicularis.

PORSENNA, LARS: king of Clusium in Etruria; in 509 BCE he undertook an expedition against Rome, to which he laid siege but could not enter.

PORUS: king of India, defeated by Alexander in 327 BCE.

POSIDIUM: temple to Poseidon in Alexandria.

POTINA: for the Romans, the local patron deity who presided over drink.

POWERS, THE: in the doctrine of Valentinus, the powers emanating from the Principle, the aeons.

POZZUOLI: a port on the Gulf of Naples.

PRÆMA: for the Romans, the local patron deity who prevented wives from refusing the caresses of their husbands.

PREFECTS OF THE CHAMBERS: chamberlains to the emperors of Constantinople.

PRESTEROS: a fabulous serpentlike animal, described by Elianos.

PRINCIPLE: for the Gnostics, the supreme God, the first aeon.

PRISCILLA: one of the two prophetesses of Montanism. See Montanus.

PRISCILLIANISTS: followers of Priscillian, a Spanish Gnostic (died 385). Priscillian preached a severe asceticism but was accused of Manichaeism (see Manes), magic, and licentious orgies. He was burned at the stake.

PROCULA: the name given to the wife of Pontius Pilate in the apocryphal literature. Her intervention on behalf of Jesus is mentioned in Matthew xxvii: 19.

PROSERPINE, OR PROSERPINA: see Persephone.

PROUNIKOS: "lascivious." Epithet given to Sophia by the Valentinians (see also Ophites) to indicate the dominance of the passions. For Simon, Prounikos is incarnate in Helena the prostitute, whose cult included obscene rites. The Nicolaitans also claimed to gather the force of Prounikos by drawing it out of the body through voluptuousness.

PROVIDENCE: As a common noun, "providence" is the plan by which God governs the world. As a proper noun, it refers to God in his capacity of overseeing the world.

PTHAH: an Egyptian god, one of the agents of Knouphis; or perhaps another name for Knouphis, representing wisdom. In Memphis, he was worshiped as the god of fire, comparable to Vulcan.

PTOLEMY: son of Lagus, a Macedonian gentleman and one of Alexander the Great's most trusted generals. Ptolemy founded a dynasty of Macedonian kings who ruled Egypt from 323 to 330 BCE.

PULTIS: a mixture of water, eggs, flour, cheese, and honey, left as an offering.

PULUTUK: Etruscan name for Pollux. See Kastur.

PUTEOLI: ancient city of Campania, in southern Italy.

PYGMIES: a fabled race of dwarfs living in the region of the headwaters of the Nile. As with the name of the Blemmyes, that of the Pygmies also refers to a real people.

PYTHAGORAS: a Greek philosopher and mathematician in the sixth century BCE. He lived in Egypt, where he was initiated into that country's religion and sciences, and then in Babylon, where he met Chaldean priests and Magi. At Crotona, he founded a school where his teaching dealt in part with hermetic mysteries, notably metempsychosis.

R

RACOTIS: a suburb of Alexandria, a quarter for prostitutes.

RAZIAS, OR RAZIS: a Jew. To escape from Nikanor's soldiers, Razis fell on his sword and, when he did not die, ripped out his own entrails and hurled them into a crowd. II Maccabees xiv: 37–46.

RUMINA: for the Romans, the local patron deity who protected the infant taking its mother's breast.

S

SABAOTH: one of the names of the god of Israel. Yahweh Sabaoth, or Lord of Sabaoth, means "Lord of hosts," or "Lord of armies." Certain Gnostics used this name to refer to the Demiurge, even to one of his subordinates, in order to mark their disrespect for the god of the Jews.

SABASIUS: the name in Phrygia and in Thrace for Dionysus-Bacchus.

SABELLIUS: a Lydian, and principal representative of Monarchianism, a heretical doctrine that affirmed that the Father and the Son were but different names for the same being.

SACHALITES: a people of southern Arabia.

SADHUZAG: This fabulous stag, with its seventy-six antler points, is described by Bochart, one of several sources used by Flaubert for such animals.

SAHARIL: one of the ancient kings of Sheba.

SAMANEANS: Hindu philosophers, living as hermits in the Samana Mountains in India.

SAMARIA: capital city of ancient Palestine, before its conquest by the Assyrians. It gave its name to the central province of Palestine.

SAMOS: a minor divinity associated with the worship of Æsculapius.

SAMOSATE: a city of ancient Syria, on the Euphrates River.

SAMOTHRACIA, OR SAMOTHRACE: an island of the Aegean Sea, where the mysteries of the Cabiri were celebrated.

SAMPSEANS: a Gnostic sect very similar to the Elkesaites.

SARRATOR: an agrarian god of the Romans; he presided over the harrowing of the fields.

SARTOR: an agrarian god of the Romans; he presided over the weeding of gardens.

SATURNINUS, OR SATORNIL: second-century heresiarch who taught in Antioch; probably a disciple of Simon. He believed that the god of the Jews was the principal of the creating angels.

SAUL: the first king of Israel. After his defeat by the Philistines on Mount Gilboa, during which he witnessed the death of his three sons, Saul threw himself on his sword.

SCHEBAR, OR SHEVAT: a month in the Jewish calendar that falls in late January to February and, according to the Jewish year (which begins in the fall), occurs in the middle of the year.

SCIAPODS: a fabulous people of Lybia or Ethiopia, mentioned by Pliny and by Philostratus as having feet that served as parasols.

SENAD: Flaubert's source Bochart mentions this animal that tears apart its young with its tongue, but does not say that it is a three-headed bear.

SERAPIS: an Egyptian god whose cult gradually eclipsed all others. Serapis is Osiris descended to Hades and judge of the dead. Famous temples to the god were at Alexandria and at Memphis.

SESOSTRIS: the name of a legendary king of Egypt, probably a compound of Seti I and Ramses II, of the nineteenth dynasty, or the seventeenth century BCE. Herodotus, in particular, ascribed to him numerous victories and territorial expansion.

SETHIANIANS: a Gnostic sect basing its doctrine on the mass of Jewish and Christian tradition that grew around the name of Seth, the last son of Adam and Eve. They believed that the lower world was controlled by Sophia. Abel, a weak creature created by the Demiurge, was killed by Cain, a creation of the spirit of evil. Sophia replaced Abel with her son Seth, whose descendants were virtuous and wise. They were endangered by the descendants of Cain; Seth reappeared in the person of Jesus Christ.

SHEBA: a kingdom established in the southwest portion of Arabia (Yemen) that lasted from the eighth to the sixth centuries BCE.

SHEM: the eldest of the three sons of Noah.

SIGEH: "silence." For the Simonians, one of the eight aeons of the Pleroma, corresponding to Ennoia.

SILENUS: foster father and tutor of Bacchus; represented as a plump, jovial man.

SILPHIUM: an aromatic resin.

SIMON MAGUS (THE MAGICIAN): also called the Samaritan. In Acts viii: 5–24, he is portrayed as a famous sorcerer in Samaria. He met the apostles in Samaria and saw in them thaumaturges of a higher science. Simon converted and was baptized. He offered to buy the power that would allow him to communicate with the Holy Spirit (hence the term "simony" for the offense of selling holy items). Though reprimanded by Peter, he propagated a Gnostic doctrine by which the angels created the world, governed it poorly, and were dispossessed by the First Power. Between the First Power and the angels, he placed Ennoia-Helena and presented himself as the great power of the supreme being. The Pleroma is sometimes said to have originated with him.

SIMON, OR SIMEON: a just man to whom the Holy Spirit appeared, saying that Simon would behold the Savior before dying, and urging him to go to the temple. Simon went on the day that the infant Jesus was brought there by his parents (Luke ii: 25–27).

SIMORG-ANKA: a fabulous bird of Persian legend; often identified with the Iukneh.

SINOPUS: a town on the northern coast of Asia Minor.

SOLITARIES: anchorites, religious hermits.

SOMA, OR SEMA: the mausoleum of Alexander and the Ptolemies in Alexandria.

SOPHIA: in Greek, "wisdom." The last, and least perfect, of the aeons in the doctrine of Valentinus. She brought about the fall of the Pleroma that occasioned the Redemption. For the Ophites, she is the mother of all living things.

SOSIPOLIS: in Elea, a legendary child transformed into a serpent, savior of the city, and so the object of worship in the temple at Ilithyia.

SOTAS: a Thracian bishop who tried to exorcise Priscilla.

SPIRIDION: bishop from Cyprus (died 348) who participated in the Nicene Council of 325.

SPLENDITENEUS: "the Ornament of Splendor"; for the Manichaeans (see Manes), at the top of the ten firmaments that, with the eight worlds, made up the universe.

SPORUS: Suetonius mentions this member of Nero's entourage.

STESICHORUS: (ca. 640–555 BCE) A Greek lyric poet who, according to Longinus, was most like Homer. Legend has it that he was struck blind for slandering Helen (wife of Menelaeus) in a poem, and that he regained his sight by composing a palinode in which he recanted by saying that it was only Helen's ghost that went off to Troy. The followers of Simon Magus related this legend to Helena of Tyre.

STIMULA: Latin goddess responsible for awakening desire.

STRIGII: mythical demons or vampires having the form of women and bitches.

STYMPHALIA: described by Flaubert's source Pausanias as "silhouettes of girls having birds' feet."

SUBIGO, PERHAPS SUBIGUS: for the Latins, a local patron deity who presided over the bride as she entered the nuptial bed.

SUBURRA: a quarter of ill repute in ancient Rome.

SUMMANUS: an ancient Etruscan or Oscan deity. A god of the night and of nocturnal thunder; also, god of thieves.

SUN: The sun was worshiped as a god in many ancient religions. For the Greeks, Apollo was the sun god under the name of Phoebus. In the Egyptian religion, Osiris was identified with the sun (Isis with the moon). Similarly, Baal or Belus was thus identified by the Chaldeans. There is much sun imagery relating to Jesus Christ (see the closing passage of the *Temptation*).

SYRINX: the nymph whom the gods metamorphosed into water reeds to save her from Pan's pursuit. It is also the name given to the flute that Pan then fashioned from these reeds.

T

TACHAS: a mythical animal that traveled rapidly underground.

TAGES: Etruscan divinity, born as a human infant out of a furrow during cultivation. He immediately began to teach divine science, how to interpret the flight of birds, and how to read the entrails of victims.

TANTALUS: in Greek mythology, a king and son of Zeus whose punishment in Hades was eternal hunger and thirst. He stood in a pool of water beneath boughs of fruit, but he could never reach either the water or the fruit.

TAPROBANA: in ancient geography, Sri Lanka.

TARSUS: an ancient city in the plain of Cilicia. Many famous schools of rhetoric and philosophy flourished there. Tarsus is the birthplace of Saint Paul.

TARTARUS: in Greek mythology, the lower world, Hades.

TARTESSUS: in southern Spain, an island in the mouth of the Betis River (today the Gualdaquivir).

TATIANIANS: disciples of Tatian, a second-century Christian apologist, missionary, and heretic. He was a leading figure—if not the founder—of the sect of the Encratites. He condemned marriage and all sensual pleasure.

TAXILLA: an ancient city on the Indus River.

TCHATAKA: a fabulous bird whose name derives from Sanskrit.

TELESPHORUS: a Greek god of health associated with Asclepius.

TERMINUS: the Roman deity of boundary markers, often dividing fields.

TERTULLIAN: (ca. 155–222), born in Carthage. The earliest of the major early Church writers of the West, he defended orthodoxy against heresy; however, strongly attracted by Greek thought, he became an adherent of Montanism (see Montanus). In much of his later writing, he speaks out vehemently against pagan customs, calling for increased austerity. In his *De Carne Christi,* he offers the view that Jesus must have been physically repugnant. In his notes for the *Temptation,* Flaubert calls him a "limited and vehement mind, incapable of ideals."

THEBAID: The region around the Egyptian city of Thebes, in Upper Egypt, long associated with the early anchorites. Strictly speaking, Anthony never lived there. It is mentioned by Athanasius as a possible retreat that Anthony at one time considered but did not choose, after his stay in the fort on Mount Pispir (now Dayr al-Maymun) and his final retreat on Mount Colzim, both in Lower Egypt. Flaubert puts the first sojourn on Colzim.

THEODAS: a disciple of St. Paul; Valentinus claimed that his own doctrine came from Theodas.

THEODOTIANS: followers of Theodosius "the tanner," a second-century heresiarch who contested the divinity of Christ. Flaubert, like many others, may have confused him with his pupil Theodosius "the banker."

THEOPHILUS: There may have been a Scythian bishop by this name at the Nicene Council.

THOMAS: the apostle who doubted Christ's wounds.

THOTH: an Egyptian god to whom the invention of all arts and sciences is attributed. He is identical to Hermes and Anubis, and his name may be for Hermes as the son of Amon-Knouphis (see Knouphus).

THOUGHT: one of the aeons in the doctrine of Valentinus.

THULE: the name given by the Greeks and Romans to the northernmost of known lands, perhaps to Iceland, or to one of the Shetland or Orkney islands, or to part of the Norwegian coast.

TIBUR: today, Tivoli; a city just east of Rome, known for its villas.

TIMONIUM: the villa in Alexandria of Anthony's family, at the end of the Posidium levee.

TITANS: in Greek mythology, the children of earth and heaven, defeated by Zeus.

TITYUS, OR TITYOS: a giant who wished to rape Leta. Zeus struck him down with a lightning bolt and bound him in chains in Tartarus, where two vultures (or serpents) devoured his liver.

TOPAZOS: an island in the Red Sea.

TRAGELAPHUS: a fabulous animal, half he-goat, half stag.

TRINITY, THE: in the Christian religion, the unity of the three divine persons: the Father, the Son, and the Holy Ghost, being of the same essence and the same substance. In other religions, a triple diety, or a union of three deities in one, as the three cabiri of Samothrace in the example chosen by Flaubert (see Axieros).

TRIOPAS: the founding god of the city of Cnidus who had a statue at Delphi; as his name indicates, he had three eyes.

TROPHONIUS: the mythical architect who, with his brother Agamedes, built the Delphic temple to Apollo. They also built the treasury of King Hyrieus and fraudulently enriched themselves. An abyss swallowed them up, and from its depths, Trophonius could be heard dispensing advice to those temerarious enough to venture nigh.

TRUTH: one of the aeons in the doctrine of Valentinus.

THYANA, OR TYANA: city in Cappadocia (Asia Minor) and birthplace of Apollonius.

TYPHON: in Egyptian mythology, the wicked brother of Osiris and the spirit of evil. He tried to seize the throne of Egypt while Osiris was away, then killed him and left his body in a casket on the Nile. When Isis found the cadaver, Typhon had cut it into fourteen parts that she re-assembled, with the exception of the *membrum virilis.* In Greek mythology, Typhon is a titan, son of Gaia and Tartarus. He sired the Hydra and the dangerous winds.

TYRE: a seaport in ancient Phoenicia.

U

UNICORN: a fabulous animal with a single horn emerging from its fore-head. Its body is composed of parts from different animals, but princi-pally the horse. In Persian mythology, it symbolized the reign of pure animals.

V

VALENTINUS: among the most influential theologians of second-century Gnostics. He spent much of his teaching career in Rome (ca. 135–60), then perhaps in Cyprus. Valentinus shared with most Gnostics (see Gnosis) the worship of the Mother Goddess whose dwelling is in the highest of the heavens in the Pleroma. She, like man, is fallen, and re-demption will occur through a divine marriage consummated between the goddess and the redeemer, a spiritual brother-husband. (See Æons, Bardesanes.)

VALENTINIANS: followers of Valentinus, whose Gnostic sect flourished long after his death. Of the Gnostic sects, the Valentinians most closely approached the doctrine of the Catholic Church.

VALESIANS: members of a sect established near the city of Petra around 240, deriving from the Montanists (see Montanus). They forbade the eating of meat and pushed the zeal for chastity to the point of self-castration.

VALLONA, OR VALLONIA: Roman goddess of valleys.

VENUS: Roman goddess of love, identified with the Greek goddess Aph-rodite. Her quality as *anadyomene* (coming from the sea) refers to the myth in which Chronos threw the testicles of Uranus into the sea, whereupon the foam drew itself around them and Aphrodite was en-gendered. The goddess wears a magical girdle that renders desirable whoever wears it. Flaubert refers to several statues of her effigies: the statue at Cnidus sculpted by Praxiteles; the one in Corinth, the Aphrodite Melaenis (the black Venus); the effigies in Attica that are similar to the squared blocks of the Hermae; and the conical (and perhaps phallic) Aphrodite at Paphos.

VERTUMNUS: Roman deity presiding over the changing of the seasons and the transformation of the vegetation.

VERVACTOR: Roman deity presiding over the fallow fields.

VESPASIAN: Titus Flavius Vespasianus, Roman emperor from 69 to 79.

VESTA: very ancient Roman deity, the goddess of the hearth; the fire lit in her name must never be extinguished. The temple and fire were tended by the vestal virgins. Her cult is at least as old at the time of Numa Pompilius (second king of Rome), who built a round, or circular, temple in her name to reflect the fact that the earth is round.

VIA SALARIA: the road leading from Rome toward the territory of the Sabini (the Sabine people).

VIRBIUS: a demon who is part of the cult of Diana at Aricia. He is identified with Hippolytus (son of Theseus and killed by Neptune), who, when brought back to life by Æsculapius and admitted into the ranks of the lesser deities, was given the name of Virbius, meaning "man twice born" (*vir bis vivus*).

VIRGO: local patron deity of the Romans; she presided over the removal of the bride's girdle.

VOLUPIA: the Roman deity of pleasure.

VULCAN: in Roman mythology, the god of fire and metalworking; identified with the Greek god Hephæstus. He was the husband of Venus.

W

WISDOM: Sophia, one of the aeons in the doctrine of Valentinus.

WORD: for Christians, the second person of the Trinity (the Son, or Jesus Christ). One of the aeons in the doctrine of Valentinus.

X

XENOPHANES OF COLOPHON: founder of the Eleatic school of philosophy, born in the third or fourth decade of the sixth century BCE.

XERXES I: king of Persia (486–465 BCE) and general against the Spartans at Thermopylae (480 BCE).

Z

ZALMOXIS: legendary hero or god in the ancient Scythian religion. He taught the Thracians to believe in the immortality of the soul by disappearing totally and reappearing three years later.

ZOROASTER, OR ZARATHUSTRA: the great prophet and reformer of the ancient religion of Iran, seventh century BCE.

NOTES

1. *My mother sank to the ground, dying:* It was after the death of both his parents that Anthony took up the life of a solitary.
2. *The fathers of Nicæa:* Claudine Gothot-Mersch points out that Flaubert's Anthony is past seventy-five years of age, since the Nicene Council took place in 325. Anthony did not attend, however.
3. *Staters, cycles, dariacs, aryandics:* ancient Persian or Greek coins, except for the cycle, or shekel, a silver coin of the ancient Jews.
4. *he environed him with the five elements:* For the Gnostics, there were five elements instead of the usual four: air, fire, water, earth, plus light.
5. *Bellerophontian sickness:* melancholy or hubris. See Glossary, "Bellerophon."
6. *Eater of Locusts:* An epithet for Saint John the Baptist, whose asceticism was extreme.
7. *Astophaios, Oraios, Sabaoth, Adonai, Eloi, Iao!:* These are the six angels created by the Demiurge. See Glossary, "Demiurgos."
8. *three great gods appear:* Brahma, Vishnu, and Siva.
9. *three goddesses:* Saraswati, wife of Brahma; Lakchmi, wife of Vishnu; Parvati, wife of Siva.
10. *the inspiring spirit of wisdom:* Ganesa, son of Siva.
11. *the Fire-Consumer:* Cartikeya, second son of Siva.

12. *The old man riding the crocodile washes the soul of the dead upon the shore:* Varouna, water deity.
13. *the master of the sun:* Sourya.
14. *The Moon-God:* Chandra.
15. *Goddess of Beauty:* Maya.
16. *I entered her womb:* Mahamaya, wife of the king of Magadha.
17. *Symbol of Jerusalem:* A symbol in this sense is the statement of a creed. Here it refers to the profession of faith adopted at the Nicene Council of 325, often referred to today as the Nicene Creed. It was significantly modified at the synod at Constantinople in 381, and it is this revised version that Anthony recites from (shaky) memory.
18. *Three hundred men strove against all Asia:* The battle of Thermopylae (480 BCE), in which a small group of Spartan soldiers under their king, Leonidas, fought valiantly against the immense army of the Persian king, Xerxes, advancing upon Greece.
19. *women of valiant heart went forth to slay captains:* Judith x–xiii (Vulgate).
20. *the antichthonus ... spheres of Aristotle:* references to ancient astronomy. The antichthonus was a planet supposed to be on the other side of the sun, always directly opposite the earth and so never visible. It is mentioned in Plato's *Convivium*. The spheres are the concentric spheres that in the cosmology of Aristotle (and others) comprise the universe. Philolaus was a Greek philosopher. See Glossary, "Philolaus."

A NOTE ON THE TYPE

The principal text of this Modern Library edition
was set in a digitized version of Janson, a typeface that
dates from about 1690 and was cut by Nicholas Kis,
a Hungarian working in Amsterdam. The original matrices have
survived and are held by the Stempel foundry in Germany.
Hermann Zapf redesigned some of the weights and sizes for Stempel,
basing his revisions on the original design.

MODERN LIBRARY IS ONLINE AT
WWW.MODERNLIBRARY.COM

MODERN LIBRARY ONLINE IS YOUR GUIDE
TO CLASSIC LITERATURE ON THE WEB

THE MODERN LIBRARY E-NEWSLETTER

Our free e-mail newsletter is sent to subscribers, and features sample chapters, interviews with and essays by our authors, upcoming books, special promotions, announcements, and news.

To subscribe to the Modern Library e-newsletter, send a blank e-mail to: **join-modernlibrary@list.randomhouse.com** or visit **www.modernlibrary.com**

THE MODERN LIBRARY WEBSITE

Check out the Modern Library website at
www.modernlibrary.com for:

- The Modern Library e-newsletter
- A list of our current and upcoming titles and series
- Reading Group Guides and exclusive author spotlights
- Special features with information on the classics and other paperback series
- Excerpts from new releases and other titles
- A list of our e-books and information on where to buy them
- The Modern Library Editorial Board's 100 Best Novels and 100 Best Nonfiction Books of the Twentieth Century written in the English language
- News and announcements

Questions? E-mail us at **modernlibrary@randomhouse.com**. For questions about examination or desk copies, please visit the Random House Academic Resources site at **www.randomhouse.com/acmart**